HARBORWOOD

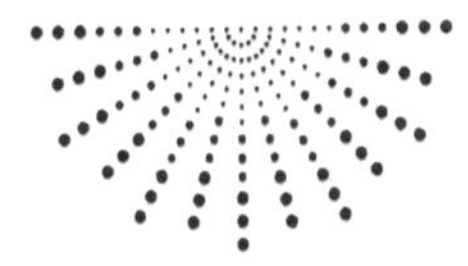

STEVEN SAWYER

DEEP END BOOKS

Editing by Megan Records

Cover Design by Ebook Launch (ebooklaunch.com)

For more information, contact at:

Deep End Books

P.O. Box 2555

Midlothian, VA 23113

www.stevensawyerbooks.com

stevensawyerbooks@gmail.com

First Printing (Boone)

ISBN: 978-0-9861473-0-2

To my dad

CHAPTER ONE

He opened his eyes to sirens interrupting the silence of the morning. They were loud, even for the city, stopping suddenly, then starting again.

He glanced around his small studio apartment, finally realizing his cell was ringing. He stretched out his arm, fumbling for the phone, but knocked into a half-full glass of something, which slipped off the edge of the nightstand, spilling onto the floor.

"Shit," he muttered, answering the call with one hand and rubbing his eyes with the other. He felt like he'd barely slept.

"Mark?" came the voice on the other end of the line.

He blinked again, trying to sit up. "Yeah."

"Mark," came his brother's voice, more urgently this time.

"Joe? What's up?"

"It's Dad..."

He fell back into the pillow. The last thing he wanted to be woken up about was some problem with his father. Dad was probably just using Joe again to complain about him not coming home often enough.

"What is it this time? Seriously, I'm trying to sleep here."

"He had a heart attack, Mark."

"What?" His eyes opened wide as he bounced back up in his bed.

"He was playing golf," replied Joe. "He collapsed on the back fairway. They medevacked him to the hospital..." Another pause. "He didn't make it."

Mark swung his legs over the side of the mattress, trying to clear his head. "Wait a minute? When was this, today? It's still morning."

"It's almost noon. He was playing the early round this morning." He heard Joe's voice crack through the phone. "He's dead, Mark. Dad died."

Mark didn't say anything, lost in a foggy stare at his reflection in the mirror across the room. Dad...died?

"Mark? Hey, are you there?"

He tried to say something, but the sound wouldn't come.

"So you need to come home, okay?" Joe continued. "Mom is going to call later, but I thought you needed to know. Are you there?"

He felt a pressure forming under his ribcage, his chest growing tighter by the second. "Okay...thanks for calling."

He ended the call, putting the phone back on the nightstand without realizing he'd put it there. He bent down, picked up the glass he had spilled, then mopped the liquid up with an old Pearl Jam t-shirt sticking out from under the bed. He stumbled over to the bathroom, closing the door even though he was alone in the apartment, barely comprehending Joe's words. He stepped into the shower and closed his eyes, feeling numb even as the water streamed over him. He turned it warmer than usual, basking in the steam curling up around him like a gas chamber. He raised his face up to the showerhead, hot streams pounding against his skin.

How could Dad be dead? A heart attack on the golf course? He couldn't place his emotion—not sad, not happy. Just numb. Was that how he was supposed to feel? Was this how everyone felt when someone close passed away? Or was it just because it was his dad, and everything to do with Dad was complicated?

He tried to remember what day it was...Saturday, he thought. Maybe Friday. No, he was pretty sure it was Saturday. He'd been out with Tyler after work at some club he couldn't remember the name of, drinking way too much and staying far too long.

He'd have to leave, get back home. He could be in Virginia by dinnertime if he rented a car and left that morning, but no, Joe had said it was already noon. The traffic would be hell getting out of the city on the bridges and tunnels. He'd need to fly; that would get him home the fastest, one of those last minute bereavement fares if they still had them.

He thought back to Joe's words.

Dad was dead.

Damn it.

CHAPTER TWO

Everyone was dressed in black, of course. Mark had wished for a dreary, rainy day, but it was clear and hot. He'd forgotten how muggy late July could be in Virginia. New York was hot, but not this humid. The men were all melting in their coats and ties, like walking through the indoor pool at the gym fully dressed.

Twelve years had been just long enough to forget. Sure, he'd been back now and then at the holidays—Christmas and Thanksgiving and such. He still stayed in touch with Mom, and he talked to Joe some, but mostly because of Lauren and the kids. Talking to Joe reminded him of Kingfisher, his dad's insurance agency, and he disliked being reminded.

Mark didn't work at Kingfisher, and for a long time he'd tried to stay as far away from the firm as he could. Joe had been groomed to take over some day, sooner than any of them realized, as it turned out. He'd recently asked Mark to work some cases on the side, and Mark had said yes, mostly just for the extra cash, but also as a favor to his brother. Mark figured Dad knew about it, but for whatever reason, it wasn't something that had ever been discussed. It was easier that way with most things.

Discussions with Dad usually went sideways fast, which was one of the biggest reasons why Mark had left home for good. Somehow it was easier to breathe being three hundred miles away. Being in the same room, the same house even, felt a bit too much like being back in that indoor swimming pool. The air was a little too thick for both of them.

Mark watched Joe's two little kids run across the grass, playing hide and seek amongst the gravestones, too young to fully realize what was going on. It was probably irreverent of them to race over the ground above the dead, but no one seemed to care. Those that would have were no longer around, their day of mourning passed. It was hard to believe Dad was now one of them. There was a part of Mark that ached to feel that young, so innocent and carefree, with everything still wide open and blue, not weighed down by whatever life had in store.

"Mark, it's really good to see you, son," said the man— Stan Carlson, he thought his name was—one of Dad's old partners, or maybe a board member at the Rotary. Dad knew a lot of people. It was funny how someone could be so friendly, so open and accessible to half the city, but at the same time barely know his own son who had lived in the same house with him for eighteen years. By all assessments, he was a pillar of the community.

Was. It was so alien to say it that way.

"Thanks," Mark answered, stone-faced. He wanted to correct the man for calling him "son." He wasn't his son. Kingfisher wasn't family, it was a business, and if he'd learned anything from his father over the years, it was that business was not personal. He supposed he should thank them all for coming to pay their respects, but he didn't feel like it. He didn't know how he was supposed to feel, but he wasn't going to dance.

Joe stood next to him, shaking hands, nodding and smiling, doing all the right things. It probably wasn't even an act. Joe was three years older than Mark, but always seemed to have more of Dad's outgoing personality. It surely guided him to the on ramp to the family business, whereas Mark had veered off to the side. Dad said Joe was a natural at selling insurance. Sure, he'd also said Mark had been a natural at throwing a baseball, but those comments had only lasted as long as his arm did, which was about forty-seven days short of eighteen years.

Things just seemed to work out for Joe. He played on the varsity football team and at a division three college, married Lauren—much to the envy of every other man—had two beautiful children, a boy and a girl, earned his business degree, then went to work at the agency. Joe's physicality on the football field seemed to naturally click with Dad's aggressive mentality. Mark was leaner, a bit more fragile looking, but graceful. He didn't necessarily have the killer instinct that drove his father.

Mark's vantage point was slightly different than everyone else's. He'd seen too many times when Dad's intensity could slip into an anger that floated just beneath the surface. Joe strangely escaped the worst of it, although even he could see the pressure that Dad exerted on Mark, occasionally amped up by drink, but mostly driven forward by an unmitigated desire to succeed.

Mom had told him some about Dad's childhood one weekend when Dad was away on a business trip. Tommy Parsons, who by all accounts had been raised by his mom, scraped by in the rough Hell's Kitchen neighborhood of New York City. His father had been an alcoholic who'd shuttled in and out of prison for much of Tommy's life before finding an early demise in a back alley behind the bowling lanes across the river in Secaucus, New Jersey. His last stint in the joint had been for assaulting his former employer in the neighborhood diner with a saltshaker. He'd messed up the man's face so bad he could hardly be recognized. All on account, Mr. Parsons had claimed, that he backed out of paying him the full overtime he was owed. Tommy had scrambled to live up to that example, often fighting his way through the neighborhood to survive. To his credit, he made something of himself, building Kingfisher from the ground up, taking on partners to expand, then later buying them out so he could run the whole show. He was an American success story.

The endless sea of well-wishers and condolence-givers eventually subsided and a group of black town cars brought the immediate family back to the house. Mom seemed to be holding up all right outwardly, but Mark could tell she was reeling on the inside. A marriage to someone as forceful as his father tended to leave a pretty big crater when they disappeared.

By all accounts, his parents had a good marriage. They seemed happy, successful, he thought they loved each other. This would be hard for her, for sure. She'd have to take time off from the flower shop where she worked part-time. She'd never had to work for the money, but it was something that made her smile and provided an excuse to get out of the house. With Dad gone, money would be even less of an issue than before. If there was one thing Mark was sure of, it was that Dad would have had a life insurance policy that was second to none.

Mark wondered if he shouldn't be feeling more, if his heart shouldn't seem so hard. He didn't know how you were supposed to feel when your father died; he suspected each person mourned and grieved in their own way. But for Mark, he just felt cold inside.

THAT NIGHT he tried to sit and watch a ballgame on TV, but found he was only staring blankly at the screen. How many nights had he sat in that living room, Dad carrying a running commentary on nearly every play to supplement the voices of the sports announcers with his own expert opinion?

Most nights they watched the Yankees, his dad's favorite team from his years growing up in New York City. Mark's too, likely by osmosis. It was one of the few things they could do without the same degree of tension. Somehow, the flow of the game connected them, diffusing the pressure of their normal day-to-day interactions.

It was their ritual, sitting together, Dad on his leather recliner,

Mark on the couch, often after a workout or dinner, especially in those years after Joe left for college and Mark was still in high school. Joe's presence in the house through high school had acted as a kind of stabilizer, and it wasn't until after he left that Mark and his dad were free to clash unabated.

But when the Yankees were on, it was like a white flag billowing from the front porch. It helped when the Bombers from the Bronx were on a hot streak, like the stretch from '96 to 2000 when they won the pennant four out of five years. Sitting in front of a game together had somehow seemed like a good luck charm, even when they had nothing to say to each other.

Just before the streak, back in '94, New York had seemed built to go the distance, after spending most of the late '80s and early '90s in obscurity with losing teams. Dad was so excited that he sprung for a satellite dish for the roof to snag every game, turning many a summer evening into a nightly party as they watched the Yanks march toward October's postseason. Until the players' strike hit in September, canceling the remainder of the season and washing away the playoffs and World Series for the first time in history.

Dad got so mad, he took a bucket of Mark's practice baseballs from the garage and fired them up at his new dish until it broke apart and crashed down onto the driveway in pieces. Mom had walked out to see what all the commotion was, but at the sight of Dad's face, she turned on her heels and walked back inside.

"Goddammit!" he'd screamed regularly that fall, often sitting in his chair staring at a blank screen, or watching pre-season football earlier than he should have. His favorite player had become Paul O'Neil, acquired in a trade a few years back from the Cincinnati Reds. He seemed to grind it out, a trait Dad admired as he was leading the American League in batting average in September when they called the season.

"Paulie had the batting title locked up, I'm telling you as clear as the day! How the hell can they let that happen?"

Mark had long given up trying to answer such questions.

Mark stared at the dark TV, thinking back to the sea of faces that afternoon, all dressed in black and lined up to shake his hand with their best canned apologies.

He wondered what was really true. What had really gone wrong with him and Dad over the years? Maybe it really was his fault, but who the hell knows?

CHAPTER THREE

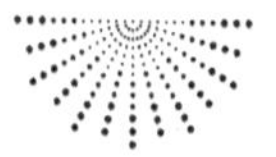

It was mostly dark when Mark woke up. He hadn't pulled the blinds, and from the early light just beginning to seep in through the windows, he could see he was in his old room. His mind searched a few beats for what was happening. It felt familiar, yet so foreign.

It had been years since he'd left home for school, but Mom insisted they keep his and Joe's room the same in case they came back for a visit. Never mind that Mark hardly ever did, or that Joe was married with a family of his own on the other side of town. Maybe it helped her feel normal. Maybe she wished for those days.

Being there made him feel squeamish, so Mark pulled on his clothes and snuck through the quiet hallway, down the stairs, and out the back door, trying not to wake anyone up. He was surprised not to run into Dad, who wasn't one for sleeping late. He'd normally be the first one up, sitting on the back deck with his newspaper, downing his first of several cups of morning coffee. Maybe it was too early?

He stopped himself at the edge of the backyard, his mind catching up to reality as he remembered the funeral. Dad was dead.

That was still hard to say, or even think, although ironically he'd wished for it at the top of his lungs in high school on more than one occasion. He supposed he hadn't really meant it—teenagers don't mean most of what they say in anger to their parents at that age—but he remembered clearly the struggle it was living with more than one man in the same house those last few years.

Now that Dad was gone, he didn't feel much relief. It wasn't anger any more, maybe not even sadness. Just numbness once again.

He turned left out of the driveway, following the sidewalk through the loop of the neighborhood. The sun was just coming up, but summer in Virginia was hot even in the morning. He walked briskly nonetheless, trying to clear his head, whatever the hell that meant. His head didn't seem to feel very clear most of the time anymore.

Dad had often said, "You need to get your head on straight, Mark." As if Mark had been some kind of hellion who was always causing trouble. The problem, he'd long ago decided, was that they just looked at the world differently. Dad's straight was Mark's crooked, and neither of them could figure out how to reconcile the difference. He swallowed hard and moved faster. Now it was too late.

His phone buzzed in his pocket, and he pulled it out mid-stride. A text from Delta. His flight back to New York had been canceled.

Shit.

He stared up at the sky; not a cloud to be seen. It figured. He clicked the airline's number at the bottom of the text to figure out what the problem was. A woman informed him of a computer glitch out of Chicago that was causing delays all up and down the east coast. Since hundreds of flights were being canceled throughout the day, it was extremely unlikely that he could get re-routed onto another carrier. She suggested he try Amtrak.

He hated Amtrak. When it wasn't crashing, it was usually

delayed worse than the airlines, and the station out of Richmond was a nightmare. It took almost as long to get in and out of the parking lot as it did to drive the whole way yourself.

Screw it, he'd drive. It would take all day, but he had the time. And it would give him a chance to think.

He closed the loop around the neighborhood until his old house came into view. Joe's car was in the driveway. He and Mom were in the kitchen, making breakfast.

"There you are," Mom said, barely above a whisper. Her face seemed drained of its color. She looked so old. She'd held strong through the funeral, but Mark wondered how she'd make it without Dad. She didn't ask him her normal questions about whether he slept well, or whether he noticed that his room was still the same, or how she hoped he'd come home for good. She just nodded and sipped her coffee.

"It was strange waking up in that room," replied Mark, just to try to make things seem normal.

She attempted a smile, but didn't really pull it off. Tufts of blue and yellow flowers drooped low in small pots in the windowsill over the sink. Normally Mom would be aghast at such a sight after her years of counseling customers in the flower shop about how to brighten up their homes, but now she didn't even seem to notice.

Mark moved behind her to get the cereal bowls. "I got a message from the airline that my flight was canceled."

"Then you can stay?" Mom said, raising her eyes expectantly at the news.

Mark shook his head. "No, I'm going to drive. I have to get back, Mom."

A darkness settled back over her countenance. "Mark, your father just passed. I'm sure your work will understand."

"I know what happened, Mom," replied Mark, a little too forcefully. "I have a life too, you know. In New York. I don't live here anymore, even if my room is still there, and you really wish I did. Okay?"

"Hey, she's just trying to help you—" said Joe from the dining table.

Mom held her hand up. "Joseph, it's okay. He's right, he can take care of himself. He's not a child anymore. If he doesn't want to spend time with his family, that's fine."

Mark rolled his eyes. "Mom..."

"No, if your life in big New York City is so great, then just go back there. You certainly left fast enough last time. I know you don't like it here. I just..." She picked up the milk carton and placed it back into the refrigerator. "I just thought you might be a little more relaxed now." She paused at the sink, staring blankly past the flowers and into the yard.

"Mom..." Mark felt the pressure in his chest tightening, his eyes turning red. He breathed deeply, then walked over and put his arms around her. "I'm sorry."

"He loved you very much," Mom whispered.

Mark tried to think of words to express how he felt. God, he didn't even know how he felt about it anymore. He used to be able to talk to her, even when things were hard with Dad. Now he couldn't find the words. Maybe it had been too many years.

The doorbell rang, followed by the high-pitched voices and laughter of Joe's kids spilling into the house in a wave of energy. He let go of his mom and bit his tongue. He really couldn't deal with everyone else right now.

He walked to the back stairway, his momentary burst of emotion quickly hardening again.

"I've gotta go, Mom."

He quickly packed his things, said a few awkward apologies and goodbyes to Joe and Lauren and the kids, then, before Mom could object any more, hopped into the rental car he'd called with the guy from the company that prided itself on being able to pick you up. Several dozen forms later, he was back on the road, heading north.

It felt good to be in traffic, amidst the other nameless faces plodding along in random cars on the freeway. He'd felt suffocated by all the talking, the sympathies, the black. A few hours of fresh air on the road felt like it might do him good.

His mind whirred with jumbles of images of Dad from his childhood, as he tried to push away the arguments and confrontations, searching for good memories, times when he and his dad were smiling. As he rolled past Baltimore, past the tall smokestack with the city's name painted on it, the scenery seemed to float by like a fog. He saw the ballparks in the distance, remembering the dozen times they'd driven a few hours north to catch the Yankees playing the Orioles.

Eventually his thoughts landed there on a baseball diamond, the place where he'd spent hours as a kid playing catch, going to games. Dad and he, sometimes Joe, practicing out in the yard until the sun sank below the horizon and it grew too dark. Somehow that was the one place where his talents seemed to live up to Dad's expectations.

THE BALL SAILED from his hands, smacking into his father's worn leather glove. Sweat dripped from underneath Mark's cap, his shoulder beginning to ache, but his glove flew up quickly as Dad threw the ball back to him again, faster than he'd thrown it. They'd been at it for nearly an hour in the backyard. When he and Joe were younger, Dad had cleared several of the trees in order to create a wide-open grassy space that could serve adequately as either a football practice field or a makeshift baseball diamond. Mark's middle school didn't have a baseball team, but the travel team was holding tryouts the next Saturday morning, and Dad had determined that Mark was going to do all he could to make the cut.

"Get your shoulders square, hold your hands higher in the set," Dad ordered, sixty feet away.

Mark nodded silently, trying to concentrate on his body angle even as he tired. He knew he had to work at increasing his skill level like Dad said if he wanted to make the team, and he really did want to. Despite all Dad's lectures and pressure to be the best, Mark somehow still loved to play the game of baseball. He was good, not great, but every once in a while he felt like it came together and he glimpsed what it felt like to excel. It was knowledge that came not only from the scoreboard above the outfield wall, but also from that special nod, that glimmer in his father's eye when Mark's performance met his lofty standard.

"My arm's getting tired," Mark called finally, after the last throw.

"Ten more pitches."

"Dad..."

"Do you want to make the team, son?"

"Yes, but—"

"Do you think those other boys want to make the team?"

"Yeah."

"Well alright then, ten more pitches. Or should it be twenty?" He stood out of his catcher's stance, putting his hands on his hips. "I've got all day here, I'm not going anywhere. That's the attitude you've got to have if you're going to be a winner, son. Or maybe I should call Coach Nance and just tell him that you're not going to make it, that you're wussing out. I'm sure they could use another skirt on the cheerleading squad."

Mark rolled his eyes and waved at his dad with his glove. "Dad, alright, I'm doing it, okay?" He sighed, gripping the ball harder in his glove, deciding once again that it wasn't worth arguing about. He hated it when Dad got like that. There was no winning. The same scrappy, sometimes reckless determination had carried him through the streets back as a kid, the hell with anyone that stood in his way.

He threw the ball with extra kick, popping it into Dad's glove with more power than his last dozen.

"That's more like it." Dad whipped the ball back to him again and punched his catcher's mitt. "Nine more. Watch your shoulder."

Perfection. Every time. That was Dad's motto. Or, if not perfect, as damn near close to it as you could get.

"Boys, dinner's ready," Mom called from the back porch, flicking on the flood lights that cut through the dimming evening sky.

"Almost done," Dad answered.

"You know, if his arm falls off it's going to be pretty hard for him to pitch anymore."

Dad grunted without turning his head. "His arm's not going to fall off Cheryl, relax." He punched his glove once more.

"Tom, food's going to get cold."

"I said we'll be in in a minute when we're done!" Dad barked back, shooting an icy stare over his shoulder, enough to send Mom back inside without another word.

"Eight more."

Mark let out a breath and reared back again, blocking out the strain in his thirteen-year-old left shoulder that grew deeper with each throw. He wasn't going to cry about it. He was tougher than Dad gave him credit for.

MARK CONTINUED ALONG THE FREEWAY. He glanced at the clock—he was making good time. He hadn't really been paying attention, passing cars on the left, moving faster than he should have, the kind of careless driving that would land him a ticket. Sometimes a long trip went by quickly when you had someone to talk to, but it seemed to work even better when your mind was lost in a haze. His car descended across the long bridge that separated Delaware from New Jersey, following the interstate back towards Manhattan.

His mind was floating through time, images still flying through his head like cards in the Rolodex that he'd played with as a kid on Dad's desk at the office. Something kept pulling at the edges of his memories. Something he'd tried to block out for a while.

His eyes drifted toward the large green highway sign approaching on the right.

Beach Exits, 1 Mile.

Suddenly he knew what it was, the thing he wouldn't give his brain permission to visit. It was her. It had always been her. Quite unexpectedly, he felt the tears fall down his cheeks. A rush of emotion overcame him.

Before he knew what he was doing, he'd turned off the highway, following the sign for the beach towns, until he'd crossed into the tiny tree-lined streets of Harborwood.

CHAPTER FOUR

He'd seen her first in the line at Groves, which stretched two-dozen deep, inching along the railing of the boardwalk. The small building's aroma of fresh-baked doughnut batter was drawing drowsy vacationers from their beach rentals like a magnet. His dad said the place had to be making a killing as the most popular doughnut shop in the quiet Jersey shore town of Harborwood. A flock of obnoxious seagulls, all too wise to the habits of the human visitors, lurked at the edges of the line, anxious to dive-bomb a lazy hand with an exposed morsel. Bikers and joggers passed by in a steady flow, casting haughty glares at the sugar addicts lined up for their morning fix.

She was further up, halfway to the front of the line. Close enough for him to watch the edges of her hair sparkling in the morning sun like grains of sand from up near the dunes, but still far enough to remain unnoticed.

He knew her from school—they'd both just finished their freshman year—but hadn't ever talked to her. He thought she ran cross-country, or maybe played soccer. One or the other. She had that fresh look to her—athletic, but natural, with hair hanging loose past her shoulders, a powder-blue, "Class of '04," long-sleeved t-shirt, and running shorts that accentuated her legs, slender and tanned from a sun-drenched summer at the beach.

Mark's chest tightened. He'd been at the shore on his family's yearly two-week vacation for a dozen days, but hadn't seen her until now. He would have noticed. She was the kind of girl a fifteen-year-old boy wanted to know.

His dad usually made the morning doughnut runs, too impatient to wait for Mark or Joe to find their way from underneath the covers. He didn't believe in late mornings or sleeping in when things could be accomplished. But that morning Dad had left before dawn for a deep sea fishing trip with a client from his insurance business, so the schedule was thrown off.

All of which led Mark to be standing in line on the boardwalk, struggling to catch his breath, ten people behind Amy Holland.

He watched her place her order, his eyes leaving her legs just long enough to see her smile at the person behind the counter. He desperately wished he could be in front of that smile.

"The line's moving," a gruff voice barked behind him.

Mark jumped, realizing he'd been staring at Amy's shorts rather than noticing the people ahead of him inching forward. He stepped a few strides ahead, glancing back at the complainer, a burly, goateed guy in an Eagles shirt.

"Sorry." It was dangerous to get between someone and their morning doughnuts and coffee. He turned back to the front of the line just in time to see Amy move away from the counter, her hands filled with a box of warm doughnuts and a Styrofoam cup.

She was turning in his direction.

His mind raced for something to say. Would she even recognize him? They hadn't had a class together, unless you counted PE, and she'd always lined up for stretching on the opposite side of the gym floor, much to his dismay.

Before he could stress about it further, Amy stopped abruptly three feet away, bending down to the boardwalk. Mark tilted his head around a lady with big hair in front of him. What was she doing?

A sugar packet had fallen from Amy's hands and she was reaching for it, trying to pry it from the gap between two boards. She had unknowingly stopped in the middle of the incoming lane of traffic on the boardwalk. A fast-moving group of bikes was headed directly toward her, out of her view from behind.

Mark's legs began to move before he could even form the words to speak. "Watch out!"

He lunged forward and pulled Amy to the right. The lead bike narrowly missed them, except for a handlebar, which caught the corner of Amy's doughnut box, tearing it from her hands. Doughnuts flew in all directions, sending the seagulls into a frenzy of feathers amongst the crowd as they jockeyed for the treats. Coffee puddled on the wooden walkway, spilling between the cracks in the boards.

"Hey!" Amy shouted, surprised by the sudden shove. Then she screamed, raising her arm over her head as a squawking bird's wing mussed her hair.

She looked at Mark standing wide-eyed with a blank grin on his face. "Thanks a lot!" she shouted. "That was supposed to be breakfast."

"The bike," Mark stammered. "It was going to hit you." He pointed down the boardwalk, but the offending riders had already blended into the crowds and were conveniently out of sight.

Amy followed his hand, raising her eyebrows at the boardwalk. She frowned. "Uh, huh. Whatever." She bent to pick up the cup and empty doughnut box from her feet, ripped in half by the birds. She shook her head. "Just great."

"Here, let me buy you some more," Mark volunteered without thinking. "I'm still in line." He looked over at the Eagles shirt guy who was passively taking in the commotion. "Do you mind?"

The man hesitated, then with an annoyed expression and a grunt, gestured for Mark to get back into line.

"Thanks," said Mark, thinking it wouldn't kill the guy to wait a few more seconds to clog his arteries.

He turned back to Amy. "Seriously, let me buy you some more."

"Are you sure?" She still seemed a bit frazzled by the collision.

Mark nodded, trying to look confident, like he treated girls to early morning doughnuts all the time. He quickly calculated the dollars in his pocket. It should be just enough to replace a box. If worst came to worst, he'd come back later for some of his own.

When she looked at him again, a faint sense of recognition filled her face. "I know you, don't I?"

Mark nodded again with more enthusiasm than he probably should have. His mouth turned dry and he couldn't find a word to speak.

"Do you go to Cooper?" she asked.

"Yes," he squeaked at the mention of his high school. He closed his eyes and cleared his throat. This wasn't happening. He had a chance to talk to Amy, and he sounded like a mouse.

"Yes," he repeated, louder. "I think you were in my gym class last year. Mrs. Bradshaw, right?"

"Yeah, I was." She paused, causing his heart to beat a bit faster.

He was talking with her, if his awkward sentences counted as a conversation.

"Mark, that's your name, isn't it? Mark Parsons?"

"Yeah," he mumbled again, not so gracefully. It was terrible. Me. Mark. What was he, a caveman? He pinched his fingernail against his thumb and forced himself to get it together.

"I'm Amy," she continued, nodding.

"Yes. I mean, right, I know. I've seen you at school." He looked out at the ocean and took a deep breath, trying to start over. "What are you doing here? I mean, do you vacation here a lot?"

"We have a house here, right over on Fourth Street, a couple blocks back. We spend the whole summer. It's my favorite thing."

Mark made a mental note that he'd just learned Amy's favorite thing. He tried to think of a hundred different things that he could say were his favorite, but all he could picture right then was

Amy, and he couldn't tell her that. Not after only two minutes of conversation. She'd think he was a stalker or something.

The counter guy saved him as they reached the front of the line. "What'll ya have?"

Mark turned to Amy. "What kind did you order before?"

"Before you knocked them out of my hand?"

"I told you there was a bike!" Mark pleaded, a bead of sweat trickling down his forehead.

Amy flashed a smile. It was the first one he'd seen so close and directed at him. It was amazing. He tried to keep breathing.

"I'm just kidding."

Mark exhaled and attempted a smile back.

"We had half a dozen glazed and half a dozen cinnamon," Amy answered.

Mark turned back to the surfer dude behind the counter. "Six glazed and six cinnamon."

"Aren't you going to order any for yourself?" asked Amy.

"Oh, right..." Mark ran the numbers in his head again. A Pearl Jam song on the radio in the background mixed itself into the aroma of doughnuts in his mind, distracting him from his addition. He could only afford a few more. "And three more glazed. In a separate box, please."

The guy behind the counter, whose name tag said "Chip," took Mark's money with just a nod and barked out the order to several of his buddies working the equipment behind him. Amy slid to the side so the next person in line could step up to the counter and Mark followed suit.

Mark stared through the glass next to the counter, trying to think of what to say. "It's quite an operation they have back there." He motioned at the rows of round-shaped batter forms winding their way around a contraption of conveyor belts as they awaited their plunge into the deep fryer.

"And very healthy for you, too," added Amy.

"At least I'm only eating three."

"Hey, those are for my whole family!"

"Uh huh," laughed Mark, starting to feel more relaxed.

"Six glazed, six cinnamon!" Chip barked. He slid a brown box onto the counter.

"And another box of three glazed?" said Mark.

"Jimmy, where's the three more glazed?" Chip hollered behind him.

"They're in the other box!" came the reply, presumably from Jimmy.

Mark tilted his head at the news. "They were supposed to be in their own box."

Chip raised his eyebrows at Mark, but didn't move or yell anything back to Jimmy.

"Just forget it," said Amy, good-naturedly. "We can separate them."

Mark imagined what his father would say in that situation. Probably refuse to move until his order was perfect. That he was paying good money and wanted his order the way he asked for it. Mark was surprised but pleased to hear Amy's relaxed response.

Even so, Mark grabbed the box with a little extra force than necessary, just to make sure Chip knew he was annoyed. He felt the doughnuts shift in the box as he grabbed it, so he held them more carefully with the other hand. It wouldn't be good if he dumped them all on the ground again.

As he turned to walk away, Amy threw her hand across his chest. "Careful...let's look both ways." She flashed him another smile. God, it was addicting.

The coast was clear, and they moved across to the other side of the boardwalk, leaning against the railing. The sun was inching higher above the water, and the gentle song of the waves hitting the surf filled the air.

Amy grasped the top bar of the railing with both hands, stepping up onto the bottom rail with her toes raised up in her sandals. She closed her eyes and tilted her head toward the sun. "Isn't it great?"

"The boardwalk?"

"The sun, the sand, the waves, the salt in the air..." She paused, taking another deep breath, as if it was the first time she'd been to the ocean. "All of it."

Mark knew he loved coming to the beach, but somehow the way Amy said it made him suddenly appreciate it even more. Her voice was filled with a passion that was contagious. He wanted to say that this was his new favorite moment, standing with her here on the boardwalk. He wanted her to smile at him again.

But he just answered, "Yeah."

Amy hopped down as quickly as she'd climbed onto the railing. She turned to Mark and the brown box he was holding. "We have to eat one now while they're hot," she gushed, opening the box top in Mark's hands. "I assume you want a glazed?"

"Sure." The truth was Mark was planning to leave his for later to eat with Mom and Joe, but the prospect of standing on the boardwalk and eating one with Amy seemed like a much better idea.

"Mmm." Amy let out a slight moan as she slowly chewed on the warm, soft batter. She looked up at Mark between bites and nodded toward the street. "Do you have a house here?"

Mark struggled to swallow his bite so he could answer. "We rent a place for two weeks over between Atlantic and First every year."

"I can't believe we haven't seen each other before. We're here all summer too. It's the best part of the year. I'm training to be a lifeguard. My parents say I have to wait until I'm sixteen, which is in February, so I can do it next summer."

Mark nodded along as the information tumbled at him like a breaking ball on the baseball diamond. He was much more comfortable on the field with his glove than talking to a girl like Amy Holland. He wished he had a notebook so he could write down all these facts. He concentrated on committing them into his memory.

"Who are the other doughnuts for?" Amy asked, motioning to

the remaining two that she'd portioned off to the side of the box. "You're not going to eat all three?"

"No!" chuckled Mark. "They're for my mom and brother. They're back at the house." He glanced across the boardwalk in that direction and grimaced. "They're probably wondering what happened to me." He was glad his dad was off fishing, otherwise there'd probably be hell to pay for taking so long.

Mom and Joe could wait. Even if Dad had been there, Mark didn't care. Getting to talk with Amy was worth it. He gazed into her blue eyes, reflecting the color from her shirt, and felt his stomach flutter again.

Amy tilted her head and raised her eyebrows questioningly. "What?"

Mark felt his face flush and quickly cleared his mind.

"You looked like you realized you're gonna be in trouble," Amy continued.

"No, it's just usually my dad would be pissed, but he's off on a fishing trip with some work clients today, so it's not that urgent." He ran his fingers through his hair that was blown in the breeze. "He really loves his morning doughnuts at the beach. My dad can be a little..." He searched for the right word. "Intense."

Amy turned away from the railing. "That doesn't sound like much fun. The beach should be relaxing. Isn't that why you come?"

Mark shrugged his shoulders, looking down at the doughnut box. "I guess." He stared back toward the street, not knowing what to say. Dad was complicated. He was usually consumed by work, and Mark often felt more like a project to fix than anything else. Sometimes it seemed easier to breathe when he wasn't around.

"Sorry if I got you in trouble. I suppose you probably did save me from being run over." She pushed the hair out of her eyes and smiled. "Wait here." She ran across the boardwalk to the doughnut counter. Mark watched her say something to Chip for a moment, then take something in her hands. She turned back, pausing dramatically to look both ways before coming back to him on the other side of the boardwalk.

"A box for your trouble, sir," she said, handing him a small, empty brown box. She lifted out Mark's two remaining doughnuts and placed them in the smaller one. She paused, looking at him sideways for a moment, as if she was trying to decide something. "Turn around."

Mark did as he was told and felt her move something pointy against his back. "What are you doing?" It tickled and he instinctively wriggled his shoulders.

"Just hold still," Amy giggled. She finished what she was doing and stepped back in front of him, quickly closing the lid of his smaller box.

Mark looked at her quizzically.

Amy took the larger box from his hands and turned toward the street. "I'm up this way. Thanks for running into me, Mark Parsons!"

Before he knew it, she was walking away from him. A sinking feeling filled his stomach. His morning had gone in such an amazing direction; he didn't want it to end. "Okay...maybe I'll see you on the beach?"

She turned back toward him, tossing her head in the breeze and flashing another heart-melting smile. "I'll look for you!"

Mark exhaled hard, raising his left hand for a feeble wave while placing his right on the railing for balance. He watched her walk away like an angel in running shorts, the breeze blowing her hair, which looked golden in the morning sun.

He stared until she was out of sight. Then he opened the doughnut box. His chest tightened again as he saw writing scribbled on the lid. Amy's words. Written for him.

Thanks for the doughnuts!
Call me - 609-555-2723
Amy

CHAPTER FIVE

Mark assumed he walked home with the doughnuts, but he didn't remember it. He might have been in the middle of the road for all he knew; he was too busy replaying the encounter with Amy on the boardwalk. He stepped in the back door of the beach house rental and was immediately barraged by Joe.

"Where have you been? I'm waiting for my doughnuts, man!"

Mark handed the small box to his brother, a distant look still in his eyes.

"Two?" said Joe, opening the box. "That's it? Where's the rest of them?"

"It's all I had money for," answered Mark.

Mom walked into the kitchen, a towel on her head from the shower. "What happened to the money I gave you? Ten dollars buys more than two doughnuts, Mark."

"I, uh...." Mark tried to think of a reasonable explanation without saying too much. "I ran into somebody on the boardwalk."

"Ran into as in crashed, or ran into like met?" asked Mom.

"Um...kind of both."

Joe stared at Mark curiously, watching his facial expressions for a clue. "Something sounds fishy here."

Mark's face reddened as he tried to change the subject. "Anyway, the waves look great today. I think we should bring the boogie boards out to the deep spot."

"Uh huh," answered Joe, still staring at him. "That's nice." He paused, his eyebrows rising suspiciously. "Where's your doughnut? Don't tell me you didn't get one for yourself; I don't buy it."

"I ate it up there."

Joe's smile grew wider. "Who exactly did you run into, little brother?"

"What? Nobody, I told you. I mean, somebody, but it's nothing to worry about. I mean..." Mark sighed loudly and looked out the window. He was just digging himself a deeper hole.

"Mark, don't lie to your brother," added Mom.

"Spill it," said Joe.

Mark sighed again. "I may have run into someone from school up on the boardwalk."

Mom looked up from what she was preparing at the kitchen counter. "Did someone knock you down? Were you bullied?"

"Mom! No, it's nothing like that."

"Do you want me to kick their ass?" said Joe, pounding his fist into his open hand.

"Will you stop? No one bullied me. Geez! You guys need to relax. I ran into a girl."

Joe chuckled out loud, shaking his head. "Dude, you got beat up by a girl?"

Mark smacked his forehead with his hand. This was why he hated to tell his family anything. Thankfully Dad wasn't here. He'd have been even worse. As a natural born salesman, his dad thought everyone in the world should be able to charm the pants off anyone they meet. Dad couldn't understand why Mark often kept his thoughts to himself, especially about girls.

Mark turned to his brother. "No one beat me up, you idiot. I was talking to Amy Holland, okay? Happy now?"

Joe's face lit up. "Amy Holland? Dude, she's hot!"

"Joseph," Mom scolded.

"What? She is, Mom," replied Joe.

"Be respectful," said Mom. "Mark, is Amy here on vacation?"

Mark nodded. "She said they have a beach house and come here every summer."

Joe made a jaw dropping expression across the table. "I've never seen her here before, have you?"

"No, I was pretty surprised," admitted Mark. He described how he tried to save her from the biker and then bought her doughnuts.

"That sounds like a nice thing to do, honey," said Mom. "No wonder she likes you."

"I didn't say she likes me, Mom. Geez. I just talked to her, that's all."

"You should totally try to find her today on the beach," said Joe. "We still have three days left of vacation. You never know what could happen." He winked with a big cheesy smile. "She could be the one!"

"Shut up," said Mark, pushing his brother out of the way. He walked into his room, his mind far away. He did want to see her again, and she did give him her number, presumably to her beach house, but maybe she was just appreciative that he replaced her doughnuts. He thought back to the smile she gave him as she walked away down the boardwalk in the sunlight. His breath quickened again just thinking about it. That didn't seem like just a 'thanks for the doughnuts' kind of smile.

"Hello, Earth to Mark." Joe tapped on the doorframe from the hallway. "Are you already off in dreamland thinking about Amy?"

"What?" Mark blinked his eyes and looked up, feeling his cheeks redden again.

Joe laughed. "It's about time you start talking to girls. I'll admit I didn't think you'd start with someone like Amy Holland, but I guess you had a good teacher." He winked and turned into the hallway toward the bedrooms. "Hurry up and get your suit on so we can try to catch some waves, will you?"

Mark tried to shake his mind free of Amy and move on with his day. He changed out of his shorts and into his swimsuit. He stared into the mirror over the dresser, combing his sandy-blond hair back a few times, imagining Amy Holland standing next to him. He pulled on a t-shirt as he headed back to the kitchen, scanning the counter for the doughnut box. He needed to copy the number down for safekeeping, but the table and counter were wiped clean, no box in sight.

"Oh no," he muttered, bending down to look on the floor under the table, but everything was clear. His stomach turned upside down. "Mom," he yelled, "Where's the doughnut box that was here?"

"What?" Mom asked from the couch, looking up from her magazine.

Mark tried to breathe, his blood pressure elevating quickly. "The box with the doughnuts I brought home from the boardwalk. It was right here. It had writing on it. What happened to it?" He tried not to completely freak out, but he couldn't hide the panic in his voice.

"I threw it away, honey. Believe it or not, I am trying to clean up around here."

"What?!" He rushed to the garbage can under the sink only to see an empty white plastic bag. He turned to his mom. "Where is it?"

"Oh, that's right. Joe took the bag down to the garbage can on the street while you were changing. It's trash day, you know."

"Mom!" Mark bolted to the door and flew down the steps. This couldn't be happening.

He turned the corner just as his brother was pulling two garbage cans toward the house. Mark was out of breath when he reached him. He opened the tops of the tall garbage cans, peering below the lid, only to see them completely empty. "What happened to them?" he shrieked.

"You just missed it." Joe pointed up the street at a rumbling sound as the tail end of a blue garbage truck turned the corner onto Atlantic.

"No!" Mark screamed, collapsing onto the street corner. How could this happen?

"What's up?" asked Joe.

"Are you kidding me?" He stood up and stared at his brother, fire in his eyes. "Why did you throw that box out?"

"Dude, I didn't do anything. I just took out the garbage like Mom asked me to."

Mark felt on the verge of tears. Shell-shocked, he shook his head. How could he have been so stupid to leave the number on the box? Amy had given it to him. To *him*! What was the chance of that happening? It was like a gift from heaven and he messed it up. He knew it was his fault, but he slammed the lid down anyway, glaring at Joe as he stormed back up the steps.

"Hey, take it easy, little brother," Joe called after him. "I think this Amy thing has gotten you on edge."

Mark tried to think of something terrible to say, something that summed up the pit growing in his stomach, but he didn't. He just walked back inside to his room and collapsed on his bed.

His life was over. Utterly, completely, over.

CHAPTER SIX

The sun was going down as Mark stepped over the cracks in the crooked sidewalk along First Street. A steady flow of people funneled onto the boardwalk against a trickle of late beach goers who couldn't bring themselves to leave the surf, even after the lifeguards had surrendered their posts and gone home.

He climbed the wooden steps and set off toward the more populated end of the boardwalk where the vendors and rides were located, and where he'd spent the better part of two weeks each summer of his life. The light in the evening sky began to shift to pink and orange, gradually creating a cloud canvas for the sparkling lights of the Ferris wheel as it rotated above the rooftops up on Ninth.

He'd combed the beach all day with Joe, hoping to spy Amy soaking up the rays on the sand or splashing in the waves, but she was nowhere to be found. He tried to summon the image of the doughnut box top in his mind and recall the digits of her phone number. He even called twenty different variations of a phantom memory, but each of them was wrong, and he eventually gave up. It was pointless.

He kept alert for her as he passed Fourth Street, not that he thought she'd be standing on the corner waiting for him, but since it was where she said her family's house was. He was banking on seeing her near the entertainment pier, that's where everyone usually ended up. He'd spent many summer evenings out on the boardwalk with Joe or occasionally with a friend that came up with them on vacation, but never with a girl, and certainly not with anyone like Amy.

He'd imagined it plenty, walking amongst the hoards of people on a busy warm summer evenings. He pictured once again walking with her, hand in hand, gazing off into the surf. His heart was fluttering again. Just relax, he told himself. She'd practically invited him to ask her out. If only he hadn't lost her number.

The crowds were growing larger the farther Mark walked down the boardwalk. Each side street brought more and more people out into the flow. Families with little ones in strollers, older couples walking slowly, groups of kids laughing together and goofing off. He scanned the faces, desperate to see a smile he recognized. There were teenagers everywhere, laughing and happy to be out from under from their parents' watch, but no Amy.

He let out a deep breath and stopped next to a fast pitch stand that let people test their speed throwing a baseball on a radar gun. He'd left his summer league team a week early to go to the beach as usual. He was supposed to be throwing more on the side with Joe, but it was hard to find the space and time with the sand and water as distractions.

Workouts for fall ball resumed next week with the rest of the team, and he needed to be ready. He'd made the freshman team the past year and was hoping to break into the starting rotation on the JV squad next spring, maybe even varsity if he was lucky, but that was a long shot. Dad seemed to have made it his personal mission to push Mark to his limits and make him practice as often as possible.

He looked around the crowd one more time, but still didn't see Amy. The line at the pitching booth had dwindled, so he pulled a couple of dollars out of his wallet and paid for three balls to throw. He stretched his left arm across his chest, then again over his head, pulling on his elbow to ease the tightness. He placed two balls on the ground and gripped the third in his left hand, naturally feeling for the laces on his fingertips.

The guy manning the booth gave a nod, and Mark stepped up to the line, waving his pitching arm in a couple windmills to loosen up some more. The last thing coach Palmer would want to hear was that Mark had pulled something throwing on the boardwalk. Speed had never been Mark's thing, but he was curious to see how fast he could hit on the radar gun, even if he was throwing cold.

Mark wound up and threw the first ball in at about half strength just to be safe. *59* lit up on the screen in red LED letters. He grabbed the second ball, reared back, and put a little more oomph into it, finishing his follow through the way Coach had taught him, head forward toward the plate and left foot up in the air.

He glanced up at the screen. *73.* Not bad for not properly warming up. He looked at the booth attendant, but he didn't seem impressed.

"Easy there, fire baller," a voice called from behind him.

Mark spun around. Amy was leaning up against the wire fence of the basketball shoot-off next to the speed gun. He ran his fingers through his hair and stood up straight.

"Hey," he managed, trying to breathe. She was wearing a white t-shirt and cut off jean shorts. He tried hard to keep from staring at her legs, but he thought she still caught him looking.

"I was hoping you were going to call me," said Amy.

Mark leaned his head back and moaned. "Okay, here's the thing...my brother...he threw away the doughnut box before I could copy your number down."

"Uh huh."

"Seriously, I really wanted to call you."

"You did?"

"Oh my gosh, you have no idea. I was looking for you on the

beach today. And that's why I'm here on the boardwalk—I was hoping to find you."

Amy nodded over his shoulder. "Looks like you're just hanging out throwing baseballs to me. Maybe I shouldn't interrupt you."

Right then the ball guy looked over at Mark with an annoyed glance. "You've got one more ball, man. You gonna use it or what?"

Mark had forgotten all about the speed gun. "Oh, no, forget it. Here you go." He handed the guy the last ball.

"Wait a minute," interrupted Amy. "What was your last pitch speed?"

Mark looked back over his shoulder at the screen, but it was blank. He tried to recall what he'd thrown last.

"Seventy-three," said the guy next to him.

Mark raised his eyebrow like he was impressed.

"It's my job," the guy deadpanned.

Mark turned back to Amy, unsure where she was going with her question. "Seventy-three."

She moved next to him, taking the last ball from the guy's hand. "I tell you what. You have one more chance to make your pitch." She placed the ball in Mark's hand. "If I'm impressed, maybe I'll forgive you for not calling."

Mark swallowed hard and gripped the laces again in his hand. He thought she was talking about more than just pitching, but he found it hard to tell what direction girls were going sometimes. "So what does it take to impress you?" he asked, warily.

Amy wiped her hand across her forehead. "It's hot out here tonight, don't you think?"

"Yeah." Mark could feel the sweat forming on his own brow whenever he spoke to her.

Amy pointed to a sign further down the boardwalk by the ice cream vendor. A digital thermometer said the temperature was 80 degrees. Things had cooled from the middle of the day, the breeze coming off the water helping some, but it was definitely warm. "Let's see if you can beat the heat."

Mark's blood pressure was rising by the moment. A nervous, high-pitched chuckle came out of his mouth before he could stop it. He looked at her, trying to tell if she was serious. She smiled at him again, sending goose bumps down his arms.

"Okay, watch and learn," he said, sounding more confident than he felt as he stepped up to the line. He gave his left arm one more long stretch. He didn't think he'd ever thrown eighty before, but he wasn't sure. They didn't always have radar guns at practice.

It didn't matter. He had to now.

He took a long breath and exhaled, staring out at the catcher's target painted onto the green tarp at the end of the pitching booth. He tried to block out the noise of the boardwalk, push back the butterflies in his stomach, the anticipation of being with Amy, and see only the glove. He lifted his right leg, rearing back once more. He threw harder than he'd ever thrown before, driving forward with his leg for as much force as he could generate, the ball sailing from his fingers, smacking hard on the target. He stood frozen in his follow through, afraid to look up at the result.

Finally he did. Two red numbers flashed.

81.

Yes! He'd done it. Pretty amazing for him.

He spun around to see the expression on Amy's face, but she was gone. Where did she go?

"Well, are you coming or not, big shot?"

Mark followed the voice and saw Amy backpedaling along the boardwalk, two storefronts down, grinning ear to ear. He smiled back, then bolted toward her, nearly tripping over two little kids on the way. He rubbed his shoulder, feeling stupid for trying so hard, but glad that he did.

"So where are we going?" he asked, catching up to her.

She looked up at him with a sexy gaze. "Where do you want to go, Mark Parsons, fireball pitcher?"

CHAPTER SEVEN

Ice cream never tasted so good as it did sitting across the bench from Amy. "You missed some," Mark said, playfully wiping a drip off her chin with his finger. His skin faintly touched hers and his whole body tingled.

She chuckled, and then took another aggressive bite into the treat. Splinters of waffle cone scattered onto the boardwalk. "Whoops!" She laughed again and tried to speak with a mouthful. "I'm a very messy eater."

"I see that." Mark had never seen a girl tear into an ice cream cone so fast. He'd only taken a few bites of his vanilla cone. Not that he was about to hold it against her.

"What do you think that says about me?" She raised her eyebrows playfully as she dove in for another chomp.

Mark pressed his brain for a witty response. "You melt easily?" Oh brother, that was just stupid.

Amy rolled her eyes, then tugged at his arm. "Come on, we have to try something." She tilted her head up the boardwalk. "Do you like to fly?"

"Uh, sure. Do you?"

"Oh, it's the best. Let's go fly somewhere tonight."

"Okay. How about California? I've never been there." He didn't really know what she was talking about, but was trying to play along. At this point, he'd go anywhere she wanted him to do.

"I was thinking somewhere a little closer." She turned and pointed up in the sky behind them. He followed her arm to the lights of the Ferris wheel dancing above them against the night sky.

"Oh...sure, we can do that." The truth was, he really didn't like heights, but that was the last thing he could bring up now. If Amy wanted him to bungee jump with her, he'd do it. Well, maybe not bungee jump, but he could certainly do the Ferris wheel.

Amy tossed her hair back. "Come on." She stood and pulled his arm again toward the ticket booth for the rides.

He stepped up and bought two tickets for the Ferris wheel, glancing up at the bright lights twirling above him out of the corner of his eye.

The attendant lowered the bar over their legs and stepped back as the ride rocked unevenly. The car was large enough for three people across, but they sat near the middle, not quite touching. Mark grasped the bar, peering up at the other cars swinging high above them.

"Are you ready?" Amy's eyes were open wide with excitement.

He couldn't tell if the feeling in his chest was the excitement of sitting next to her, or if he was about to be ill. The two seemed similar sometimes. He prayed that he wouldn't get sick at the top and puke all over her. That would be even worse than saying something stupid.

Before he could finish his thought, the ride jerked forward with a start. Amy let out a short scream as she slid toward him in the car, her hip and shoulder pressing against him. His breath quickened and he held the bar so tightly, he thought his knuckles might be turning white. He turned to Amy, her face desperately close to his, the night breeze blowing loose strands of hair across her nose, her eyes closed like in a trance.

Mark's mind raced for what he should do next. The truth was, this was the closest he'd sat to a girl he liked before. He knew enough from talking with the guys at school and movies that she was probably expecting him to make a move. But what? He didn't want to make her mad or rush things, but it had been her idea to go on the Ferris wheel, and she didn't seem to mind him being so close.

As the carriage rose higher into the air, he looked at her hand lustfully as it rested on her knee, wondering if this was a good time to hold it. Just as he was about to move in, she pointed to the sky.

"Isn't it amazing?"

He stared out in the direction she was pointing. He'd been trying not to look down, but now he realized he could see everything from up there. The boardwalk, the beach, the ocean. It all stretched out in every direction.

"Wow." It was amazing. He tried to relax and take it all in and not be so consumed with Amy for a few moments. "Hey look, the doughnut shop."

"The scene of the crime," laughed Amy.

"What crime?"

"The one where you faked a bike crash just to hit on me." She lowered her face and smirked. Even with the breeze, her head was so close he could smell her hair. It smelled like apples.

Mark rolled his eyes. "Come on, you know there was a bike. I didn't even see you there until I got in line."

"Uh, huh. Likely story. I bet you say that to all the girls you pick up at the beach."

"Give me a break," said Mark. "I don't ever pick up girls on the beach." He looked down at the people walking below them as the Ferris wheel began its decline, then back at Amy with a sly smile. "Just on the boardwalk."

"What?" Amy opened her mouth in fake shock and poked him in the ribs with her elbow. "I knew it. All this mild-mannered, nice-guy routine is just an act." She shook her head with a smile.

"Yep," Mark continued. "I'm a real ladies' man. I'm surprised you haven't noticed me earlier at school."

"Apparently I'm behind the times," laughed Amy. "It's a good thing I've got you all to myself up here." She inched closer, slowly leaning her head on his shoulder.

Mark was sure his heart was going to explode as he tentatively reached over and took Amy's hand in his. He held his body as still as humanly possible, afraid that any small movement would end the moment.

When their car reached the bottom of its rotation, Mark no longer wanted the ride to end. He wondered what would happen if he refused to move, if he just sat there with Amy's head resting on his shoulder. They'd have to pry him away.

Thankfully, their car continued around, shooting higher and higher like a spaceship into the night. He felt the warmth of Amy's body next to his. He rested his chin on her head, breathing her intoxicating apple smell. He stared out into the sea stretched out in front of them like a vast painted canvas in the cool night air with glittering lights all around them. It was like a dream. Maybe it was. If so, he silently prayed that he would never wake up.

As if on cue, the ride jerked to a stop at the very top of its rotation. Mark instinctively released Amy's hand and grabbed onto the bar of the car as it rocked back and forth high in the air.

"Relax, it's just stopped for a second," laughed Amy. "Wow, you're not nervous or anything, are you?"

Mark exhaled and tried to play it cool. He searched for something smooth to say, but just grinned.

"Look, a cruise ship," shouted Amy.

"Where?"

"Right over there, way out in the sea." She pointed again out into the great expanse of blackness, the water nearly indistinguishable from the night sky.

Finally he saw a cluster of blinking lights moving left to right. "Oh...there. How do you know that's a cruise ship?"

"It's big. That's not a regular fishing ship, or even a sailboat.

They only have a few lights. That one's far out to sea. It must be huge."

Mark stared at the cluster of lights. He still couldn't make anything out, other than seeing the movement. "I wonder where it's going."

"It's heading south, to Florida or the Caribbean, I'd bet. It probably just left port from New York."

Mark imagined riding on the giant cruise ship, steaming toward Jamaica or some other exotic location. He could swim in one of those fancy infinity pools Mom talked about that seemed not to have an edge, with water flowing over the sides. He could picture Amy next to him in her swimsuit, but he pushed the image out of his mind before he got carried away. For once he was with the real thing.

"You seem to know a lot about boats," he said.

Amy nodded. "My dad likes the water. We rent a sailboat here every summer and take it out over on the bay side. It's fun. Do you like sailing?"

"I don't know, I've never been." He thought of his dad on the fishing charter earlier in the week. He and Joe had gone with Dad a couple years back, but Mark didn't like it. He hadn't expected all the rocking. Dad said the sea was particularly rough that day, told him to "man up" and catch some fish. Instead, Mark puked over the side twice and spent the rest of the trip lying on a bench inside the stuffy cabin. Dad didn't invite him fishing again after that.

"Sailing's a lot like this, but on the water," smiled Amy, looking around. "Fresh air, wind blowing on your face. It's great. You should come with us."

Mark felt his stomach turn again, thinking back to the fishing trip. "Maybe."

The ride slowed as they descended again toward the Earth. "That was fun," said Amy as the car rested in place and the attendant unlocked their safety bar. She gave Mark's hand one last squeeze.

"What now?" asked Mark as they stepped onto the boardwalk.

"Let's just walk." Amy slipped her arm through his and they moved away from the rides and began a slow stroll along the boardwalk.

Despite the swell of people all around them, it felt to Mark like they were the only ones on the boardwalk. Every sparkling store sign was just for them, announcing their arrival as they progressed along the path. It was so unlike all those other nights that Mark had walked over the same boards, past the same small shops and stands, wistfully watching other sets of lovers moving together through the night, their cares seemingly lost in the breeze.

But tonight, it was him. With her. Two bright lights, twinkling in the night like ships at sea, moving slowly south, toward a future that was at once uncertain, yet so exhilarating and bright.

CHAPTER EIGHT

As they walked, they chatted and laughed about little things that didn't really matter but somehow meant everything at the same time. Amy pointed out all her favorite shops she liked to stop in with her parents. Mark showed her the spot where he fell on the boardwalk and got a two-inch splinter of wood in his knee when he was four.

He wasn't sure if time was standing still or moving fast, but as they walked, the crowds seemed to thin. He hadn't told his parents what time he'd back to the beach house, but at that moment all he wanted to think about was Amy. He'd gladly deal with whatever consequence Dad might impose for being out late. They stopped in front of the big hotel where the storefronts ended and the boardwalk narrowed.

"Come on, I want to show you something," called Amy, walking down the steps to the sand.

Mark glanced around to make sure no one noticed. The beach was officially off-limits after dark, but he knew sometimes people walked around anyway. Once he'd gone down with Joe with a flashlight to look for sand crabs until a beach patrol cop chased them down and kicked them off. But sneaking down with Joe wasn't anything like going with Amy.

She paused at the bottom of the steps, slipping off her sandals and stashing them underneath the last stair. She took his hand and led him down the path that cut through the dunes alongside a spindly wood and wire fence, the salt air blowing slightly harder as they moved closer to the water. The lights and sounds of the boardwalk receded behind them, replaced by the gentle echo of the surf.

"Where are we going?" asked Mark. He stared down the beach, only partially cloaked in darkness due to the boardwalk lights behind them.

"Over here. Relax, nobody's down here."

Mark thought back to what she had said on the Ferris wheel. "I'll bet you take all the boys down here, don't you?"

"You know it. A different guy every night, actually." She nudged into him with her shoulder. "Wait, is this Wednesday? There might be someone else waiting for me. Do you mind?"

"I do, yes," said Mark. He laughed, but it was something that had crossed his mind. Maybe she did have someone else. While he'd never had a girlfriend before, Amy was different. He knew she'd gone out with other guys at Cooper. Most guys thought she was hot, although he also knew enough to realize that everything he heard in the locker room wasn't true. Most of it was just the other guys trying to talk themselves up and look cool. But still, he didn't really know that much about her. He thought she'd gone out with Jeff Stabler last year, but wasn't sure how serious it was. Either way, tonight she was here with him and not Jeff, and that was a good thing.

They approached a dark shadow in the sand between them and the ocean. As they drew closer, Mark realized it was the lifeguard stand, turned over on its back.

"Help me lift it," said Amy, bending down to the sand.

Mark placed his hands over the edge of the wood where red block letters said Watch Your Children and lifted. The chair was heavy, but the two of them set it upright without much trouble. Amy scrambled up the short ladder and out of sight. Mark looked around again to make sure no one was watching, took a breath, and followed her onto the white wooden bench.

She squeezed up against him, gripping his arm tight with both hands. "I love looking into the sea at night. It seems so endless, so full of possibilities."

"Yeah," replied Mark, trying to follow along. "It's hard to imagine that it just keeps going, all the way to Europe...or Africa...or whatever." He couldn't remember what was directly across the Atlantic from New Jersey.

Amy chuckled. "Wouldn't it be nice to just float away?"

"From the beach, or life in general?"

"I don't know, just get away from the way things are." She sighed.

"You don't like how things are?"

"No, I just mean sometimes life seems kind of stuck. This is actually one of the best nights I have had in a long time."

He looked down at her and took a deep breath. "I kind of know what you mean. There are times I can't stand my family. Well, mostly my dad, I guess."

She was staring at him, but not in a judgmental way, like Dad did. More like she was genuinely interested in what he was saying. "You don't get along with him?"

Mark laughed nervously. "You could say that. He's really different than me, always working, acting like that's the most important thing."

"It's not."

"I know, right? But it sure seems like it sometimes at my house. About the only thing we have in common is baseball. He loves to see me play, which is good. But sometimes it's all we can agree on."

"Do you like playing baseball, or is it just for your dad?"

"No, I do, actually, I really love it. It's the one thing I feel like I'm good at. Pitching. My coach thinks I have a lot of raw talent.

Dad says I could get a college scholarship one day if I keep working hard, especially since I'm a lefty."

"Is that important?"

"Kinda. There's a lot more right handed pitchers out there, just like there are mostly right-handed people in general, so it's a good weapon to be left-handed."

"But why?" asked Amy.

"Because left-handed pitchers are better at getting out left-handed batters. The ball comes in at them closer and at a harder angle to pick up."

Amy turned her head like she was confused. "But aren't there fewer left-handed hitters, too, since there are fewer left-handed people? That doesn't make any sense."

"Well..." Mark tried to think about how to explain things more clearly. Everyone knew being a southpaw was important in baseball, and what he'd said was the right answer, but she was turning it all around on him somehow.

"That's okay," said Amy, laughing. "I'll take your word for it. It's good to be a left-handed pitcher. What about hitting? Are you good at that?"

"Hitting I'm okay at, but pitching is really my best thing. There's nothing like being out there on the mound with the game in your hands."

Amy nestled closer and squeezed his arm. "Nothing?"

Mark laughed. Up until now, he'd swear pitching was his favorite. The past two days felt like everything was changing. "You're definitely giving it some strong competition."

"I hope so," said Amy. "All the other boys usually like it here."

Mark frowned, but tried to chuckle. He tried not to be paranoid.

"I'm just joking," she giggled. "Seriously, you need to relax."

"Right..." He tried to think of something else to talk about. "So what do you want to float away from?"

Amy turned quiet, the only sound coming from the pounding

of the surf. For a moment, he wondered if she'd heard him. He was about to ask her again, when she spoke.

"My mom is sick. Which makes things kinda hard at my house sometimes."

Now he felt bad for asking her the question at all. "Oh, I'm sorry. I didn't mean to—"

"No, it's okay. I don't mind talking about it. She's awesome. We're really close. My dad too. She was diagnosed with leukemia two years ago. She goes up and down. Sometimes she seems completely healthy, other times she has to have treatments and is stuck in bed for days at a time. It just drains the energy from her."

"That's terrible."

"Yeah. I hate seeing her like that. She used to be so vibrant, the kind of person that would do anything and always trying to have fun."

"She sounds like someone else I know," said Mark.

"I know. That's what Dad says, that we're cut from the same cloth. Which I think makes it hard for him too, when she has her bad spells. It's really hard to see her beaten down by the disease. But we're powering through. Mom loves the ocean, which is why we still spend the summers here. She was an art teacher before she got sick, and she still loves to paint scenes of the ocean and the beach and the boardwalk. I think it helps her cope."

Mark realized he didn't know as much about Amy as he thought he did. He hadn't had anyone in his family with a serious illness. His arguments with his dad probably seemed pretty trivial. "Do you have any brothers and sisters?"

"Nope, it's just the three of us. Some kids say they wouldn't want to be the only kid in their family, but I don't mind it. We're like three friends who love to spend time together. It's fun."

"Wow, that's cool. Joe is three years older than me. He's going to start college at William and Mary in the fall. We get along pretty well, but he's not around as much now as he used to be, even less come this fall. He's a lot more like my dad, I think, so they don't argue as much. Dad seems to be grooming him to work at his insurance company."

"What about you?"

"Me?" Mark paused for a moment, deciding how he wanted to answer. "Nah. I'm going to be a pro baseball player." He laughed, mostly because he'd never said it out loud. It was something he often told himself privately, but most people would think it was a joke since he wasn't even on varsity.

"I bet you will," Amy answered, hopping up from the bench and jumping down into the sand. "Turn around."

"What?"

"Just turn around," she giggled. "Look up at the boardwalk."

"Okay..." he said, staring up at the lights. "I don't see anything up there..." He turned back toward Amy just in time to see her leap into the dark waves with a scream.

"What are you doing?" he called, jumping off the lifeguard stand in surprise. He looked down at his feet and saw her shorts and t-shirt lying in the sand. "Oh my god," he said out loud.

"Don't just stand there," Amy yelled over the sound of the waves. "Come in!"

CHAPTER NINE

Mark's heart was pounding through his chest again. He was almost frozen there on the beach, filled with a mix of excitement and fear as Amy swam half-naked in the ocean in front of him.

"Come on, Parsons," he said to himself in the night. "It's now or never." He stripped off his shirt and shorts, and then dashed down to the water in his underwear. He let out his own wild scream as he charged into the surf, the cold water hitting him like a smack in the face.

Mark scanned the dark water, his mind suddenly remembering the scenes from *Jaws* and how sharks fed in close to shore at night when the fish were running. He tried to make Amy out through reflections from the boardwalk, when a flash of white zipped past him below the surface, brushing his leg.

Before he could stress about sharks any longer, Amy surfaced next to him, eyes aglow like tiny fires in the moonlight, her face a wistful smile.

"Isn't it great?" She took both his hands in hers as they bounced up and down in the small waves.

Mark just nodded, speechless, watching her swim next to him

like a mermaid in the ocean. He was dumbstruck, staring at her breasts glistening in the water, the darkness of her nipples pushing through her wet see-through bra. Despite the coldness of the water, he felt himself wanting her. Locker room talk and conversations with Joe flooded his mind, and he wondered where this night was going.

It was difficult to catch his breath in the chill of the water, but he started to get used to it. They began to chase each other in the waves, playfully splashing and swimming back and forth as he gradually relaxed.

"Watch out!" Amy yelled, then disappeared beneath the water. Mark turned just as a giant wave crashed into him, sending him reeling backwards and off of his feet. For a moment it seemed like he was in a washing machine, twirling into unnatural positions in the swell. His back smacked against the sand on the bottom of the ocean as the wave released him, and he quickly pushed himself back up to the surface, gasping for breath.

He wiped the water from his eyes and searched the dark water for Amy's bobbing head. He didn't see her; maybe she'd been knocked down by that wave too.

"Gotcha!" Amy pulled up behind him, wrapping her arms around his neck. She rested her hands over his chest. It felt good.

"Hey, thanks for the advance warning on that wave."

"That came out of nowhere, I swear," she laughed.

"Just like the bikes, I guess." He leaned his head back next to her face, her breath warm on his cheek. "Even?"

"Even." She squeezed him tighter, her breasts pressed against his back. He didn't ever want to leave that spot, wrapped up in Amy like a blanket. And for a long time, forever it almost seemed, they rode the tide, silently bobbing up and down in the water, locked in a warm embrace.

Mark thought again of the ship out at sea, and how he was now part of that sea, floating effortlessly with a mermaid on his back. He felt alive. Perfect. And when he remembered back to that moment years later, he wondered if perhaps it really was.

"Hold on," he whispered, taking in a deep breath and pushing off the sandy bottom with his toes. He dove down beneath the waves, Amy's arms still clinging to his shoulders. He kicked out toward the sea for several beats before shooting back up to the surface.

"Where are you going?" she giggled, pulling herself around to face him.

"Anywhere you want," he answered, tingling all over as she wrapped her legs around his waist. He stared at the water dripping from her dark lips, only inches from his. Every part of his being longed to kiss her, but he laughed instead. He thought she wanted him to kiss her too, but didn't really know how to make the first move. His only real kiss had been to Jessica Marks after the eighth grade spring dance. It was awkward, though, and neither of them seemed to care for it much. But Amy was different.

"What?" Amy asked, parting her lips into a smile that crushed him. "Are you cold?"

"No," he answered, leaning forward, unable to resist any longer. He pressed his lips gently against hers, pushing past his doubt. She tasted wet and salty like the sea. He pulled back slowly, staring into her eyes so deeply it felt like they penetrated all the way through him.

Was this love? Could it even happen so fast? It was just a kiss, but he'd certainly never felt this way before.

He squeezed her body tight, kissing her again, harder. Her mouth opened, her tongue dancing against his lips. He followed her lead, struggling to keep his breath.

Another large wave swelled up, lifting them off their feet. They were carried up and then down, pushed in toward the shore. They released their lovers' grip, standing to catch their balance in the wave.

Amy shrieked playfully and paddled to shore. She scurried up the beach to the lifeguard stand and pulled on her clothes over top of her wet underwear. Mark did the same, while not-so-casually eyeing Amy's glistening curves in the light. He knew she saw him watching, but she didn't seem to mind.

"What time is it?" Amy asked.

"I don't know. Probably late."

"I should get back. Daddy always waits up when he knows I'm out."

Mark wrapped his arms around her again, pressing her lightly against the wood of the lifeguard stand. He didn't want to leave the beach. The moonlight must be magic. It was the only way to explain what had happened.

"I guess you're right," he mumbled while bending his head down and kissing her again. God, he didn't ever want to stop kissing her.

"He's going to want to meet you, you know," said Amy.

"Who?"

"My dad. And my mom. But Daddy's always protective about who I'm dating."

"Oh, all those guys..." Mark had that feeling creep back into his mind, but then also realized she'd said they were dating. Is that was this was?

"Stop. You know what I mean." She wiped her wet hair from her eyes. "Don't worry, you'll like him." She looked out at the ocean and turned back to him. "Hey, we could go sailing. That would be fun, no?"

Mark thought back to the fishing trip with his dad. But that wasn't sailing. Surely it would be better than that. Plus, Amy would be there, and that would make things better automatically.

"Sure, let's do it," he said.

They walked back up the edge of the dune where they'd stowed their sandals and then up the boardwalk. Mark insisted on walking her to her house, turning onto Fourth Street and then up two blocks. Amy stopped under a tree on the sidewalk as they neared her house.

"He's probably waiting up in the front room. I'll go in the side door. It's quieter; maybe he fell asleep."

Mark nodded. He didn't really want to meet her dad for the first time late at night with his daughter dripping wet.

"I had a great time." She rose up on her tiptoes and kissed him softly.

Mark wanted to say that he wanted to see her every day for the rest of his life. That he never wanted to let go of her hand. That he wanted to see her smile every second he breathed.

"Me too," he replied instead, in perhaps the world's biggest understatement.

Amy stepped backward, away from him, arm outstretched, but still holding his hand. "I'll talk to you tomorrow."

"Let's go sailing," he answered, with more certainty than he felt.

"You'll like it," said Amy.

"Sure. What time?"

"You will, trust me. Three o'clock."

"Okay."

"Goodnight, Mark Parsons. I'm glad you ran into me."

"There was a bike."

"I know," she said, grinning.

"Goodnight."

"Bye." She let go of Mark's hand and he watched her slowly back away, glowing beneath the streetlights like an angelic firefly on Fourth Street. He watched her until she turned and waved at her house, then ducked down a side path.

Mark forced himself to breathe, pulling at the wet shirt stuck to his skin. He turned in the direction of his beach rental, floating along the empty streets like he was still in the water with Amy on his back, bobbing up and down in the waves. He stared up at sky, emblazoned with a billion stars, sucked in the night air, and smiled.

CHAPTER TEN

It was late when Mark awoke the next morning, his head still spinning. He'd dreamt about Amy all night, and as he opened his eyes, he wasn't completely certain if it had been real. It was like a dream he'd had many times before, but when he dropped his feet over the side of the bed and onto his still-wet clothes clumped on the floor, he knew that this time, it was actually true.

He sat for a moment, smiling at the memory of swimming with her in the ocean. Maybe he had never stopped smiling. It was possible. He looked forward to seeing her again today, but it would be hard to match last night.

It had been midnight by the time he found his way home the night before. Joe was still up, watching a late night *SportsCenter* to see the highlights of the West Coast ballgames. Mark hadn't felt like talking, so despite Joe's protests, he'd slipped down the hall to his bedroom and surprisingly fallen fast asleep.

He threw on some dry clothes and wandered out to the kitchen. Mom was cleaning up the dishes, and Dad was at the breakfast table, finishing off reading the business section in the newspaper.

"There's the sleepy head," said Mom.

"Where the hell were you last night?" Dad barked. "We almost sent Joe out looking for you."

Joe sat up from reading a magazine on the couch. "How was your date, lover boy?"

"Sorry, I lost track of time with Amy on the boardwalk, that's all," Mark answered, pulling a cereal box from the cupboard.

"From the look of the soaking wet clothes you were wearing, it looked like you might have fallen off the boardwalk, little brother."

For once, Mark didn't even mind Joe's ribbing. This time it was for something that actually had happened.

"So who is this girl that you've run into?" Dad asked. "Someone from school?"

"It's Amy Holland," Joe answered for him.

Mark shot him a dirty look. He didn't mind telling Dad, but he didn't need Joe to talk for him.

"Amy Holland, huh?" Dad repeated. "Is she in your grade?"

"Yeah," said Mark.

"Holland..." repeated Dad. "Is that Chuck Holland's daughter? The history teacher? Think I ran into him when I tried to sell the community college a group policy a few years back."

"I'm not sure," replied Mark. Of course he would think he knew Amy's dad. Dad's favorite saying was that he never forgot a face or a name, and that it was one of the keys to being successful in the insurance business. Mark didn't know what her dad's job was. Amy had mentioned her mom used to be an art teacher before she got sick, but not her dad.

"Gotta be," Dad continued. "Seemed like one of those bleeding heart liberals. Probably from out west in Berkley or someplace." He placed his paper down on the table and stood to look down at the street below the porch. "So, this Amy...is she a looker?"

A looker? Who even says that? "Uh huh," answered Mark. The

less information he gave them the better. He just wanted to get out of the house and find Amy on the beach anyway.

"She's really cute," elaborated Joe. "She was one of those freshman girls that all the junior guys were noticing. She has a really nice a—"

"Joseph!" scolded Mom again. "I told you to be respectful. How'd you like it if someone said that about me?"

"Mom! Eww!" Mark and Joe howled in unison.

Joe moaned. "Why do you have to even say that?"

Dad walked over to their mom and hugged her. "Well it would be true. You do have a nice ass."

She slapped him on the arm, wriggling free from his grasp. "Tom, at least try to set a good example for the boys, will you? We're trying to turn them into respectable men."

"Oh, don't worry," said Joe. "Mark's becoming a man alright, based on how he looked last night."

"Will you shut up," said Mark, slurping down the last bit of milk from his cereal and dumping the dish in the sink. "You're all crazy." He stepped to the porch door, and then remembered Amy's invitation. He turned and faced his parents. "Oh, and Amy wants me to go sailing with her family today on their boat. Is that okay?"

"Is she going to help you raise the mast?" laughed Joe.

Mark just glared at him.

"They have their own boat, do they?" asked Dad. "Maybe they do need a policy after all. Boat coverage is one of the most overlooked coverages around. Did you know that 73 percent of people—"

"Tom, please, they don't care," interrupted Mom. "What time, honey?"

"Huh?" responded Mark. He was already picturing himself sailing into the sunset next to Amy in his mind.

"What time did they invite you to go sailing?"

"Oh..." Mark racked his brain for when Amy said to meet. "Three o'clock, I think. Most of the marinas are over on the bayside, so I should probably get to her house earlier. Okay?"

"I suppose that sounds nice. You're sure her parents will be there?"

"Yes, Mom. Her dad is the one driving the boat. They'll definitely be there."

"You don't drive a boat, son," corrected Dad. "You can steer it, till it, navigate it, but you don't drive a sailboat."

"Whatever. So I can go?" Mark was getting exhausted by this conversation. He didn't know why he even asked for permission for stuff like this. He was almost sixteen and should be able to do what he wanted.

Mom glanced at his dad, as if to get his sign off on the idea.

"We're leaving for home tomorrow, and you need to pack up all your things. I don't want to be stuck loading the car by myself while you carry on with your new girlfriend. I've got to be home by two for a conference call."

"Geez, Dad, it's just a boat ride, what's the problem? I'll pack up when I get back."

"Damn straight you will. Have you even gotten any throwing in? Camp opens next week, you know, and you need to be ready. Your competition for a starting spot on varsity isn't sitting on the beach with their girlfriend, you can bet on that. You haven't worked all this time just to piss it away on a week of fun, have you?"

"I'll get my throwing in, Dad, relax."

Dad's fist slammed down on the counter, the anger seeming to pull him up out of his seat. Mark reflexively tensed at the sound.

"Don't tell me to relax. I'm just looking out for you, son. You've got a golden opportunity in front of you. If I had half the talent you have in your left arm, I wouldn't be selling insurance, that's for damn sure."

"I'll throw with him later, Dad," said Joe, moving closer to the table, coming to Mark's rescue. He could usually diffuse the tension when he was around. For some reason, Dad always believed it when Joe said it. Not so much with Mark. It was going to be very different at the house when he left for college in the fall.

"Let the boy go sailing, dear. Baseball isn't going anywhere," said Mom.

"Not going anywhere?" Dad said, starting to wind up again. "Time is slipping—"

Mom folded her arms on the other side of the counter and gave Dad a look that said she'd just about run out of patience with him, so he stopped. Dad listened to her, too, most of the time. She knew when to keep her distance during those times when he really raged, when the old Tommy from the streets bubbled up too close to the surface.

Dad gave Mark one more hard stare, gradually exhaling, lightening the color of red on his face, then gestured with his hand out toward the ocean. "Fine. Just behave yourself. Listen to her father, unless he starts spouting off some left-wing political crap, and please don't get the girl pregnant."

"Dad!"

"Tom!" hollered Mom. "That's enough."

Joe burst out laughing. "Oh, boy, now we're talking." He patted Mark on the back as he walked by. "Always remember these family memories, bro. They're precious times."

Mark walked onto the porch, his cheeks flushed. Dad was such a jackass. He sat in a deck chair and stared off in the direction of the ocean.

He thought about what Dad said about leaving tomorrow. It was too soon. He'd only just met Amy. He didn't want to leave. You never knew what would happen when they both settled back into their regular lives. Would she still be interested in him when they were back at school? Maybe he was just a short summer fling. Maybe Jeff Stabler was waiting for her. He was a junior after all, and a captain on the soccer team. How could Mark compete with that?

He thought about fall baseball workouts starting next week. Dad was right, he hadn't been throwing enough. Not at all, actually, since he'd met Amy. Other than the fast pitch on the boardwalk, and that was stupid, as he nearly threw his arm out. Coach wouldn't be happy.

He had to try harder. There wasn't any excuse for not keeping up with his training. Dad was right about that, too. He'd worked too hard to let it slip away. But life suddenly seemed different with Amy in the picture. Maybe it was the summer, or the sun and the sand, but she was clouding his brain like nothing ever had before. Not that he minded.

As he sat on the porch, the warm morning sea breeze blowing through his hair, it felt like he was right on the edge of something. It reminded him of the beginning of the baseball season, the whole year spread out ahead of him filled with exciting possibility, but also uncertainty.

He wondered what was going to happen next. He certainly wouldn't have predicted this week would turn out the way it had. All he was sure of, what he suddenly felt consuming every fiber of his being, was he wanted to be next to Amy Holland every second of every day.

CHAPTER ELEVEN

The sun was still high in the sky as Amy craned her neck around the porch post to see up the street. She wasn't nervous for Mark to meet her parents, just excited. She still found it hard to believe he and his family could have been coming to Harborwood all these summers and she didn't know about it.

Even though the small town was a popular family destination, it was fairly unusual for two families from Virginia to regularly visit the Jersey shore instead of going to the Outer Banks, Virginia Beach, or even farther south like Myrtle Beach in South Carolina. She recognized him from school, she'd seen him in the halls, but Cooper was huge and there were a lot of kids in her grade that she didn't know. He was a little shy, but in a cute kind of way, and she'd always had a thing for guys that played sports.

The truth was, she could have passed him a hundred times and probably not even noticed. Freshman year of high school had been a bit of a whirlwind: going to a new school, figuring out where to fit in, not to mention Mom's illness. It was a lot to take in, which is probably how she had so quickly fallen into Jeff Stabler's arms. But that was definitely over. He'd grown much more interested in himself than her, or maybe it had always been that way and she just hadn't realized. She privately suspected he'd gotten a little too friendly with Maggie Welch a few times under the bleachers after soccer practice too.

Yes, Jeff was definitely over.

She didn't know if she believed in fate, but there was something special when Mark bumped into her on the boardwalk. She couldn't get him out of her mind. She'd always considered herself a free spirit. Daddy said she got that from Mom, but somehow it felt so easy to be herself the few times she'd been with Mark. Maybe that's why she'd stripped down and swum in the ocean like that. It had been a wild thing to do, even for her, but somehow she felt safe with him. It was so cute how he'd seemed flustered, and it was magical floating together in the waves, holding onto his back. It wasn't hard to tell that Mark had liked it too.

Their beach house was on the second floor, which gave her a good view of the street and some advance warning before he got there. Most of the houses in town were split first floor and second floor, with either different owners, or the same owner that rented each floor out separately. When she spied him bouncing up the sidewalk nearly a block away, she shot back inside and tried not to squeal as she told her parents he was coming. She sat down and attempted to look calm when his footsteps came up the stairs and he knocked on the screen door to the covered porch.

She hurried to the door, wearing a red bikini top and her favorite cutoff jean shorts, her hair pulled back into a ponytail for a change since they were going to be on the boat. She wondered how she'd feel when she saw him again. Was it just a passing moment on the beach the night before where she'd let her spontaneity get the best of her?

But then she saw him standing at the door, wearing long blue board shorts and a grey baseball t-shirt, his hair slightly tousled—like he'd tried to make it look nice but it had been taken by the breeze on the walk over—and grinning wide when he saw her approach the door. When he looked at her, she felt her heart grow warm. She smiled a bit sheepishly, almost embarrassed to let him see how she felt. It had only been a few hours since they'd been together, but her toes were still tingling.

"You made it!" she exclaimed, pushing her private thoughts aside.

"Three o'clock," Mark answered.

"Ready to sail?"

"Absolutely."

A commotion sounded behind the door, and a flash of fur shot between Amy's legs, nearly knocking her down.

"Mandy!" she shouted, as the large yellow dog leaped up on Mark's chest, its front paws nearly reaching his chin.

"Whoa," said Mark, trying to keep his balance. "Hi there...Mandy. Good girl."

"It's a boy, actually," laughed Amy, reaching over to grab the dog's collar and pull it back to the ground.

"Isn't that a girl's name?"

"Normally. Mom named him after Mandy Patinkin."

"Who?"

"The actor. He's one of her favorites."

"Oh," said Mark, sitting on a porch chair. He petted the dog's ears as it nuzzled his head between his knees. Amy hadn't thought about whether or not Mark liked dogs, but she hoped he did. They'd always had one growing up and Mandy was a big part of the family.

"Friendly, huh?" said Mark.

"Very. Do you have any pets?"

Mark shook his head. "No. I'd like one, but my dad says they're too much work."

"Hmm. That's true, but they're worth it." She squatted next to Mandy, rubbing his back with long hard strokes. "Yes it is." She talked in a silly baby voice. "You're a very, very, good boy, aren't you?" Patting the dog on the rump, she stood up. "Come inside, I'll introduce you to my parents."

"Okay." Mark followed her through the doorway and into the

living room which connected to the kitchen just like most of the other beach houses in town.

Amy turned and spoke in a low voice. "Mom's not feeling great, so I don't think she's going to come on the sail, but I want her to meet you."

"Oh, well I don't want to bother her if she's sick," said Mark, stopping in the hall.

"No, it's okay, she's reading. She's just not up to spending all afternoon out in the sun on the water." Amy moved down the hallway and nodded her head. "Come on, it's fine."

At the last minute, she wondered whether it was too much for Mark to meet her sick mom so soon, but she continued to the door anyway. She sensed he could handle it, and she really wanted Mom to meet him.

She opened the door to the bedroom that doubled as a small study. Bookshelves lined two walls behind a couple of reading chairs. Mom was sitting on one of the chairs with a yellow pillow behind her head, paging through a book.

"Mom, this is Mark."

Mark stepped forward and extended his hand. "Hello, it's nice to meet you."

"Hi, Mark. It's so fun with y'all vacationing here at the same time as we are. Amy says you're in the same class at Cooper?"

"Not the same class, but grade. Yes, ma'am," answered Mark. "We've come here for a couple weeks every year for as long as I can remember. We love it."

"It's wonderful, isn't it?" Mom said, gazing peacefully at the sunshine pouring through the open window next to her chair. "Fills your soul with light. That's what I always say. There's something about the sea air and the sunshine."

Mark nodded.

"Well, who's ready for an ocean sail?" Her dad's voice came from the doorway behind them. Everybody always said he looked perfect for his job as a college professor, with his tall frame and slightly receding dark blond hair. His face, with his round-rimmed glasses and a short beard, seemed to be locked in a constant warm smile.

"Daddy, this is Mark."

Mark shook his hand. "Hi, Mr. Holland."

Amy thought Mark looked a little nervous. She wondered if she'd scared him by saying her dad would be up the night before when she came home wet from the ocean. He was up waiting for her, but luckily she'd snuck into her room and dried off before he knocked on her door to check.

"Very nice to meet you, Mark. And please, call me Chuck." He put an arm around Amy's shoulders. "You've made quite an impression on my little girl the past few days. She's been talking about you nonstop."

"Daddy!" said Amy, turning to gawk at him. She felt her cheeks turn red, but tried to hide it. She *had* been talking about Mark a lot, but still she didn't want him to know that.

Not yet.

"Thanks for inviting me on your boat," replied Mark.

"Happy to have you," Dad answered. "It looks like a beautiful afternoon. I checked the weather, and there should be a good wind blowing and only light clouds. A great evening for sailing."

"It's perfect," said Amy. She smiled and wrapped her arm inside Mark's.

"Rachel, are you sure you don't want to come, sweetheart? I can put the awning up to keep the rays off your face." Dad reached over and adjusted the pillow behind Mom's head.

"I think I'm just going to stay here and rest. You guys enjoy yourself, though." She looked in Mark's direction and smiled. "Take care of them out there, Mark. They're precious to me, both of them. It's very nice to have met you."

"Okay," Mark replied. "I'll do my best. It's nice to meet you, too. I hope you feel better."

Amy started to grow antsy. The sea was calling to her. "Let's go!" she exclaimed, tugging Mark's arm toward the doorway. "I can feel the wind on my face already."

CHAPTER TWELVE

While Mark helped her dad haul a large cooler out of the house, Amy grabbed a bag and put the dog on a leash.

"She's coming on the boat?" Mark asked.

"*He's* coming on the boat," said Amy.

"Oh, right. I just didn't know dogs could go on boats."

"Sure they can," answered Amy. "Mandy's a great swimmer." She bent over and rustled the dog's ears again. "Aren't you boy?"

Everyone piled into Dad's Jeep, and they drove ten minutes over to the marina on the bay side of Harborwood. Rows and rows of boats in all shapes and sizes lined the docks next to the parking lot. There were fishing boats and medium-sized yachts with two-story decks that she'd always eyed enviously, wondering what it would be like to voyage on one across the ocean.

Dad led them down a dock to the left with mostly sailboats, stopping next to their rental, which was one of the smaller-sized boats. "This is it," Dad proclaimed. "Nothing fancy, but she gets the job done." He stepped over a thin metal railing onto the back section of the boat. "Let me get her opened up and then you all can board." He pointed up to a flagpole on the end of the dock with a dozen multicolored flags flapping gently. "Looks like there's a decent wind."

"That's a good thing, I guess, right?" asked Mark.

Amy chucked. "Considering it's a sailboat, yes. No wind means we don't move, which can get pretty boring and wavy when you're on the ocean." She looked at him sideways, remembering his story about fishing with his dad. "You're not going to get seasick, are you?"

"Hopefully not," Mark replied. Mandy barked, resting his front paws on the edge of the boat. "Looks like he's ready to go."

"He loves it on the water," said Amy. "It's like sticking his head out the car window. He loves the breeze on his face."

"Alright, everyone ready to board?" Dad asked, emerging from a small cabin in the middle of the boat. It wasn't very big, but Daddy rented it, or one just like it, for the whole summer. They took it out on the water once or twice a week when the evenings were clear and cooler. There was a small cabin with three rectangular-shaped windows on the side. It had a couch, a table, a foldaway stove, and a toilet with a blue liquid like an airplane, and it smelled gross. Amy refused to use it unless it was an extreme emergency. There was also a bed in the bow that, technically, you could sleep in. Dad had slept overnight there once a couple years ago, but she had no desire to try.

After Dad opened a latch in the railing, Amy hopped onto the boat, followed by Mandy, who barked excitedly on the leash. Mark stepped on carefully behind them, carrying the cooler. She watched him catch his balance as the floating dock shifted under his weight, and he almost fell overboard. She giggled as he set the cooler down on the floor, quickly sitting on a bench along the stern.

"You really haven't been on a lot of boats before, have you?" she teased.

"I'll be fine. Just getting used to it." It looked like he was trying to be tough, but she could tell he was a little unsure.

Dad came back to where they were sitting. "Everyone all set?"

They nodded.

"Okay, then, let's head out. Amy, do you want to untie the lines and push us off?"

"Aye, aye, captain," she replied, jumping out of her seat and stepping back over the railing to the dock. She bent down and untied several ropes from metal cleats on the dock and tossed them onto the boat. Dad pulled the start cord and revved the small motor on the back of the boat.

"I thought it was a sailboat," asked Mark.

"We have to motor out from the marina first," Dad answered. "Then we'll shut it off and raise the sails. You can help if you like." He looked up to the bow. "All set, Amy, shove us off!"

She walked up the dock to the front of the boat and leaned into the bow. Dad simultaneously powered the motor in reverse, and the sailboat slowly drifted backward and out of the dock slip. She walked alongside for a moment, guiding the boat so it didn't smack into the wooden dock, then gracefully stepped on board just like she'd done dozen of times.

Once on the boat, she leaned over the side and pulled up several rubber cylinders.

"What are those?" asked Mark.

"They're bumpers, so the boat doesn't run up against the wood when it's docked." She walked back to the stern where Mark was sitting. "Pretty cool, huh?"

He nodded. "You seem to really know what you're doing."

"Daddy taught me. It's fun."

Dad looked over at them and smiled. "Amy's a top-notch first mate, Mark. She's loved the water ever since she was a baby."

Mandy barked approvingly, his fur blowing in the wind.

Amy laughed. "Yes, you're a good first mate too, boy."

They motored slowly past the rows of docks in the marina, into an open part of the harbor, beneath a huge bridge, and then further into the open ocean.

AMY WATCHED Mark from across the stern seats. He seemed to be enjoying himself. Daddy was demonstrating some of the finer points of sailing—how to steer with the tiller which moved the rudder, which ropes trimmed the sails, when to watch for the boom swinging across the deck when they came about—all the things that seemed very natural to her, but were a new experience for him.

"It's kind of fun," he said, smiling over at her. He seemed more relaxed as they headed in a steady course parallel to the shore.

"I know. I told you it would be."

"It's not like a fishing boat. There's not as much rocking."

Dad smiled. "That's because we're moving. A fishing boat often sits in one spot, so you feel the tide much more. I've always found this to be more relaxing."

Mark nodded. "My dad likes the thrill of the hunt in fishing, I think."

"Yep," said Dad. "Some folks like that more. Personally, I like to feel the wind in my hair, see the water rush past without a motor roaring. Nothing but the wind and the water."

"And us," added Amy.

Dad smiled. "Yes, and us."

She turned to Mark. "Come up to the bow. You have to see how it feels to be up front." She turned to Dad. "Is that okay?"

He nodded. "Just hold onto something and bring a float cushion. It gets bumpy sometimes out here on the open water. I don't want anyone going overboard."

She nodded, grabbing two square, yellow seat pads that were also flotation devices, and took Mark's hand, leading him along the side to the front of the boat. There were railings along the side for them to hang onto, so she wasn't worried. She'd done it lots of times before.

Mark squeezed her hand tighter as they reached the bow.

She smiled back at him, his face filled with uncertainty. Somehow his following her despite his concern seemed romantic. "It's fun, relax."

She crouched down in front of the mast, sitting with her back supported against the front edge of the cabin and the float cushion like a lounge chair. She patted the spot next to her, and Mark sat down slowly. She snuggled under his shoulder so he could hold her with his arm, then closed her eyes, listening to the sound of the water rushing by them, a slight spray misting their faces.

"Wow," said Mark. "This is awesome."

She opened her eyes only to see that he was staring at her. "You're supposed to be looking at the water, silly, not me. Isn't it beautiful?"

"Yes," he replied, not taking his eyes off her. He squeezed her tighter, then looked cautiously behind them.

Amy raised her chin up and kissed him. "Don't worry," she whispered. "He doesn't mind. He likes you."

"Uh, huh," said Mark, kissing her back. "Right up until the minute he turns the boat real fast and hits me with that metal thing on the sail..."

"The boom," said Amy.

"Right. And *boom*, I tumble into the ocean, never to be seen again."

Amy laughed. "That's only happened once."

Mark smirked, tickling her ribs with his finger. "Knock it off."

She wiggled in his grasp and laughed loudly.

"How's it going up there?" Dad called from the stern.

Amy waved her hand up high in a peace offering. "We're good, Daddy. Keep sailing."

"See, I told you," whispered Mark.

Amy rolled her eyes. "As long as you don't plan on having sex up here or anything, I think we're fine. Daddy's pretty relaxed."

Mark's cheeks blushed, and she laughed again. It was so cute how he got embarrassed about things. The only two other guys she'd dated had turned out to be jerks. They weren't cautious, they never got embarrassed, they only wanted to push the envelope as far as they could, mostly it seemed, to see if she'd let them in her pants, which she hadn't, much to their dismay.

She had described most of what happened to Mom, who was always a good listener and never judgmental. Mom told her she was too good for such guys. She said Amy needed someone who respected and valued her for who she was, not just someone to fool around with. That all sounded right to Amy, so she dumped them.

But Mark—he seemed different. In a good way. Somehow she could feel it.

"I like your dad," Mark said, interrupting her thoughts.

"You do? I'm glad. Me too, he's great."

"He's much more relaxed than mine."

She nodded. From everything Mark had said, his dad seemed to be an uptight workaholic that pushed him too hard. She could almost see the pain in Mark's eyes whenever he talked about him.

"You're lucky," said Mark.

She nodded again, then rested her head on Mark's shoulder, not knowing what else to say.

"Who's ready for crabs?" Dad called from the stern after they'd rode the breeze for close to an hour.

"Crabs?" asked Mark. "Are we going fishing from here?"

Amy smiled. "No, dinner. We brought soft-shelled crabs in the cooler. It's fun, we can just drop the pieces overboard when we're done."

"Just don't go swimming afterward," warned Dad. "It might draw sharks."

Mark laughed nervously, his eyes open wide.

"You *do* like crab, don't you?" asked Amy.

"Well," Mark answered slowly.

"Oh, no!" She should have asked him. She just figured that if his family came to the beach every year, they must like seafood. And crabs were the best kind.

She turned toward Dad. "Well, I guess we might have something else—"

Mark pushed her gently on the shoulder and smirked. "I'm just joking. I love crab. It's cool, I just didn't know you could eat them on a boat."

Amy rolled her eyes. "Maybe there still is time for Daddy to knock you overboard to test out his theory about the sharks."

CHAPTER THIRTEEN

It was nearly dark as they pulled back into the slip at the marina. They all helped unload the boat, and then Dad drove them back to the beach house. Amy rested her head on Mark's shoulder in the back seat until they turned onto Fourth Street.

"Well, it was nice to meet you, Mark," Dad said, shaking Mark's hand when they got out. "I hoped you enjoyed the sail. You looked good out there. You might be a seaman yet."

Mark grinned. "It was awesome. Thanks for having me."

Amy looked out at the darkened sky toward the boardwalk. "We're going to go on a walk, Daddy. Okay? It won't be long."

Dad raised his eyebrows. "Uh huh." He looked over at Mark. "Take good care of my Little Bear, okay, son?"

"Dad!" Amy exclaimed.

He laughed, holding his hand up apologetically. "I mean my daughter. She doesn't like it when I call her that in public. Sometimes she still seems like my little girl. But you hear what I'm saying, don't you, Mark?"

"Yes, sir," Mark answered, squirming a bit.

Amy covered her eyes. "Daddy, please." She tugged on Mark's arm. "Come on, let's go."

Mark stopped, pointing toward the Jeep. "Here, let me help you bring the cooler up to the house."

Dad waved them off. "Nah, Mandy and I've got it, you two go for your walk. Just watch out for that last step, there's an ocean over there you know." He paused, grinning. "You might get wet." He shot her a knowing glance.

Amy blushed this time and tugged Mark's arm. "Come on. Bye, Daddy."

They strolled up to the boardwalk, her arm wrapped under his. It felt like they were in an old movie, with the glow of the streetlights over the boardwalk, the sound of the surf pounding on the beach just barely audible over the hum of the crowd and the shops.

"So, Little Bear?" asked Mark, grinning.

Amy groaned. "I wish he hadn't said that in front of you. When I was little, my favorite stuffed animal was Winnie the Pooh. I used to take it everywhere. When I got a little older, I started hating it when he called me 'Pooh Bear' so I made him shorten it to just 'Bear.' Normally I don't mind it too much, but it's usually not in front of anyone."

Mark chuckled. "It's cute. It's nice that he loves you like that."

"Yeah," she replied. "I can't really complain."

"I have to leave tomorrow, you know," said Mark.

She closed her eyes and tugged herself closer to him with her arm. "I know." He'd told her earlier. She wasn't leaving for another week, but he had to get back sooner for baseball practice. He seemed to be pretty serious about it, and as much as she wanted him to stay, she wanted him to be happy and do his best for his team.

She wished she'd met him earlier in the summer, but she realized he'd only been there for two weeks. She tried to think of what it would be like spending the whole summer with him, wondered where things would have led, but she pushed it out of her mind as pointless.

"But we'll see each other at school, right?" he asked.

"Sure."

"Sure, as in good, or sure as in, unfortunately?"

She stopped walking and looked up at him. "Sure, as in, I sure can't wait to see you all year in school." She tried to think of how to say what she was feeling without revealing too much of her heart. "It's just kind of weird."

Mark's face turned down. "Weird?"

"No, that's not what I mean. I feel like I just met you here, in this fantasy world at the beach. But the weird part, the *good* weird part, is that in real life we actually live in the same town, go to the same school. We might even have classes together. It's hard to imagine we'll have the chance to be together so much."

Mark nodded. "It'll be nice, though, right? I mean, I guess if you don't want to see each other, we could take it slow..."

She reached up and kissed him. Hard this time, pulling her body tight against his. She could feel his warmth and it made her feel on fire. She hadn't been with a boy like that before, she'd never wanted to, but suddenly she wondered where this would lead. She'd messed around a little with Jeff, but not all the way. In that moment, she was surprised to find herself wondering what it could be like and wanting Mark to be the one.

"I'll miss you," she said softly.

"It's just a week."

"But you'll be busy with baseball, I'll have swimming club, we'll have homework."

"You can come watch me pitch," he volunteered. She sensed it was as much a question as a suggestion.

She smiled. "Mark Parsons, fireball pitcher. I guess I could work that into my schedule."

They started walking again, in silence now, as if they'd used up all their words and anything else would ruin the moment. The fact of the matter was she didn't know what it would be like dating him at school. Her friends would be shocked. Most of them still thought she would get back together with Jeff. Mark was going to hit them out of left field.

They reached the end of the boardwalk, then turned onto the side streets until they came back to Fourth and her beach house. Was it really just yesterday that he was kissing her sopping wet under the street lamp? It seemed like weeks. Months, maybe. Was this what it felt like when you were in love?

As he kissed her goodbye, she stared up into his eyes and winked. "See you at school, Mark Parsons."

"See you," he said, drifting slowly away from her, like the tide was pulling him out to sea. And she knew, deep in her heart, that he was the one, and her life would never be the same.

CHAPTER FOURTEEN

The past flooded back as Mark slowly cruised the streets of Harborwood. It had been years since he'd been there. Everything was different, yet strangely familiar. He rolled to a stop at a red light and lowered the windows. The sea breeze filled his nostrils, an unmistakable combination of air and salt water. He recognized some of the buildings, the names of the streets, saw the place where Joe had liked to pick up sandwiches in the morning for lunch on the beach.

The summer was in full swing and the streets were busy. Families loaded down with chairs and umbrellas trekked back to their rentals or cars, teenagers and a few grisly lifers rode old bikes with wide handlebars and banana seats, weaving between the sidewalk and parked cars on the street, a couple with surf boards draped behind them.

This was how he'd spent so many summer weeks growing up. Tanned, crusts of sand stuck to his body, carelessly spending his days living under the sun and the surf. So different from his apartment now in the city. Pavement, glass buildings, faces as hardened as the sidewalks. As if the lives that marched in a fast, steady beat along the city streets were wearing body armor, tough exoskeletons from the elements. It was the polar opposite of the beach, where everyone seemed open, clothes peeled off, at one with the sun and the waves.

He turned right onto Atlantic, maneuvering between a couple of kids on bikes holding surf boards and doing their best West Coast imitation even though they were stuck in New Jersey—not unlike what he and Joe had done. The Ferris wheel peeked out from above several buildings on the boardwalk. Before his mind could drift too far back too fast, his stomach rumbled in distraction, convincing him to pull into a rare open on-street parking space and grab a bite.

He strolled a couple of blocks up to the ocean, drifting in a general direction without really knowing where he was headed. He paused when he reached the boardwalk, staring at the surf coming and going against the golden sand. God it was beautiful. He suddenly felt like he'd missed something, like any summer without at least a taste of the ocean and all that came with it was not quite complete, like it could recharge your soul and point you in the right direction.

The sun still hung in the sky, but it was after five as he stared over the water. The beach was starting to thin out. A few stragglers still lay in their chairs, dragged closer to the waves to let their feet get touched by the receding tide. A group of teenagers played soccer up higher on the beach. A dad with two dancing little girls worked to stretch their kite string into the sky, although it kept nose-diving back into the sand. He watched the waves break and retreat from the land, just like it had done for years, centuries, millennia maybe. Knowing it was all still here was comforting somehow, a constant amidst everything else that had changed in his life.

A kid passed with a yellow pizza slice, reminding Mark's stomach that he hadn't eaten. He turned back to see Nick and Normans right behind him, home of the best pizza on the board-walk, hands down. The smell of the warm dough called to him.

He paid for a couple of slices and a soda, then started walking, absorbing the sights and sounds of the boardwalk. The old-fashioned streetlamps lined the wooden boards, ready to light up the walkway like a ball field. Seagulls circled overhead, biding their time for a snack.

He turned at the fishing pier, walking all the way to the end where it stretched out over the water. A handful of old men were positioned with their fishing rods, watching time pass by with the waves like they'd probably done most of their lives. Occasionally one would reel in his line to check the bait, then bravely cast back out into the depths.

Memories of Dad flooded back, even the sickening fishing trip he'd hated. For all his faults, Mark had to give Dad credit for leading the family to the beach and making it a tradition. It was some of his greatest memories from his childhood.

For a moment, he didn't feel any anger toward Dad, only loss.

CHAPTER FIFTEEN

Mark stared at the grizzled faces of the men fishing. They seemed to resemble the weathered pier they were standing on: the old pylons held up the boards, resisting year after year of wind and the waves, but were still affected by the salt and the spray. Beach life, ocean life, it got in your blood. He knew that clearly from just the two short weeks over the summers.

There were moments when the ocean drew you in like a magnet. Like a drug. It made you never want to leave, made you feel like that was where you needed to be, like where you *had* to be. He figured it was one of the reasons so many families made annual pilgrimages to the ocean for vacation. Maybe it was the same in the mountains, but he wasn't sure. There was something amazing about being so near to nature, to the elements, maybe to God.

One of the old men got a tug on his rod and stood to reel in, the others on the pier glancing in his direction at the momentary excitement. Eventually, the end of the line appeared, a wide fat flounder wiggling on the hook. Mark remembered some of the names of the fish from the nauseating deep-sea trip. It was funny how some things stick in your mind. A sly grin formed in the corner of the old man's mouth as he unhooked the fish and placed it in a cooler at his feet. It seemed simple enough. In theory, Mark could see how Dad had enjoyed fishing so much, but for him it just never caught on.

"Something nice about finding a fish on the end of your line, isn't it," a voice said calmly behind him.

Mark jumped out of his thoughts and turned his head. His eyes opened wide in surprised recognition at the man standing next to him.

"Mr. Holland?"

"Hello, Mark. I thought that was you. And you know it's Chuck. How are you, son?" He reached out and shook Mark's hand.

Mark's mind raced. "I'm okay," he stammered. "What are you doing here?"

"Me?" Mr. Holland grinned, looking out into the ocean. "I live here now. Year-round. Moved to Harborwood two years ago after Rachel passed." His face turned down slightly, but just for a moment, as if he'd grown distant enough not to feel the pain as intensely as it once had been. "Amy's mom," he clarified.

Mark felt a pinch in his chest hearing Amy's name out loud. Or was it about her mom dying. Maybe both. "I'm so sorry," he managed to say.

"Thanks. It was her time. I think you knew her in about the middle of everything. Some good days, some bad. After Amy graduated high school, it got mostly bad until the end."

Mark's mind turned back to the funeral, of everyone in black. He saw his dad again on the fishing boat, reeling in the marlin. It must have showed on his face.

"What's wrong, son?"

Mark suddenly realized he was crying. His face flushed. He felt angry for showing so much emotion. Certainly not to a guy like Mr. Holland, whom he hadn't seen in years, but he couldn't help it.

"My, uh..." He tried to find the words, but he hadn't had any practice saying it. Maybe there was no good way to do it. "My dad just died last week too."

"Aw, Mark..." Mr. Holland rested a hand on his shoulder. "I'm real sorry to hear that."

Mark brushed his arm to his nose and nodded. "We just had the funeral yesterday in Virginia. I'm heading back home." He looked over at the man who had once felt like a father to him. He remembered the long talks they used to have at Amy's house in high school. They'd grown close in a short amount of time, as Mark found her dad much easier to talk with than his own.

"I can't believe I'm talking to you." This was crazy.

Mr. Holland smiled. "What are you doing in Harborwood? Do you live nearby?"

Mark shook his head. "No, well, I mean New York, so not too far, I guess. I was supposed to fly home, but the flights were all messed up, so I decided to drive. Needed some time to think. I was on the highway..." He tried to think of how to explain why he was there, but honestly he didn't really know himself. "For some reason I just turned off and ended up here. It's weird."

Mr. Holland leaned up against the railing, staring farther out to the sea. "There's something comforting about this place. It's full of people, but yet at the same time peaceful." He turned back to face Mark. "It's been a long time, Mark." His eyes looked kind in the evening light. "What are you up to these days?"

Mark's stomach turned. Another question he didn't know how to answer. He forced a chuckle, tried to smile. "Well...not exactly what I'd hoped I'd be doing." He looked back over at the old men. They seemed to know exactly what they were doing. Just fishing, and that seemed to be enough.

Mr. Holland chuckled. "It happens. Don't beat yourself up."

"I don't know how life became so complicated," said Mark.

Mr. Holland nodded his head. They were quiet for a full couple of minutes before the older man pointed out to the sea. "You see that fishing boat out there?"

Mark narrowed his eyes to see over the top of the waves.

"Two o'clock off the end of the pier."

He caught a glimpse of a boat moving across the ocean. "Yeah, I think so."

"There's something about fishing, about being out on the waves, putting in your line. You don't always know what you're going to pull up. Sometimes you can do everything right and still end up with nothing. Other times, some dumbass could drop his line over the side with no technique or skill and get lucky with the big one." He paused, looking back to the ocean.

Mark nodded. He thought he followed what Mr. Holland was saying, and he didn't think he was talking about just fishing.

Mr. Holland looked back over at Mark. "You get to be my age, it hits you a little harder, patterns like that in life. You go through something like you just did, losing your father, or a wife, and your feelings are more raw." He placed a hand back on Mark's shoulder. "It's not just about how many fish you catch, Mark. Sometimes it's important to just stay in the boat, keeping your line in the water. You follow me?"

Mark nodded, feeling another tear slip down his cheek. He wished he could have had these kind of quiet talks with his dad. No pretense or posturing, just an honest heart to heart about something besides selling insurance or throwing a baseball. He remembered the first time he went out on the sailboat with Amy the summer they met. He could sense right away how her family had something deeper than he was used to at his house, something warmly comforting and secure.

"You should come by and see Amy."

Mark jerked his head up in surprise. "Here?" The last he'd heard, Amy was married and living on the west coast. San Diego, he thought it was, or Santa Barbara. Jack Collins had told him a few years ago.

Mr. Holland seemed to read the surprise on Mark's face and smiled. "Yep. She's living here too now, believe it or not. Moved back east a year ago this November. To be with me, I think, but also to be around something familiar now that her mom was gone too."

Mark tried to process this new information. He'd been shocked to run into Mr. Holland on the boardwalk, but certainly never imagined that Amy lived there. He didn't really believe in fate or coincidences, but what were the chances? He tried to think of the right way to phrase the question pounding in his head.

"Did her husband move back here too?"

"Nah, that didn't last, I'm afraid." Mr. Holland answered. "Not that I minded so much. I never was too keen on Dylan. Wasn't right for her. I told her that from the beginning, but she didn't want to hear it. Amy did what she wanted." He looked over at Mark. "I'm sure you remember that."

It was Mark's turn to chuckle. Yes, he certainly remembered. Amy was a force of nature, usually in a good way. But she didn't fit into a lot of molds. She wasn't afraid to go against the grain. "Yeah," was all he answered, grinning.

"She got that from her mother, you know," Mr. Holland said, still staring out at the waves. "A wild spirit, just like Rachel...but that's part of what made them both so beautiful."

"Yeah..." Mark answered again, beginning to squirm, unsure of where this was going. He suddenly felt uncomfortable, knowing Amy was living right there in Harborwood. He glanced around casually. Maybe she was on the boardwalk with her dad.

Mr. Holland laughed. "Don't worry, she's not going to sneak up on you, son. She's down at the clinic until closing tonight."

"Clinic?"

"She opened her own veterinary hospital over on Seventh Street when she moved back. Used money from the divorce settlement. Probably the best thing that came out of that marriage, taking half of a surgeon's assets. He's very good at what he does, from what I hear."

"Oh yeah?" said Mark. He vaguely remembered hearing she'd married a doctor.

"That's right. A boob man."

Mark raised his eyebrows.

Mr. Holland chuckled. "Dylan's a plastic surgeon. Made a fortune on silicone implants."

Mark coughed. "Huh."

"Only problem was he couldn't seem to stay away from his patients."

"Oh," replied Mark. "I can't see Amy standing for that very long."

"Put up with it longer than I imagined she would have, to be honest with you. But it hurt her, Mark. She lost a little of that sparkle from her eyes." He pursed his lips like he was fighting back anger. "But she's getting better." He took a step from the railing. "I think it might do her good to see you."

Mark tried not to show it on his face, but he grimaced anyway. His heart was racing. It was too much right now for him to take in. Not this week. He wanted to run, but searched for what to say without sounding rude.

"I'm sorry," Mr. Holland said, shaking his head, letting him off the hook before Mark could answer. "I don't know what's wrong with me. You have enough going on right now with you father passing and all. I guess I'm just as susceptible to get caught up in nostalgia as anybody else. I have fond memories of those years you were around, you know that, don't you, Mark? I always considered you like a son. I've never seen my daughter happier."

Mark smiled weakly. He didn't know what to say. "It's okay. I just don't think I'm up to it right now. I've got to be getting home."

Mr. Holland extended his hand again. Mark shook it, then without really knowing why, pulled the old friend in for an embrace. He didn't let go for a little while, or maybe it was Mr. Holland that didn't let go. But for a moment it felt good to just be hugged. Eventually he pulled back.

"You take care, Mark." Mr. Holland bent down to pick up his fishing rod. "Maybe we'll run into you again sometime."

"Thanks."

"You're always welcome. Look me up next time you're in town. We'll go for a sail. I'm in the same house on Fourth Street we used to rent. You remember where it is?"

Mark nodded, his mind flush with images of standing on the corner, sopping wet, with Amy that night they first kissed.

"I remember."

CHAPTER SIXTEEN

Training for fall ball normally had a relaxed air to it, at least it had Mark's previous year at Cooper. It was kind of like the grapefruit league in Florida for the major leaguers in spring training. A gradual integration back into the flow of the baseball season, slowly stretching out the arms, bringing bat speed back into place.

But this year something was different. Maybe it was the heat wave sweeping through the region, turning Virginia into a late August sauna, or maybe it was Coach Palmer taking over the team from Coach Jenning, who'd finally retired after being at the helm for nineteen years. While they'd never won states, Cooper had played in several sectional title games. Coach Palmer wasn't what you'd call a sentimental man, he seemed to be more of a football coach mentality than anything else, but he knew the players and generally seemed to have everyone's best intentions at heart.

On Friday, the end of the first full week of camp, Mark was in the second batting group around the cage, then spent twenty minutes in the far bullpen getting his throwing in. Adam Tresselmeyer, Tressy to his teammates and just about everyone else, was wearing the catching equipment. Coach Palmer was standing behind the plate, separated from Tressy by the protective mesh draped over the tunnel like an oversized mosquito net.

Mark felt the fluid motion as he released the ball and the solid pop into the leather of Tressy's glove. It felt good, and he wondered if it was just his imagination, or if he was throwing harder than he had in the spring. He thought back to the boardwalk, how he'd hit eighty on the gun and whether that was a hormone-induced fluke or a growing trend.

His dad and Curt Parker, the team trainer, had been telling him for a while that everyone grew and strengthened at varying intervals, and if he kept working at it and focused on the strength program as he should, good things would happen. Mark thought he noticed a glimmer of a grin emerging from under the brim of Coach's cap, and felt a surge of energy flow through his body as he hurled the next one in a smidge harder, prompting a grunt from Coach.

"Okay, hit the showers, boys, nice work," Coach barked, closing his notebook and stepping around the net toward the artificial mound Mark had been throwing from. Mark pulled up the net and walked over next to him.

"Looking good, Parsons," said Coach. "Looking real nice." He turned to the backstop. "Whacha think, Tressy?"

The catcher nodded, tucking his mask under this arm. "Wait till you see the curve he's been dropping, Coach. I think we might have a winner here."

Coach looked up and chuckled. "Is that so?"

Mark shrugged his shoulders and nodded. "Working on it."

"Well maybe if we can get some of that fire in the game situations, we might be able to use you this year, Parsons." He turned off toward the main field and called in the rest of the team to the showers.

Tressy elbowed Mark in the ribs. "Looks like we might have some fire moving in *our* direction right now. Check it out." He nodded toward the edge of the field. Mark looked up and saw

Amy standing against the fence post, her arm raised in a faint wave. Mark felt his heart flutter and a low burn fill his heart.

Tressy raised his eyebrows and looked up at Mark incredulously. "You gotta be shitting me. Get out of here, Parsons. No way."

Mark grinned and tried to look confident. "Watch and learn, Tressy," he said, veering off toward Amy, eating her up with his stare as he grew closer.

"Hey Mark, you're going the wrong way," another player's voice jeered at him playfully from the field behind him. He sensed a buzz among his teammates watching him and felt a part of him well up with pride and expectation.

"Hi, stranger," Amy said as he walked closer.

"Hey."

"I figured you only pitched well under pressure on the boardwalk, but looks like you might be legit."

"Yeah, well, sometimes." Mark ran his hand through his hair, wiping the sweat onto his workout pants. "When'd you get back?"

"This morning," replied Amy, leaning toward him over the low fence. "I missed you."

Mark felt his body burn again, all those feelings from the beach racing back. Amy kissed him, holding it a second longer than she needed to as a bevy of whoops sounded behind them from the field. Mark could feel his teammates' eyes boring into them but he didn't turn around. He hadn't mentioned Amy to any of them yet. A part of him wondered if maybe it all really had been a dream, and he didn't want to be overly presumptive as to how life would be back at school, despite her having said all the right things.

But as their lips parted, his body tingling, he felt a rush of what he thought must be love, or at least the closest he'd ever come to it. He smiled and laughed as he squeezed her tight.

"What?" Amy asked.

"Nothing, I was just really wondering how it would be when we saw each other again."

"And? How did it go?"

Mark grinned and pulled her close to him, his hands on her hips. "It was perfect."

THAT KISS at the ball field melted away any doubts that may have lingered in Mark's mind about Amy's intentions being just a summer fling at the beach. In fact, their infatuations not only carried over from summer, but seemed to grow by the day.

Tressy and the rest of the baseball team had only been the first to view their newfound affections for each other, but word soon spread as they walked the halls of Cooper High together, often hand in hand, much to the surprise of their fellow classmates. There had been rumblings the first few days that Jeff Stabler was raising a fuss to his friends, threatening to kick Mark's ass, but soon even those rumors seemed to subside as the student body seemed to grow more used to the idea that Mark Parsons and Amy Holland were a couple and not just a passing fad. By all accounts, they were very much in love.

"What's the shortest side of a quadratic triangle?"

"Umm..." Mark squirmed against the arm of the couch, running his foot along the inside of Amy's tanned leg. "The left side?"

"Stop it, we need to study this."

"I think we've got it," said Mark, moving his foot higher up her leg to the edge of her running shorts. Studying with Amy had become one of Mark's new favorite pastimes, although it was doubtful a whole lot of studying got done on most days.

She brushed his foot away and sat up straight on the couch. "Your parents are right over there."

"So?"

He slid his foot a little higher, brushing the edge of the nylon leg of her short.

Amy's eyes widened in mock disbelief. "Mr. Ziegler isn't going to be so understanding if you flunk the geometry test tomorrow, and I don't think your dad will be very happy either."

Mark frowned and put on his best hurt face until Amy sighed and leaned toward him, kissing him softly.

"Doesn't look like much studying going on to me here," Dad said, striding into the room without an ounce of hesitation.

Amy pulled back quickly, her face blushing faintly. "Hi, Mr. Parsons."

"Dad..."

"Hello, Amy," Dad replied. "Don't stop on my account. Looks like it was just starting to get somewhere."

"Dad!" yelled Mark, as Amy's face grew a shade redder.

She closed her book and gathered some papers into her book bag. "It's okay, I've got to get home anyway."

"No, wait, we're not finished yet."

"We can finish at lunch tomorrow. Geometry isn't 'til fifth period." Standing from the couch, she kissed Mark quickly and moved to the hallway. "I'll call you later."

Mark set his jaw in annoyance. "Okay...." He glared at his dad, now pulling something from the desk on the other side of the living room, then walked Amy to the front door. "Bye."

"Bye."

Dad walked up behind him on his way to the kitchen. "She leaving already?"

"Yeah, I wonder why, Dad."

"Hey, you should be studying anyhow."

"I was."

"Didn't look like it to me, son. Besides, you know where your focus should be now, on your books and the field. Not getting tail."

Mark stood silently, his mind boiling over. He was never quite sure what to say in moments like that. The words seemed to tumble out in perfect rhythm for Dad, like he was on a lifelong sales call with a silver tongue. Most of the time things stayed mixed up in Mark's head, a cluster of dark colors and emotions when Dad was involved.

"I think you need to consider cutting back the time you're spending with that girl," Dad added, seeing Mark had nothing further to say. "She's a distraction, and you can't afford distractions right now."

"What are you talking about?" said Mark, indignantly.

"The Holland girl, she's a distraction. You need to be focusing on pitching."

"Amy?"

Dad nodded. "Unless you've got another one hidden up there under your bed that I don't know about."

"She's not a distraction, Dad. And my pitching is doing fine."

"Uh huh."

Mom walked in the front door with an armful of grocery bags, but stopped short when she noticed the expression on Mark's face. "What's going on?"

Mark ignored her and turned a stormy face back to Dad. "I'm not spending any less time with her. She's only the best thing that's ever happened to me in my entire life, and you're not going to ruin it, Dad!"

He turned on his heels and marched up the stairway, ignoring his dad's voice behind him. He didn't even know what he was saying, his head clouded with anger. He could put up with a lot of things from Dad, but there was no way in hell he was going to let him get in the way of Amy.

CHAPTER SEVENTEEN

"Top five favorite movies. Go."

"Um...*Gladiator*, *The Bourne Identity*, *The Lord of the Rings* was pretty good...How many is that?"

Amy smiled. "Three."

"*American Pie* was hilarious." He thought for a moment, trying to concentrate on the curving road up ahead of him. "Uh, *The Matrix*. How about that?"

"Interesting," said Amy.

"Your turn."

"Hmm, I probably should have thought ahead before I asked you that question, huh?"

"Probably."

"*American Beauty*, *Good Will Hunting*, *Fight Club*, *Notting Hill*, and...let's see, it's hard to narrow it down to just five. I'd have to say, probably, *High Fidelity*. Honestly anything with John Cusack in it. Did you ever see *Say Anything*?"

"Say what?"

Amy giggled. "No, *Say Anything*. It's the name of the movie."

"No, I don't think so. Is it new?"

Any shook her head. "No, it's old. But it's so sweet. We have to watch it."

"Okay, I'll take your word for it."

The road wound up the mountain like a snake, mirroring the stream that ran alongside to the right. He was driving Amy's Jeep Wrangler, a present from her parents for keeping her grades up at the close of her junior year. It was a red, used '99, but it was fun. He'd driven it a few times, but with the warm mid-May weather, they'd taken the doors and the top off. It nearly felt like they were on a motorcycle, the wind blowing through their hair. Amy had pulled hers back into a ponytail and was wearing one of Mark's old Yankee hats to keep it from flying around in her face.

"So do you think your parents will be mad if they find out?" Amy asked.

"Probably." Mark tried not to think about it. He'd told his dad that he was going camping up in the Blue Ridge Mountains with a few guys from the team, not by himself with Amy. For an instant he imagined Dad's face if he found out, blowing a gasket and grounding him for life.

"I think it's for the best that they don't," he added, reaching his arm over to Amy's seat, squeezing the back of her bare neck gently. "You didn't tell yours either, did you?"

"No, they think I'm over at Heather's, although it would have been fine if they knew. I told you, my parents trust me. And for some reason, they seem to really like you too."

"I've got 'em fooled good."

"Yeah, I keep trying to tell them you're all wrong for me, but they don't listen."

"And what do you think? Am I corrupting you?"

Amy purred, leaning her head back into his hand. "Possibly."

The trees seemed to be growing taller, darker somehow as they entered the Shenandoah National Park, following the narrow paved roads deeper into the park area. Mark glanced at the map he'd printed off before they left, but mostly went by memory from times he'd come up to the mountains for overnights with Joe. One of the advantages to having an older brother was that he could take you along on fun trips like camping if you were nice to him.

Amy looked up at the sky. "It's getting cooler."

"Yeah."

"Do you think it's going to rain?"

"Don't say that."

The forecast said there was a 20 percent chance of thunderstorms in the evening. Every time he went camping it seemed to rain, as if the tent was some kind of primitive signal that drew the precipitation, but there was no way he was going to cancel the trip for a 20 percent chance. He'd planned out every detail, the packing list as well as finding a time to get away when there wasn't a baseball game scheduled.

A small part of him felt bad lying to his parents, but a much bigger part of him longed to spend the night out in the darkness with Amy. He didn't know exactly where things would lead, but he could imagine plenty he'd like to happen, and he knew she was looking forward to it as well.

He'd had to devise a cover story with Tressy in case his parents asked about him, as unlikely as that was.

"So you're taking her up into the woods, just the two of you?" Tressy had teased him.

"Yeah," answered Mark as they packed up their things after practice the week before.

"And you're sure she doesn't suspect you're a psycho killer or anything like that?"

"Pretty sure."

"Sounds like somebody's gonna get some action," laughed Connor Smith from behind the lockers.

"Alright," said Mark.

"So you know what I'm going to say..." started Tressy.

Mark shook his head, knowing what was coming next. He supposed some conversations were called "locker room" talk for a reason, but he didn't really want to hear it. He just wanted to cover his tracks and get to the weekend with Amy.

"Be good," continued Tressy.

"Well we know that isn't going to happen," chimed in Connor. "Or then again, maybe we don't. Parsons is a starter and not a closer, after all..."

"Yeah, yeah," said Mark.

"If you can't be good, be careful," Tressy added.

"Oh, I think Mark's pretty careful," said Connor, laughing harder.

Mark finished zipping his duffle bag and waved them off, walking around the corner out of the locker room.

Tressy and Connor could barely get the words out as they hollered around the cement block walls. "And if you can't be careful, name it after me!"

By the time they turned off onto the gravel road that led to the campsite Mark had picked, a few raindrops were already hitting the windshield.

"Unbelievable," he muttered.

"Should we stop and put the top on?"

"No, I think it's just a sprinkle for now. It's not far up the bend here."

"Don't stress," Amy counseled, her hand on his knee. "It'll still be fun if it rains, okay?"

"I know."

"Worst case we'll just have to spend more time in the tent together." She squeezed his thigh. "And that wouldn't be so bad, would it?"

Mark chuckled, shifting in his seat while still trying to pay attention to the curves in the road and not let his mind wander to the ones in the seat next to him.

Amy didn't seem to be much of a camper, but she'd acted excited when he'd suggested it and was up for the challenge. As perfectly as he'd planned and imagined things, the rain wasn't going to help. The campsite was nestled in the woods off by itself, the kind he preferred to larger campgrounds with dozens, if not hundreds, of other people several yards away. In fact, Amy's Jeep's four-wheel drive made the job even possible, as some parts of the road tended to be gravel or dirt which could get hard to pass if there had been rain recently.

They rolled up to the site, a cleared square area about thirty by thirty with a spot for the tent, a metal fire grate, and a picnic bench. Also unlike most of the larger campgrounds, there weren't any toilet facilities or showers, a fact he realized he might not have shared with Amy. He tentatively glanced at her face as they stepped out of the Jeep, but she seemed to be all smiles, even as the raindrops came down harder.

"Okay?" asked Mark.

Amy nodded. "It's beautiful."

"Come on, let's get the tent set up and the roof on the Jeep before everything gets soaked."

The forecast didn't hold, and soon the skies opened just as they threw the last of the sleeping gear into the tent and got the soft top zipped up tight on the Jeep. A campfire was out of the question, and darkness was already setting early with the stormy weather.

"Hurry up!" giggled Amy as she pulled off her shoes and jumped into the tent, the rain now falling hard. Mark tumbled in behind her, collapsing on the soft down sleeping bags.

"Twenty percent my ass," he muttered, shaking his head, mentally discarding his perfect plan to woo his woman in the woods. He was just glad he brought the rain fly for the tent. He hoped it didn't leak. "This is a mess, I'm sorry. It really wasn't supposed to rain."

Amy slid over and wrapped herself in his arms. "I told you it's fine. This is fun."

"It is?"

"All I wanted was to be with you."

Mark exhaled, reminding himself that being in the tent was

the part of the trip he was most excited about anyhow. He was mostly worried about disappointing Amy and her not having a good time.

"I am a little hungry though," she added.

Mark closed his eyes. He was planning to cook burgers and hot dogs over the fire. "Um..." he said, racking his brain for alternatives.

"What were we going to have for lunch tomorrow?"

"Peanut butter and jelly sandwiches."

She tried to hold back a giggle but failed. "Perfect!"

"Oh my gosh, this is a total disaster."

"No, really, it's good. I like PB&J."

Mark rolled over on the sleeping bag and put his hand to his head. "Yeah, real romantic."

"Hey, what did I tell you?" She turned and planted her warm lips on his, his body quickly responding.

As the rain pelted their tent on all sides, their bodies pulled tighter together, feeling for each other through the shadows.

"Don't stop," Amy gasped, as Mark pulled his head up for air.

"Are you sure?"

"Yes."

Even as every piece of his body screamed out for her, he pulled back, propping up on his elbow. As much as he'd hoped that it would be the night they went all the way, he knew neither of them had before. Sure, he'd brought protection, and in an instant his mind whirred to think of where he'd packed it, relaxing only when he remembered it was in the duffle next to his feet.

"I want you to be ready," he said, slowly wiping a strand of hair off her moist face, staring into her eyes in the low glow of the flashlight that shone from the corner of the tent. "I just don't want to mess this up by getting the signals wrong."

He hadn't known where the night would go, but he hadn't seen Amy Holland coming either. These past two years were the best days of his life, and they'd both agreed to go slow, waiting to make sure that things were right, that they were ready.

Amy sat up, pulled her t-shirt off, and then seductively slid her shorts down to her toes.

"Come on, fireballer," she purred. "I'm not going to say it again. I'm waving you home."

Mark's face lit up as he followed suit with his clothes and fumbled in his bag. He suddenly felt dizzy with desire and emotion, his mind racing with memories of how they had found each other, that first night swimming with her in the waves in Harborwood, floating on the surf as one. As he moved his body on top of hers, he kept his eyes open, wanting to see every part of her as their bodies slowly rose and fell in the night, each crying out in pleasure and pain until finally crashing down like a wave to the sand.

"I love you," he whispered, sliding beneath the warm fibers next to her. He pushed his lips against hers and felt the soft curves of her skin. "I love you so much."

They held each other, falling asleep to the patter of rain against their tent, basking in the warmth of their bodies held close together. The smell of her against his skin, flush with the knowledge that she was his, and that they surely had been made for this moment, made to be together.

CHAPTER EIGHTEEN

They'd forgotten all about the sandwiches. Amy woke up in the dark tent, unsure of exactly what time it was, but starving and needing to pee badly. Both of them had fallen sound asleep after making love, even though it was early. She slipped on her shorts and a sweatshirt, sliding on her shoes as she quietly unzipped the tent.

The ground was soft, but the rain had stopped, the night sky revealing a dazzling display of stars between the branches stretching over their clearing, silhouetted in the darkness. She moaned at the prospect of no toilets, but managed to stumble a few steps into the undergrowth and finish while trying not to think about whatever wild thing might be waiting for her in the bushes.

As she walked back into the campsite, she sat down on top of the picnic table, feet up on the bench. She breathed in the cool night air, gazing at the tent where she could faintly hear Mark's breathing only a few feet away. Somehow she knew her life had changed in those moments of passion. A piece of her felt different now, like she'd carved out a corner of her soul for this boy that had entered her life two years ago.

She hadn't truly made a conscious decision that they would go all the way while camping, but she suspected she knew deep down. She wondered what it meant, that she had given herself to him completely. It wasn't quite what she'd expected, but somehow it felt right—terrible and wonderful all at once—but more than anything else, it had cemented him in her heart. She found her mind wandering more and more in recent days about what life would be like beyond high school, and wanting Mark to be a part of it. She wondered if sex would change things, if it would become awkward, but somehow she knew, in a deep place within her, that they were made for each other.

Her stomach rumbled and she nearly giggled, thinking again of the sandwiches. She stood and carefully opened the Jeep door, pulling the cooler from the back until she found a Ziploc. She turned her head at the sound of the tent zipper, Mark's head emerging from the entrance.

"Amy?"

"Hey, I'm over here, by the car."

"Are you okay?"

"Yeah, just hungry." She laughed, realizing that they were whispering since it was the middle of the night, even though they were completely alone.

Mark pulled his shoes on and walked over to her. "I didn't know where you went."

"Did you think I'd been eaten by a bear?"

"Maybe." He leaned over and kissed her, then laughed.

"What?"

"Peanut butter."

"And jelly. You should have one, it's good."

He yawned. "It's like the middle of the night."

Amy leaned into the car and looked at the clock. "Two thirty, actually." Her brain was starting to move faster, even at the late hour. "It's the perfect time for a snack."

Mark grunted. "You wore me out."

"But in a good way, I hope."

"Very good." He leaned against the car and pulled her close to him. She stuck her finger in his mouth until he licked off a dab of peanut butter.

"Are you sure you're okay?" he asked.

"Yeah," she nodded, folding her body closer into his. "I wanted it. I wanted it to be with you."

He smiled, burying his chin against her hair, resting on her shoulder. "I'm glad."

"I love you too," she whispered into his ear.

And before she knew it, they were on each other again, pushed up against the cool metal of the Jeep, hands touching each other's body everywhere, soaking each other in under the moonlight.

CHAPTER NINETEEN

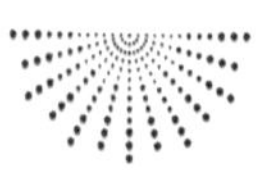

Baseball had become part of what defined him, both in his mind and from the perspective of others. Mark had entered high school as a timid, lanky kid who loved to play ball, but had little hopes that he'd make it far. Then something happened his sophomore season. Something clicked for him. Maybe his fingers grew a bit longer. Maybe it was the months of training with the team in the weight room and greater flexibility that helped his elbow tendon elasticize. Maybe his focus just increased. Maybe it was confidence that came from knowing someone like Amy Holland loved him.

Whatever it was, he'd morphed from an inauspicious skinny kid trying to make junior varsity to someone who earned a spot relief appearance for varsity in a midseason game his sophomore year. The game was already well out of hand when he'd entered, with Gainesville Prep out in front by six. Mop up duty, Dad used to call it. But regardless of the score, Mark came in facing the heart of the order, the three, four and five hitters who were, in large part, responsible for taking Gainesville five outs from the state championship the previous season. Then, in the blink of an eye, he struck out the side on nine quick dazzling pitches, changing speeds and dropping his curve over the plate like a master.

After that that day in relief, he had it. The ball danced from his fingertips to the catcher's glove, and he was special. Dad said just because he was having success now didn't mean that he could stop working. "Never stop working." That was Dad's motto. Frankly, it got old. His dad never seemed to work enough, and he was plenty successful. Not successful enough for his taste, but that's where Mark and he diverged.

Except when it was time to step on the mound. That's where everything seemed to become clear and slow down, even things with Dad, who was almost always there, watching him pitch. He said he loved to watch Mark pitch more than almost anything. And Mark believed him. Most of the time it didn't seem like Dad thought much of the rest of him, but the pitching, that was where they clicked.

The curve had become his bread and butter, with a rainbow arc that started at the batter's nose and ended at his toes. It was his pitch that sent even the biggest sluggers flailing at air in the batter's box. But it was also the toughest pitch to throw, twisting his arm in unnatural directions in order to get the maximum amount of torque on the ball.

That curve, or more generally his left arm, was his ticket to the show. The huddle of pro scouts that often camped out behind the home plate screen all said so, their radar guns aimed like a firing squad. For a lot of hurlers, they came to measure the heat, but Mark was different. He'd never punch ninety-five on the guns. That eighty-two he'd thrown for Amy on the boardwalk was not far off from his all-time ceiling, but he had something even better —a graceful tumbler that dropped in at a steady seventy-eight miles per hour and sent the opposition trudging back to their bench, wondering what just happened.

He'd thrown the pitch hundreds of times—thousands, really.

Until the last one.

"Gentlemen," said Coach Palmer, standing in the corner of the locker room, a foot propped up on a folding chair, the team fanned out around him, each on one knee, listening intently. "This is where our season starts to come together. We've had a good start, a nice run here, but Drayton is not a team to be taken lightly. We know where they're soft, but to be honest with you, it's not much. We need to play strong and tight on defense, make the simple plays, strong throws, be patient at the plate. We know Hallfield is starting, and he can be wild early. Wait for your pitch, don't try to do too much, let your teammates pick you up."

He paused, scanned the young faces slowly, his eyes landing on Mark's. "Parsons, we're counting on you to keep it close. Let your defense do their job, put the ball in play. Keep that rainbow dropping. Tressy, keep him honest out there."

Coach didn't say it out loud, but everyone knew that much of the game was riding on Mark's shoulders. Drayton was one of the best hitting teams in the state and if he didn't keep the score low early, there was no way they'd be able to come back. He took pride in the fact that he'd developed into Cooper's most consistent starter, and that he was being counted on to deliver.

As they jogged out of the locker room, crossing the crunch of the gravel in the back parking lot separating the ball fields from the school building, he tried not to think about the half-dozen scouts rumored to be in the stands, looking at several players from Drayton but also at him. He knew it was a golden opportunity. Dad had made that crystal clear at least a hundred times over the past week. He'd be sitting in the stands too, and probably Mom. Joe said he'd wanted to try to get home to see the game, but he was tied up studying for finals.

Mark strolled out to the mound for warms-ups as the home team, catching a soft toss from Tressy and bending over to sift the rosin bag through his fingers. He fidgeted with his cap, adjusted his cup through his uniform pants, and let his eyes wander through the stands that were buzzing a little more than normal. The newspaper had been billing this as the biggest matchup of the year so far, and there was a little extra tension in the air. He caught a patch of blue over the home team dugout and saw Amy sitting between her friend Heather and Mom. She smiled down at him and waved. For a moment, his mind wandered, thinking of only her and not the scouts or his dad. He felt himself riding the waves again with her on his back and he smiled.

"Mark!" Tressy barked out at him. "You with me?"

Mark raised his head and focused back on the task at hand. He pulled the brim of his hat lower to his eyes like he'd seen his favorite Yankee, Andy Pettitte, do on the mound and tried to concentrate. This was here. This was now. Let's play some ball.

By the seventh inning, things were getting tight. Mark was still on the mound, having held Drayton to two runs over six and two-thirds. He'd just walked their leadoff hitter, who was now dancing off the first base bag. Mark spun and threw a quick pickoff attempt to first and the runner slid back in just under the tag. Had to keep him close. A foul and a quick strike brought the count to two strikes.

"Here we go now, Mark," Tressy called from behind the plate.

"Bring the rain now Mark," said Taylor at shortstop.

Mark stared in, glaring underneath the low brim of his hat, feeling the surge in the crowd, sensing the pivotal moment in the game, knowing all eyes were on him, but trying hard to block it out, to see nothing but the glove and the two fingers Tressy held down for the pitch. Curveball. His pitch. His ticket. Time to close the door on the inning.

He set his glove at his waist, glanced at the runner on first, then dug his first two fingers into the ball, his thumb spread wide underneath, and raised his right knee above his belt. He saw the glove, pictured the ball flying to the plate in a brilliant arc that would leave the batter swinging through nothing but air.

But as his hands separated, and his left arm sailed past his ear, his wrist pushing the ball into a death spiral, it happened. He felt it immediately in his left elbow. A pop, followed by a pain like a knife. The ball sailed harmlessly high and outside into Tressy's glove, but Mark didn't even care. Nothing but fire flared through his body, pulsing from his left elbow.

And just like that, he was done.

He knew it as he cradled his pitching arm in his right hand, the field, his teammates, the crowd, all set in a blur. He barely noticed Coach and Curt Parker, the team trainer, running out to him on the mound. Curt was talking, but everything was too cloudy for Mark to understand the words. Time had slowed down, the only thing breaking through was the throbbing in his elbow.

He saw Amy in the third row, standing, staring out at him walking off the field. He saw her tan legs, her blue shirt. She raised her hand, moved toward him, called out, but he ducked into the shelter of the dugout, sat down on the wooden bench, and cried.

CHAPTER TWENTY

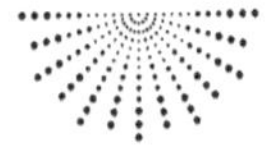

Joe used to joke he could sense their dad coming before he saw him. Like a storm moving in on the breeze, the trees seemed to bend in warning of his approach. It was true on that day, too, as Mark felt the sheer force of Dad's presence bursting into the waiting room of the orthopedic clinic.

"Parsons. Mark Parsons. I'm his father." His voice boomed, still down the hall at reception, but snaking its way around the corners and into his exam room. Curt Parker had dropped him off, knowing Mark's family would be close behind.

Mark closed his eyes, the room slowly fading to black. He tried not to think about his father as he lay flat on his back on the table, his left arm numb but throbbing next to him, as if disconnected from his body. The ice pack was wrapped around his elbow like a scarf, working to reduce the swelling so the doctor could get an MRI to better inspect the damage.

The door opened and Dad burst in, his eyes wide, but steady, like he was about to close a big deal. He stopped just inside the door, surveying the damage, piercing directly into Mark's arm with his eyes, deciphering the problem to be solved.

"Dad."

"How's it going, champ?"

"Not good."

"The elbow?"

"Yeah." Mark took a deep breath. "I heard something pop. I think it's bad."

"Uh huh. You heard a pop," Dad repeated. "Are you in pain?"

"Nah. It's just cold now."

Dad walked over to the table and tapped on the wrap, as if he was testing its stability. "Ice."

"Yeah."

The door opened and a doctor walked into the room while he knocked in a fluid motion. He nodded to Mark's dad and walked up to the table. "How are we doing, Mark?"

"Okay."

"What do you think, doc," asked Dad.

"Well, we need to wait until the swelling goes down until we'll be able to take a proper MRI. I hate to speculate until we can see the test."

"Uh huh," said Dad again, nodding along, like he was waiting for a punch line.

"I'm done, aren't I?" Mark said softly.

Dad's eyes opened wider. "You don't know that. You heard the doc, they need to take tests. It's too early." He sounded more like he was trying to convince himself.

Mark looked pleadingly up at the doctor.

"Like I said, Mark, we can't know for sure without the test."

"But?" said Mark.

"But..." the doctor hesitated. "If I had to guess, I'd say it sounds a lot like a torn elbow ligament."

Dad closed his eyes. "Damn."

Mark pursed his lips. It wasn't surprising. He already knew. Somehow you can feel when things in your body break that are serious. He was done. A torn elbow ligament meant shutting down from ball for months, a year even. Maybe Tommy John surgery. Lots of rehab. His high school career was essentially finished.

He glanced up at his father's face, which was white like he'd just heard about a cancer diagnosis. This would crush him, even though it wasn't even his life, his career that would be over. Despite playing years of football, Joe had somehow made it through his high school and college career without any major injuries. Like it was expected that if you worked hard enough, if you willed it hard enough, you could sustain things. That you could prevent an injury from happening. It had never been said out loud, but getting injured was a sign of weakness.

A knock sounded at the door. Everyone looked up, trying to break out of the trance in each of their minds about the reality of the situation.

It was Amy.

"Can I come in?" She wore a tentative, yet empathetic look on her face.

Mark stared down at the floor. He didn't know what to say to her, didn't even know if he wanted her there, seeing him broken down.

"Uh, doc, this is Mark's girlfriend, Amy. Do you mind?"

The doctor nodded. "Of course, come on in, Amy. We were just finishing up."

She walked over to the table, placing her arm around Mark's shoulder. "How you doing?"

Mark slowly shook his head.

Dad cleared his throat. "I'll let you kids be alone. Mark, I'll be in the waiting room." He followed the doctor out of the exam room, his steps unsteady and slow, as if he'd just identified a body at the morgue and there was nothing left to say.

Mark felt the tears coming, welling up inside him, ready to burst.

Amy pulled his head up, looking tenderly into his eyes. "It's going to be okay."

The first tear streamed down his cheek as he shook his head again. "I'm done. It's over."

She nodded, still staring into his eyes. "I love you. Whether you pitch or not."

Mark turned away. He felt like he was going to throw up. He didn't know what to say.

Amy leaned into him sitting on the exam table, pulling him toward her and wrapped him tightly in her arms. That's when the floodgates opened. She held him for a long time as he sobbed. He hated himself for acting so weak, but he couldn't help it. The emotion poured out of him, his body heaving in her arms.

CHAPTER TWENTY-ONE

If he stared at the ceiling in his room long enough, Mark could imagine just about anything. He saw fighter jets flying across puffy clouds in the white sheetrock, giants chasing villagers across a field of snow, even himself back out on the mound, his elbow still in one piece, firing off strikes to opposing batters. Amy was waving from the stands, bending over to give him a wet kiss in between innings after he'd struck out the side, Dad bragging to all his insurance buddies that Mark was his son and how proud he was. But when he blinked his eyes, the vision faded, sinking back into the seams of the wallpaper and the dream that it was. Just a mirage of the life he'd thought he would have, not the reality that was now his, one that did not include baseball.

His dream of going to the majors, visions of being drafted, signing with a pro scout, were as good as gone. All the hours and hours he'd poured into his training were washed down the drain the instant that he let go of that last curveball and the tendon in his elbow snapped like a rubber band.

Coach Palmer had stopped by, Tressy and a couple of the guys too, offering him their best wishes, but pretty soon everyone acknowledged that it didn't really matter, even though they didn't say so out loud. The connection between a baseball coach and a player didn't work very well when that person didn't play baseball anymore. Mark wondered if his relationship to his teammates would change, like old middle school friends whose interests diverged onto separate paths, gradually becoming acquaintances and then just recognizable faces passing in the hallway.

Amy had come by and called on the phone, but he didn't want to see her. Mom was sad for him and tried to say all the right things. She had a comforting way about her that made him feel safe. Or maybe it was just the contrast she held in comparison to his father. Mark wondered who was taking the news worse, his dad or himself. It reminded him of a horse owner who'd bred and trained his stallion, only to have it pull up lame the week before the Preakness or the Derby.

"How's it feeling today?" Dad would volunteer on some mornings as they crossed paths at the breakfast table. Or, "I saw in the paper that the team beat Jackson Southern last night. Must have been one hell of a hitting performance, three round trippers I think."

Mark couldn't help but feel responsible for the void that haunted their conversations, like the elephant in the room, how he'd spit the bit to let everyone down. Dad never said it either, but Mark could read it all over his face. Just a little more distant, a bit more disconnected, an awkward pause before he spoke, the hint of anticipation that never was realized.

After their second doctor's appointment, this time to an elbow specialist up in DC at Georgetown, Dad seemed to switch to a different approach.

"So I was talking with Roger Henry yesterday. He said he heard of two kids down in Florida that came out of Tommy John throwing harder than they were before the surgery."

Mark didn't respond; he just stared at the trees passing by out the window.

"I think with a couple years of rehab, we might be able to get back on track, maybe get into the junior college circuit. Sure, it'll be a setback, but you've always been a quick healer. I think it might be possible. What do you think?"

Mark sighed, stole a quick glance at his father, who stared ahead behind the reflection of his sunglasses as he navigated his BMW down the freeway, in between the DC traffic to get back home.

"I don't think so, Dad."

Dad was silent for several moments, perhaps collecting his thoughts, lining up his rehearsed second stanza of his sales pitch guaranteed to close after years of experience with far greater challenges than his son next to him in the car that day.

"Son, life isn't going to be handed to you, you have to take it."

"Uh huh."

"God knows you have talent; you're a hell of a pitcher, Mark."

"Thanks."

"A hell of a pitcher," he repeated, this time sounding farther away, like he was remembering flashbacks of Mark's successes on the mound.

"Dad, I think I've had enough. It's not going to get better. You heard the doctor."

"People hear what they want to hear."

Mark shifted again in his seat, knowing almost what was coming before it was said.

"I'm not going to let you piss this opportunity down the drain, son. It's too important."

"Dad—"

"No, let me finish. This isn't some kid fantasy, you have a legitimate chance to get drafted, or even to play division one ball."

"Had," clarified Mark. .

"It's still out there, Mark, you just have to want it. Do you think I got to where I am in life by just waiting for people to hand me things? Hell, nothing was handed to me, even before I was your age. I had to scratch and claw for everything I had. But you're different, you have a head start, living in a nice house, a good school, great coach, quality training program.

That's the start of something big, Mark, but you can't just give up on it."

"I tore my UCL to shreds, Dad. My elbow is dead and I'm not taking a tendon from my leg and working for two years at something that probably won't even happen. I'm not you, okay. I know you want it, but I don't."

He stared back out the window, trying to hold in the tears. Dad adjusted his sunglasses, shifted uncomfortably in his seat, but stayed quiet and never brought it up again.

The days turned to weeks, but that last conversation with Dad seemed to have worn them both out, and neither appeared to have the energy to even try again. They were in the same house but operating like two ships passing in the night, just an occasional blip on each other's radar, but making no attempts to engage.

Mom tried to make the peace, to keep spirits up, but neither Mark or Dad were making her efforts easy. To make matters worse, college applications were now coming due and suddenly Mark was being asked questions he'd never given much thought to. The only schools he'd even looked at were the ones that had offered him scholarships, but he'd never been heading to college, he was going to get drafted and report straight to the minors with a healthy signing bonus. Even Dad had gone along with that philosophy, staying strangely silent on the matter even when Mom had pressed him. College could wait as a fallback, but a pro career would not.

Now, the scholarship offers were long gone and Mark could barely process what to do next.

CHAPTER TWENTY-TWO

It was after five when Mark pulled into the driveway, returning from the grocery store for Mom before she came back from her Friday evening gardening club. He was surprised to see Amy's Jeep parked in front of the house, and then picked her out from behind the hanging baskets, sitting on the front porch swing.

"Hey," he said, carrying a plastic bag onto the porch.

"Hey, yourself."

He moved slowly up the steps, as if he wasn't in a big hurry to get closer.

She looked out at him, her eyes filled with expectancy, following his movements with an air of hesitation. "What's in the bag?"

Mark glanced down and shrugged. "Eggs, milk, bread, something else, tomato sauce, I think."

"Planning on cooking?"

He set the bag down on the porch and leaned against the railing. "Nah, just stuff Mom asked me to get."

"How are you doing?"

"Fine."

Amy tilted her head, looking over at him cautiously. "Yeah?"

"Uh huh."

"Good. As long as you're fine."

"How are you?" said Mark, biting on his thumbnail.

"Oh, I'm fine too, except for one thing."

He looked up. "Oh? What's that?"

"I seem to have lost my boyfriend. Have you seen him?"

"Very funny."

"Not really."

He sighed. "What are you talking about?"

"I don't know, Mark, why don't you tell me?"

"Tell you what? You're the one sitting on my porch talking in some crazy code. What's the matter with you?"

Amy's eyes narrowed. "I got a letter today."

Mark's eyebrows rose. "Oh, yeah, from your boyfriend? Maybe it'll tell you where he went."

"Very funny. No, it was from a school." She paused, as if to gauge his response, which remained blank as a washed chalkboard. "I got accepted to Oregon in their pre-veterinary school on a partial scholarship."

Mark stared out across the driveway over the roof of his car. "Nice," he muttered, finally.

"What?"

"I said that's nice." He turned and looked into her eyes. "Congratulations. You deserve it. I'm sure you'll have a great time."

"Mark..."

"Yes?"

"I don't want to go. I don't want to be in Oregon. I want to be with you. You know that. Just like we talked about."

He shifted uncomfortably against the railing. "Yeah, well, a lot of the things we talked about aren't really working out, you know?"

"That's not what I meant."

"Yeah, well that's how it is. I'm not sure what you want me to say."

"I don't want you to say—" she started.

"I can't wave a magic wand and make it all perfect again, Amy. I can't fix my elbow that's all torn to shit, and all those schools that wanted me so bad are long gone." He felt himself step closer to her, his voice growing louder, his blood boiling. "And I sure as hell can't keep you from going to Oregon or help you figure out where your boyfriend went. I thought, call me crazy, that he was sitting right here in front of you, but I guess that's not good enough for you anymore."

"Mark..."

It was as if the conversations with Dad in the car, the mindless wandering around the house, were all coming to a head right there on the porch. "Why don't you just say it?" he finally blurted out.

Her lip quivered slightly, then she straightened up before she spoke. "Say what?"

"That you don't want this anymore. That I'm not good enough, that you're just looking for an excuse to move on, asking me for permission to get out of here."

"What are you talking about? Is that what you really think? That I care about the fact that you blew out your arm? That I was only in this because of your pitching?"

Mark looked off the porch silently.

"Well, is it? Is that what you think?" she repeated, her voice louder.

He shrugged.

"You are unbelievable. Can you take just a moment and get over yourself? I don't care about whether you play baseball. It was never about baseball, Mark. It was always about you, about us, what we have together, what we had together, until you started falling into this shell of yourself, this sad, broken guy who can't seem to get past the fact that he hurt his arm, that he's never going to be able to live up to his father's expectations."

Mark flinched, shooting her a glare at the mention of his dad.

"You know," Amy continued, "maybe you should have some

of your own expectations and focus on what's really important to you. What's standing here right in front of you."

He felt a burst of anger. "It's not just some stupid injury, you know that. Pitching was my thing, it was my future! If anybody was to understand what I'm feeling, I thought it would be you."

Amy shook her head, her breathing unsteady. "Of course I care about it, Mark, because I care about you. I want you to be happy, but I care more about our future together, not just on the baseball diamond."

He scoffed, his brain racing, fighting back emotions and tears. He shook his head, speaking before he even knew what was coming from his lips. "Maybe Dad was right."

Amy looked up, her eyes red. "Right?"

"About us being a bad idea. That you were too much of a distraction."

She opened her mouth but nothing came out. She just stared at him incredulously.

He peered back over the car. "Maybe you *should* go to Oregon. It's probably for the best. This was never going to work, anyway."

He saw the tears rolling down her cheek out of the corner of his eye, but his mind felt closed, constrained like a great weight was pulling down on him. He could barely breathe, let alone look over at her. He knew what he'd said was wrong, knew he didn't want her to leave. More than anything he wanted her to just hold him close, wrap her arms around him and never let go. He wanted to forget he'd ever picked up a baseball, forget he'd ever had a dream of being drafted and playing in the pros.

He thought back to that first day, standing in the line at Groves, how beautiful she looked in the sunlight that morning, the tan on her legs, the glow of her face in the ocean breeze, the fun they'd had talking on the boardwalk, how every ounce within him felt happiness. He'd been so amazed to see her then, a feeling that carried over into every day since, so grateful she was in his life.

But as he stood straight against the porch railing that afternoon, he didn't say any of those things to Amy. He just fought back the tears and stared out into the distance, barely even hearing when she said goodbye, stepped past him through the yard, into her Jeep and out of his life.

MARK WALKED off the pier and back down the boardwalk, the breeze at his back, the sky slowly burning to pink. Why had he not returned for so long? Life's events seemed to get in the way, conspiring against him—his injury, breaking up with Amy, distance with Dad—and before long, they'd skipped a summer of coming to Harborwood, then another.

Why had he even stopped? Probably just feeling overly sentimental about Dad. He never dreamed he'd run into Mr. Holland. Was that fate? Coincidence? He didn't know. Maybe there was no difference.

He reached his rental car and started the engine. He stared at the street signs, trying to remember how to get across the Bay on the bridge that hadn't been there when he was growing up. He drove a few blocks, turning away from the ocean to the next intersection, his mind in a daze as he watched two gulls turn aerobatics beneath the clouds.

A car honked behind him as the light turned green. He had no idea which way to go, so he pulled over to the curb to check directions on his phone. Right on Atlantic, left on Seventh. Seemed easy enough. He turned to check his blind spot when a big black nose stuck into his car window.

"Whoa!" Mark startled.

"Casey, come back here," a man's voice called. The dog's head jerked away from Mark's open window as its owner leaned down. "Sorry, don't worry, he's friendly."

Mark nodded. "No problem."

He watched the man and the dog enter the door to the building off the sidewalk. He leaned forward to see the sign. *Harborwood Veterinary Hospital.* Mark's eyes opened wide, his blood pressure rising. A voice in his head whispered, or was it screaming, that this must be Amy's clinic. He stared at the steering wheel, trying to breathe. He didn't know if he was ready to face this.

He turned back toward the building, his eyes moving to the large window past the door. In the dusk, the lights were on in the office, making it fairly easy to see in. The man and his dog were at a counter, speaking to a receptionist behind the desk.

He took a deep breath, until he saw a door open from behind the desk. A woman walked out, her back turned to the window as she opened a file cabinet. Mark didn't need to see her face, he felt it deep down.

It was Amy.

Before he could think about it any longer, he stepped on the gas, jerking the wheel away from the curb and accelerating into the lane. Horns blared and brakes screeched, but Mark didn't look back. Not at the cars. Not at the clinic.

He didn't want to see Amy. Not today. Not ever.

He'd worked too hard to forget about her all these years. It didn't matter that she wasn't married anymore. Those days were gone.

Harborwood, the beach, the waves, Mr. Holland, Dad, Amy.

It was time to move on.

CHAPTER TWENTY-THREE

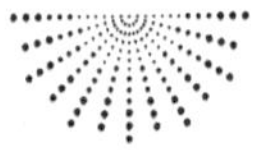

By the time Mark returned the rental car, it was close to nine. Tunnel traffic into the city from New Jersey had been murder, and he'd been alone in his car for the past three hours—he didn't want to go back to his apartment. He called two of his buddies, Percy and Tyler, and they agreed to meet at DJ Murphy's, a popular after-work and weekend haunt.

Even though it was a Sunday night, DJ's was still buzzing when Mark walked in at nine thirty. There was no sign of the guys, so he took a seat at the bar, nodded to Kelly, the perky waitress behind the counter, and started on a beer. The Yankees were in the top of the seventh against Kansas City, the manager in the midst of a chess match of opposing middle relief pitchers, trying to get to their closer who was lights out. It was getting to him that usually spelled the problem, and in Mark's opinion, was the biggest reason the Yanks wouldn't make the playoffs.

Kelly bounced back and forth, maybe a little more than she needed to. Mark thought she might like him, but he'd never made a move. He wasn't really sure why.

"Come here often, big boy?" a voice called in his ear. Tyler laughed, grabbing his shoulders in a hard squeeze. Mark's beer splashed a bit on his jeans. He looked up at Tyler with an annoyed glance.

"Oh shit, sorry."

Mark set his beer down on the bar before he spilled any more. "Thanks. That was real helpful."

"Nice," said Percy, following behind. "Hey, brother." He sat down on the other side of Mark. "I'm sorry about your dad, man."

"Yeah," said Tyler. "You doing okay?"

Mark shrugged without answering.

"I think he needs another, one, Kel," said Percy, waving his hand to the tap.

"Make that three," said Tyler.

"Funeral was tough?" asked Percy.

"Yeah," answered Mark, trying not to think about all the black again. "It was hot as hell."

"I thought you were coming back yesterday?" asked Tyler.

"I was, but the flights got all screwed up, so I drove."

Tyler nodded. "Wasn't it in Virginia? What did you do, stop off in Chicago?"

Mark shook his head. "New Jersey, actually."

Percy raised his eyebrows, questioningly. "Jersey? For what?"

"I stopped in Harborwood."

"Oh, boy," said Percy, knowing enough of Mark's history to be concerned. He was a friend from college who'd moved to New York about the same time as Mark did. They'd shared an apartment in Brooklyn for a few years until Percy had gotten serious with Sheri. When she moved in, Mark quickly got his own place. They still saw each other a lot though. P was one of the few people Mark could really talk to.

"What's in Harborwood?" asked Tyler, at the same time as he gave a slight nod to the girl down the bar who was making overly obvious googly eyes at him. "Isn't that down the shore?" Tyler was a friend of P's from high school, but had quickly become a tight part of their circle. He was a real ladies' man, the one the girls usually gravitated to when they went out. He partied a little harder than the other two, but he was a loyal friend and harmless.

"Just strolling down memory lane?" asked Percy.

"I guess."

"But..." Percy looked across at Mark. "I sense there's more to this story."

The girl down the bar slowly unzipped her light jacket, revealing a low-cut tank top. Tyler gave her some cheesy expression that somehow always seemed to work for him.

"Dude, not now," scolded Percy.

"Right...sorry, man. I can't help it, these women just come at me." He turned his back to the girl and looked at Mark. "So what happened in Harborwood? Did you hook up or something?" Tyler's definition of something significant happening in life was whether or not you hooked up with a girl on the weekend. Or on a weekday. Not that Mark was averse to getting together with girls, but Tyler was a one-track record.

"Shut up," said Mark. "No, I didn't hook up with anyone. But I did run into Amy's dad."

"You're shitting me," said Percy, leaning back from the bar. "Just by chance?"

Mark nodded.

"Amy's dad..." said Tyler. "Oh, wait, Amy, like that girl from high school, Amy?"

Percy sighed and smacked Tyler with the back of his hand. "Yes, that Amy, stupid. Will you shut the hell up? It's like you're on tape delay. I'm trying to talk to him."

Percy took a long drink of his beer and looked back at Mark. "So what happened? Did you talk to him?"

"Yeah."

"About Amy?"

"About her, about my dad, about a lot of stuff. He's easy to talk to. It was kind of nice, until he told me about Amy."

"What about her?" Percy asked.

Mark looked down at his beer. "Oh, just that she's living in Harborwood now."

Percy's jaw dropped open. "What? I thought she was in California?"

"Wasn't that girl married?" asked Tyler, trying to keep up.

"She got divorced."

"Oh my god," said Percy, throwing back the last of his glass. "Kelly, we're going to need a lot more beer. This is serious."

The girl at the end of the bar began peeling off her jacket all together, eliciting a noticeable groan from Tyler, who'd faced forward again.

Mark took a long sip from his glass, trying to make things feel cloudier, if that was possible. The only time he approached Tyler's drinking habits was when he felt down. He wasn't sure if that was worse than drinking to have fun, but he sensed tonight could be rough.

"So did you see her?" asked Percy.

"Nah." Mark thought back to sitting in his car outside of the veterinary clinic. "Well, sort of, but not really." He described watching her through the window and then hightailing it out of town.

"Whoa," said Tyler. "That's messed up. So she's like, single now?"

"I guess," said Mark.

"But you were just passing through, right?" said Percy. "That was all a long time ago."

Mark nodded. "It was."

"When was the last time you talked to her?" asked Tyler.

Mark tried to do the math in his head, the numbers slowly mixing together with the growing beer buzz. "Twelve years, I guess. Just after high school."

"You never saw her after you broke up?" asked Tyler.

"Nope. She moved west when she went to Oregon. I was still in Virginia, then in Boston." He took a drink and stared through the back of the television set as the Royals squeeze-played a run home in the eighth. "She got married to some doctor she met in school, and that was it."

"Hey Kel," Tyler called to the waitress on the other end of the bar.

Kelly walked over to them, leaning her petite but shapely figure against the wooden counter in a way that said she knew exactly what she was doing. She'd worked there for a while and always seemed to get good tips.

"What's up?" she asked.

"Mark just ran into his high school sweetheart at the beach after twelve years," explained Tyler.

"Oh, wow," said Kelly.

Mark rolled his eyes and smiled weakly at Kelly. "I didn't run into her."

"Okay," said Tyler, "He ran into her dad, and then he stalked her from his car."

Mark punched Tyler in the shoulder. "Will you shut up." He shook his head. "That's not what happened."

Kelly grinned, staring into Mark's eyes. "So you didn't talk to her?"

"No..." Mark tried to find the right words to explain why he hadn't. "It's been a long week."

"His dad just passed away," added Percy softly.

Kelly's expression melted, and she leaned a little closer to Mark. "I'm so sorry, I didn't know. That's terrible. Was he sick, or was it sudden?"

"Heart attack," said Tyler.

Percy smacked him in the head again. "Dude. Let him answer."

"What? It was a heart attack," said Tyler, grimacing. "Why's everybody hitting me?"

Kelly reached out and clasped Mark's hand. "That's awful. I'm so sorry, Mark." She pulled back from the bar. "Here, this round's on the house." She filled their glasses and smiled again before moving back down the bar to help another customer.

After another hour drinking, Mark felt sufficiently numb. Percy took a call from his wife, probably checking on him to see why he was coming home so late on a Sunday night. Tyler had ended his resistance and was now sitting with the hottie at the end of the bar who was laughing loudly at something he'd said.

Mark shook his head and headed to the restroom to take a leak. When he walked back out to the bar, Kelly intercepted him next to a high top table she was clearing.

"You okay?"

Mark nodded, the room only slightly spinning in front of him. "Yeah."

"I'm so sorry about your dad," she repeated, looked up at him, her eyes sparkling behind the locks of long black hair.

"Thanks." Mark grabbed her hand and squeezed it.

"You know, if you ever need to talk to someone, or get a bite, I'm off on Wednesdays."

Yep, she was definitely hitting on him now. Even in his half-drunken state, Mark could see that. Or maybe it was a sympathy offer, he wasn't sure.

"Thanks," he said, reaching his arm around her in a short hug. She kissed his cheek, but he pulled back. He didn't even feel like trying to hook up with Kelly right now. He was tired. He needed to go to bed. He wanted to be alone.

CHAPTER TWENTY-FOUR

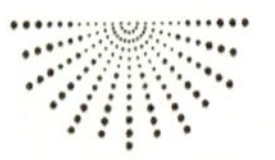

When high school ended, his baseball career in shambles and most of the better schools no longer an immediate option, Mark swallowed his pride and worked for the summer at his father's insurance firm with Joe. He'd known from the start that it was a bad idea, but he didn't have anything else, and Mom and Joe had convinced him that it could be okay. Dad hadn't discouraged the move, although he hadn't really encouraged it either. After weeks of wandering along in the fog that had become their relationship at home, it just kind of happened, both of them dubious about its prospects, but neither determined enough to embrace or decline its convergence.

Mark quickly remembered what he already knew—insurance made his stomach ache. It wasn't really due to the job; he actually didn't mind the work. It could be interesting, meeting people, recommending the best coverage for their needs, making sure their assets and loved ones were taken care of.

He'd helped out before off and on over the summers during high school. People told him he was good at it, too, and not just because he was the boss's kid. He'd had some novel ideas about how to run things more efficiently that he passed along to Joe and seemed to improve things. But it was always a little too suffocating with the old man. He always did something just a little bit not right, at least the way Dad saw it.

That summer after high school, working full-time, things came to a head. He'd been mostly filing claims, but Joe also gave him a few random sales calls now and then when it was needed. Mark had run into an older couple that was borderline for needing an update to their whole life policy. They'd shared with Mark how they'd been having a tough time, so he didn't push too hard, letting them move on in peace. He thought it was the right thing to do, but Dad didn't see it the same way.

He remembered, like it was yesterday, his dad calling him into his office to talk about what happened with the policy. He was sitting behind his wide oak desk, holding court like something out of *The Godfather*. A 300-pound marlin, Dad's most prized fishing trophy, hung mounted on the wall above his head. "That was a layup son. A meatball pitch."

"Sure, Dad," Mark had started off saying, sitting down but not wanting to get into it. He'd had a version of this conversation with his father dozens of times, be it about baseball, work, school, or anything else—the same dance even if to different music.

"You gotta have more killer instinct," Dad continued to bluster, like he was reading off his normal script for how Mark was a screw up. "That old couple could have been solid money. You don't just turn that kind of thing away. That's not how I've built this business, by being weak. Do you understand?"

"Yeah, Dad." Mark stared absently at the fish on the wall. He wondered what it had thought, as it was fighting through the waves, hauled out of the deep by his dad's never-ceasing thirst for the hunt. For an instant, he pictured his own face on the head of the giant fish, a hook and a line snagged into his lip, being dragged through the office, knocking into filing cabinets and sliding over desks, papers scattering to the floor.

Then something snapped.

Mark wasn't even sure why. Maybe it was the end of high

school, blowing out his arm, or Amy moving away. He hadn't spoken to her since that day on his front porch weeks ago, although he figured she must be getting ready to head out to Oregon soon since it was nearly Labor Day. Maybe it was all those things combined, but right then, he didn't want to listen to any more of his dad's bullshit.

"I understand, Dad," Mark said, standing up in front of the desk. His mind began whirling and he barely registered the words pouring from his lips. "But you know, maybe I don't care about the business over everything else in life. Maybe I don't want to be a complete asshole like you. Those people didn't need another stupid insurance policy. Did you ever think about that?"

For a moment it was like time stood still. Mark's words hung frozen in the air. A part of him wondered if he'd really said them out loud or just imagined it. His father sat unmoving, a pen held still in his hand, a spear that might hurl across the desk at the blasphemer who dared question his authority. Then his eyes narrowed as he looked up at Mark and his face darkened like a storm, bubbling in a rage about to boil over.

"Sure, I get it, Mark. Nobody's forcing you to work here. Some of us are born to be winners, and other are losers. Just like on the baseball diamond. Maybe you just don't have what it takes."

He looked back down to his desk and scribbled something on a notepad as if he'd already forgotten Mark was standing there. "You take after your mother," he said finally, looking up and meeting Mark's eyes. "Nothing but a pussy."

MARK DIDN'T GO BACK to the agency after that confrontation with Dad. He'd had enough. High school was over and there was nothing to stop him from being his own man and setting out alone. Within a week, he was moved out of the house and living with Shawn Hanson, a friend from school, at his cousin's farm in

Massachusetts thirty miles outside of Boston. Shawn had said they could use him through the harvest, and driving a tractor and throwing hay bales seemed easier than thinking about Dad, Amy, baseball, and where his life was headed—or where it wasn't.

He actually didn't mind the physical work. It kept his mind off things and reminded him of evenings spent training and putting in time out on the ball field. Shawn and his cousin's family were decent enough folks and easy to get along with. They were grateful for the help and even though he didn't make a ton of money, it was something. After ten hours working in the fields, his body was usually so tired that all he wanted to do was get to bed early before starting all over again at five the next morning.

He and Shawn bounced around the small town through the winter, mixed with a few weeks working in the kitchen at a ski resort. They bar hopped on the weekends, chased girls, and acted generally irresponsible for the first time in Mark's life. They helped again at the farm in the spring, but by summer, Mark had realized he didn't want to throw hay bales forever, so he enrolled in computer programing classes at the local community college. Once he realized he had a knack for it, he moved to full-time in the fall.

By the spring semester, his grades were high enough that his professor encouraged him to apply to transfer to Boston University in the fall. He surprised himself by getting in, turning down his parents' offer to pay for it. He never talked to Dad about it, only Mom, but he knew it must have irritated him to no end, and that more than made up for the extra pinch to Mark's own wallet. The last thing Mark wanted was be dependent upon his father for anything. That was why he'd left home in the first place.

He ended up rooming in an off-campus apartment with Percy, expanded his major to computer science and marketing, and graduated in five years, counting his time at the community college. Percy accepted a plum job offer at a law firm in Manhattan and he convinced Mark to follow him and room together in New York rather than stay in Boston. Mark bounced between several entry-level jobs, enjoying his independence but never really catching on to one place that felt right.

It wasn't lost on him that he was living in the same city where his dad was born and raised, but he pushed any thoughts about following in Dad's footsteps out of his head. He wasn't his father, regardless of which city he lived. He was going to forge his own path, whatever that might be.

CHAPTER TWENTY-FIVE

He'd woken up late and hung over the morning after DJ's, and spent what was left of that morning and most of the afternoon eating cereal and watching movies on HBO. Other than a funny Billy Crystal movie about throwing your mother from a train, he watched mostly depressing stuff. And drank. A lot. He called in sick Monday and then again on Tuesday, barely venturing out of his apartment.

On Wednesday, he managed to drag himself out into the world, but fell asleep on the subway, missing his stop and waking up somewhere deep into Queens. He finally made it to the office, but didn't accomplish much. Luckily his boss, Marvin, was on vacation with his boyfriend in the Caymans, so everyone was operating on a slightly looser leash than usual. Running advertising databases for online retailers wasn't exactly hard work, but it was steady pay and most of the time he only moderately hated it. Best of all, he'd written his own background code into the database that automated most of the tasks for which Marvin thought he was responsible. On most days things hummed along practically by themselves with only limited oversight on his part.

Mark knew he was overqualified, but he was privately proud of himself for taking the initiative to master the system and keep it under wraps. Sure, if he'd been more ambitious, he would have used his creativity to move into a more challenging position, but for some reason he found it easier to just use it to coast where he was.

Percy was always giving him crap about not leaving. Even though Mark's degree had taken a year longer than it should have from BU, Percy knew Mark was sharp and could work at any number of tech startups in the city if he chose to apply himself. P was one of the few people that knew about the freelance programming Mark did at night on the side or the many business ideas that floated around in his brain.

If Mark kept at his side work consistently, he'd be doing great, but most of the time he didn't. His side gigs went in spurts, moving forward in great bursts when he felt inspired and motivated, but then slogging by for weeks or months when he got bored or distracted. He wasn't sure why. He knew he should be doing better, but he told himself it was fun knowing there was more to him than met the eye, that he was holding back for the right opportunity. But with each passing month, which were quickly turning into years, he felt a growing unease that he needed to get his act together.

Mom had called twice during the week, checking up on him. The first call he'd ignored, for the second he made some kind of lame excuse to hang up after a few minutes. Joe had emailed about needing help on a project for Kingfisher, something about tracking someone down in the city with paperwork to sign. Mark had been moonlighting once in a while for Joe too the past couple years, since he was in New York and a lot closer to certain cases than Virginia. It was brainless, and he only talked to Joe. The extra spending money was nice too.

More than anything, though, it seemed like he was just drifting. This week was just more dramatic than usual. It felt like things had come to a head in his mind. So much was wrapped up around Dad over the years, he wasn't sure how to untangle it. He knew a couple people from college had said talking through their issues to a counselor helped, but it seemed lame.

Mom kept asking him if he was going to church. He lied and said sometimes. He didn't really know how that would help much either, although he knew it seemed to for some people. Joe, for instance. They'd never been a particularly religious family growing up. Sometimes they went to services at Easter or Christmas, but he never really understood why. He didn't think Dad believed much in any god who had more power than he did. In Mark's mind, if you didn't believe, going through the charade was just a waste of time, but there seemed to be lots of people growing up in Virginia that went to church just because it was what people did.

Joe had a similar take, or at least Mark had thought so, until he came home from college. Suddenly his older brother seemed different, and he didn't think it was just from dating Lauren. She was from Florida and one of those born-again types that went to church every Sunday. Joe had started going most of the time too and even seemed to like it. It was one of the few things he and Dad never saw eye to eye on, but Joe didn't seem to care. Now he said it was important to him to raise his kids with a faith they could believe in. Maybe he was on to something, but as Mark sat down on the couch in his apartment, flipped on the TV, and took a drink of beer, he didn't really know.

The phone rang, and as if on cue, the caller ID said it was Joe. Maybe he really was connected to a higher power.

Mark groaned, but muted the TV and clicked answer. "Yeah."

"Hey there, buddy."

"Hey. What's up?"

"How are things, you doing okay up there?"

"Yes, I'm fine. Just like I told Mom. What do you guys think, I'm going to jump off a bridge or something?"

Joe gave a nervous laugh. "No, we're just checking on you, little brother, that's all. It's been a hard couple weeks for all of us, you know. It's just that you're up there by yourself and we're down here. We have each other to talk to through things, that's all."

"Okay, well, I'm talking to people. Don't worry."

"Good."

Mark sighed. "We're talking right now, although I don't know what about. Didn't you say you needed me to do something?"

"Yeah, actually, I do. Are you up to tracking somebody down?"

"Sure. Why not." He switched off the TV and moved to his desk. "Hang on, let me get a pen."

"Okay, great. It shouldn't be too hard," continued Joe. "It's just a background check, interview, the usual paperwork delivery deal. A pretty basic beneficiary payment from a term life policy. The beneficiary is there in New York on the Upper West side, I think..." He paused. "Yeah, near West 87th Street. Donna Paris. Think you can do that?"

"Like right now?"

"No, just in the next couple days. We need to have the paperwork signed so we can clear this out of the system under the deadlines. Some stuff got backed up with Dad, and, well, we need to get them cleared up."

"Okay, I got it."

"Great. I'll email you the summary and a FedEx packet with all the paperwork should get to you in the morning by ten. If you could set something up with her tomorrow, the next day at the latest, that would be great."

"Uh huh," said Mark, jotting down the time and circling it on his notebook.

"And Mark?"

"Yeah?" This was getting old.

"We should talk more often, you know. You could come down for a long weekend, Lauren and the kids would love to see you. This hasn't been easy for Mom either. She could use your support."

He knew it. That's what this was. Mom had been peppering Joe to get Mark to come down more often. She probably wanted him to move back home, maybe even work at the agency with Joe.

Well that wasn't happening. His life was in New York, and his present job notwithstanding, he was going to find his own way.

"Okay, I'll talk to you tomorrow, then," said Mark. He'd do another one of Joe's little errands, but that was all. It was Dad's business, or at least it had been, and that alone was reason enough to stay away.

CHAPTER TWENTY-SIX

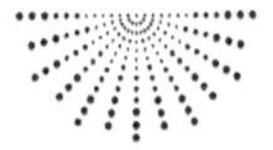

Mark walked back up the block, rechecking the address in his phone. Number 228. He must have passed it. He scanned the numbers of each building until he came to a small brown door tucked neatly into a recessed section of wall between a nail salon and a dry cleaner. He walked into the tight entryway, scanning the wall plate above the mailboxes for the right apartment.

He'd half-expected the woman to live in a doorman building. He glanced over his shoulder out at the street. It was kind of an up and coming neighborhood; maybe they hadn't reached the doorman status yet. Besides, there wasn't enough room in the tiny entranceway to work one anyway.

"D. Paris," he read, then pressed a round button.

A long pause came and went with no answer. He pushed it again, longer this time.

"Yes?" a voice answered amidst loud static.

"Hi. I'm Mark Parsons, I'm here to see—" The interior door buzzed loudly before he could finish.

"Donna Paris," he finished, as he opened the door. He checked his phone again. Apartment 3B. He didn't see an elevator, so he started up the stairs. The building was not what he'd call fancy—he wasn't sure if he'd even call it nice—but it had an endearing feel to it. Maybe it was the way the brass railing turned in a coil at the end of each staircase, or the molding along the ceiling and floor. It needed some restorative work, but clearly whoever had constructed the place had high intentions.

There were only three apartments on each floor, and when he turned the corner on the third landing, he easily spotted the blue door marked 3B and knocked.

"Coming!" a voice yelled from inside. This time he could clearly make out a feminine quality without the static. He heard a couple locks turn and the door opened. A woman appeared in front of him, a very attractive woman, hair pulled back into a ponytail, face flushed, and a towel around her shoulders. She looked like she came straight off the set of a shampoo commercial.

He tried to focus. "Hi, I'm Mark Parsons with Kingfisher Insurance. We'd emailed earlier about some paperwork?"

"Oh, right," she said, nodding and sounding slightly out of breath. "I'm Paris, nice to meet you." She extended her hand. Her skin was soft.

Mark scrunched his eyebrows in confusion. "Oh, I, uh, thought your first name was Donna. Donna Paris?" He glanced toward his bag like he should check his files. It was just his luck that the pretty one was the wrong apartment. "Do I have the right place?"

She smiled. "That's me. I'm Donna, but most people just call me Paris." She waved her arm. "Come on in."

Mark eyed the towel around her shoulders. "Sorry, did I catch you at a bad time?"

"No, not at all." She threw the towel on a table. "It's perfect. I was just finishing a workout."

"Yoga?"

"Kickboxing."

He raised his eyebrows slightly and she must have noticed.

"It's fun, ever try it?"

"No. I'm more of a team sports player," Mark answered.

"Soccer?"

"Sometimes, but mostly baseball." He grimaced, then reflexively rubbed his left elbow and corrected himself. "Softball now."

"Oh, nice. I love kickboxing. It's great cardio. Here, have a seat, I'll be right with you."

Mark sat on the couch and considered Ms. Paris with her skin-tight yoga pants that left little to the imagination. A loose-fitting tank top revealed the majority of a black sports bra that seemed to be working overtime.

He pulled his mind back to the task at hand, surveying the good-sized apartment. "What exactly do you do?" The room was full, slightly cluttered, but in an organized way that made her seem busy. Not huge, but decent sized for Manhattan where anything over three hundred square feet meant significant dollars, even more so with a view like she had.

"I deal drugs."

Mark did a double take. "You what?"

Paris smiled. "Prescription drugs, that is. To doctors. I'm a pharma rep."

"Oh..." Mark exhaled. That made sense. He'd seen the squads of attractive women in the waiting room at his doctor's office many times. She certainly fit the bill. "What kind of drugs do you sell?" For some reason, the only thing he could think of was Viagra, but that was probably from all the commercials he saw on TV. The man and the woman sitting in the bathtub at the base of the Rocky Mountains. Or maybe that was the other drug. They all seemed the same.

"Heart medication—you know, Beta Blockers, ACE Inhibitors, that kind of thing." She looked up from the counter she was writing on. "Do you have a science background?"

"No, just wondered." He didn't know what the hell she was talking about. It sounded like a foreign language to him.

His eyes watched her move around the small kitchen. He couldn't tell if she was tidying out of habit, necessity, or just flittering around so he could watch her. He tried not to stare, but there was no denying that she was unusually pretty. What was he doing here? He remembered the paperwork.

"So I have some forms to fill out and a few questions for you to answer," he said, pulling a couple manila folders from his bag. He spread them out on the coffee table.

Paris plopped down on the couch next to him, her ponytail flipping around to partially cover her smile. "Okay, what have you got for me?"

"Well," answered Mark, trying to concentrate, "most of this is just background. Certification that you are who you say you are, that you knew—" he leaned down to see the name at the top of the file folder. He kept forgetting it. "Doris Murphy."

Paris nodded. "Right."

Mark looked up at her. "Did you know Doris Murphy?" He remembered this from working with Dad in the past. Insurance was a mix of boring accounting, high-pressure salesmanship, and a bunch of very personal questions about history and health.

"Oh!" Paris chuckled. "Right, sorry. Yes, Doris Murphy was my aunt. My mother's older sister."

Mark nodded. "And you were close?" He paused for her to answer, but when she didn't, he clarified. "To Doris..."

"Yes, we were. At least we used to be, when I was younger. She didn't have any children, and I spent a lot of time at her house before I went to college."

"And Doris left you as the sole beneficiary of her life insurance policy." Mark picked up another one of the folders, inspecting a page with a yellow tab marker. This time he did actually remember what he was going to ask, but he wanted to make it look like he was doing his job correctly. "One hundred fifty-seven thousand dollars."

Paris gave a nervous smile. "I know, can you believe it? I was really surprised when I got your call." She picked at a throw pillow at the end of the couch with her fingers. "Well not your call, but the call from your office." She looked up at him. "That wasn't you, was it?"

"That was probably," Mark shifted his jaw for a beat before completing his answer, just long enough to be noticed. A thousand images shot through his mind in an instant. "That was probably my dad."

"Oh, that's nice. Is it a family business?"

"Kind of...well, my brother works there too, so I guess it is. He, uh, well, Dad passed away a few weeks ago."

Paris dropped the pillow, sitting up straight in her seat. "Oh shit..." She covered her mouth. "I mean, I'm so sorry. I didn't know."

Mark tried to smile, waving his hand. "That's okay. I'm just not used to having to say that yet. I'm helping out, since we're both in New York and the office is in Virginia. I don't usually make these kind of calls."

"Well, you're a natural." She gave him a hypnotizing, perfect-teeth smile that made him blink.

"Thanks." He moved two stacks of papers closer to her on the coffee table. "If you could just sign on these spots with the yellow highlights." He stood while she signed and stepped over to the window to give her some space.

On the wall next to him, he noticed a black and white picture of the old Yankee Stadium. That was a bit unusual for a hot girl's apartment. He nodded at the picture. "You a fan?"

"Absolutely," she answered, looking up from the papers. "Who doesn't love the Yankees?"

"Sox fans."

"Well, besides them." She finished her signatures, then walked over next to him. "I try to get to a few games a year."

He couldn't help but raise his eyebrows. "Really?" This girl was getting more interesting by the minute.

"Yeah, really. What, you think just because I'm a girl I don't like sports?"

Mark grinned. "Of course not. I know you like to box...and kick."

She nodded. "I do. I used to be friends with someone close to the team. They'd get me tickets whenever I wanted them. It was pretty nice."

"Wow, that's my kind of friend. What kind of person are we talking about here? Ticket agent, front office person, hot dog vendor?"

"Um...well..." He thought he saw her face flush a bit as she contemplated an answer. "More like a second baseman."

Hold the phone. A player? Now it was his turn to turn feel flush. He already felt like he was swimming in the deep end talking to this beautiful woman, but if she'd dated professional baseball players, he was really feeling out of his league.

"So like...Robby Swinson?"

Paris sighed and shook her head. "Jack Best. It was a couple years ago before he was traded to Cleveland. It was...interesting. But I met a lot of fun people and still know a bunch of people with the team. My sister, Paige, and I are going to the game tonight, actually. They're playing the Braves in interleague."

"Wow. I'm impressed." That sounded stupid, but hey, he was. He felt like an idiot trying to talk to her now or thinking that she was flirting with him. He clearly didn't stand a chance.

She shook her head. "Sorry. I shouldn't name drop like that. It's no big deal."

"No, it's fine. That's really cool." He moved back to the table and gathered up the forms. "Well, I think you can figure out the rest of this. We just try to make sure you don't have any questions for a claim this size." He turned back to her. "It's not that complicated, really."

He pulled a general Kingfisher business card out of his shirt pocket and scribbled his name and number on the back. "Sorry, I told you this was just a side thing." He smiled and handed her the card. "If you have any concerns, don't hesitate to give me a call."

"Okay, well thanks for the personal touch. And I'm really sorry to hear about your father. I'm sure he'd be happy that you're helping with the business." She touched his shoulder lightly with her hand.

Mark felt a tingle run through his body as her hand touched his shoulder. She moved it away, but only after it had been there a little longer than it needed to be. Was she flirting with him? Nah, probably just trying to show some sympathy because of his dad.

He smiled and shook her hand again. "Well, thanks for your time. Let us know if we can do anything else to help." He was still shaking her hand and he had to force himself to let go. She still felt amazing, but he felt like an idiot.

She laughed and showed him to the door. "Nice to meet you, Mark. Thanks for coming up."

He nodded. "Go Yanks!" he called, as he started down the stairs. He heard her giggle as she shut the door. Good grief.

CHAPTER TWENTY-SEVEN

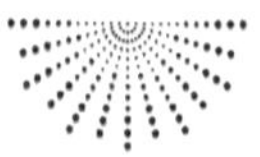

Mark hustled back to his office after delivering the paperwork to Donna Paris over lunch. His boss, Marvin, was back from his vacation and things were moving with more of a skip than they had been when he was out. It was nice while it lasted.

"I need those campaign updates before you leave today, Mark," Marvin said. He gave one of his extra-second condescending glances that meant he thought they should have already been done by now. Mark got an hour for lunch, but that didn't stop Marvin from expecting more.

Mark felt even less patience for his boss than usual, now that he had a tanned glow about him from his vacation. Screw you Marvin, he thought as he scanned the insurance files into his computer on the sly.

When he was done, he tried to clear his mind and go through the latest ad campaign interface screens. Each retailer had its own ad group in different online networks, which each had different sized creatives, which each had varying degrees of performance. All of which had to be tracked, optimized, and reported up the ladder.

It was boring, but he'd been doing it for a couple years and it wasn't that hard, especially with his automation programs.

Percy always kept telling him he needed to get out of that place and spread his wings. Maybe go into business for himself. That was easy for Percy to say. He'd gone on from BU to get his law degree and was now making good money downtown.

Mark's cell phone buzzed on his desk, and after a quick glance to make sure Marvin the Terrible wasn't walking his way, he answered the call from Joe.

"Hey."

"Hey bud, thanks for taking care of that project for me. I got your scans you sent through. You're overnighting the originals?"

"Yeah. And it's no problem. Believe me."

"What are you not telling me?" asked Joe.

"If you saw her, you'd know that you wouldn't need to be thanking me," replied Mark with a laugh.

"Really...that good-looking?"

"Yes."

"You don't even know how good-looking I was thinking."

"Whatever you were thinking, it's better. Think Bar Refaeli."

"What's that, some new Manhattan hot spot?"

"Dude, you've been married too long. She's a supermodel. Look her up, if your wife will let you, that is."

"Yeah, yeah, rub it in. Well, all in a good days work for the single man, I guess. I'll send you a check in a few days. Think of it as a gift from Dad."

Mark was silent. He didn't know how to respond to that.

"Hey, I'm sorry, I was just kidding. That wasn't cool. You know what I meant."

"Yeah."

"Anyway, so you gave her all the paperwork? Everything was good from the policy standpoint?"

"Yeah. She signed everything, no questions. I gave her—" Mark's phone beeped in his ear. "Hang on, I've got another call."

He looked at the screen and saw a local number he didn't recognize. "Hello?"

"Yes...hi, is this Mark?"

It was a woman's voice.

"Speaking."

"Oh, hi. It's Paris, from earlier today? Donna Paris. You were at my apartment going over the policy with me?"

Mark felt a pinch in his stomach but ignored it. "Oh, hey. I was just talking about you."

She laughed. "Oh really? All good I hope."

"Yes, I mean, it was about business. I'm actually on the other line with my brother going over your policy as we speak. Is everything all right? Do you have a question about it?"

"Yes, I mean no." She laughed. "I mean, yes, I do have a question, but not about the policy."

Mark really caught his breath this time. What was she calling for? "Oh, okay. What's up?" He tried to think of something witty to say. "I hope you don't need a sparring partner. I'm not very good at kickboxing. You'd probably kick my ass."

Paris laughed. "Fear not. No ass-kicking required. Actually, I don't know if you remember, but I'd mentioned that I'm going to the Yankee game tonight with my sister. Well, she just told me that she's bringing her boyfriend, Cary, so I need to get some extra tickets, and well, I thought maybe you'd like to join us."

Wait a minute, was she asking him out? How was this happening?

"Mark?"

"Uh, yeah, wow. That sounds like fun. I'd love to."

"Perfect! We're going to meet at Stan's, across from the Stadium around six. Do you know where that is?"

Did he know where Stan's was? It was kind of an unofficial institution in the Bronx, a dirty sports bar under the elevated subway tracks. It used to be directly across the street from the old stadium before they tore it down. Now it was a block or two away, but still served as a pre-game drink place for many of the pinstriped faithful.

"Of course, that sounds good. Thanks for asking me."

"Yeah, no problem. It should be fun. Okay, I'll see you then."

"Okay, bye."

He set the phone down, staring absently out the window. It buzzed again, Joe's face covering the screen. He picked it back up. "Hello?"

"Hey, I'm still here."

"Oh, right..."

"Dude, are you okay? Who was that?"

"You're not going to believe this..." Mark began. Now that he was about to say it, he wasn't sure he believed it either.

CHAPTER TWENTY-EIGHT

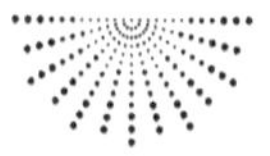

The mass of people streaming off the elevated "4 train" subway line spilled onto the sidewalk like a flood, the loud chatter of the throngs echoing off the grimy buildings that sat under the train platform, the entranceway to the baseball mecca that was Yankee Stadium in the Bronx. The old stadium was now flattened and turned into a parking garage and a grassy field, but the newest monolith sat across the street in all the glory that 1.5 billion dollars could bring.

It was still one of Mark's favorite places to be. Despite growing up in Virginia, Dad's New York roots had brought him to several games as a kid. Now that he lived in the city, Mark tried to go to half a dozen games a year. One of the benefits of being single was although he still didn't make a ton of cash, he didn't have a lot of extra expenses with a wife or family like Joe or Percy. That left plenty of spending money for going out. There were times when he started to wonder if he was getting too old for it all, but he usually ignored those feelings and tried to enjoy things while they lasted.

As Mark reached River Avenue, rows of street side shops were filled with memorabilia and spray-painted murals of baseball greats were everywhere. In any other location, Stan's would be an eyesore, but since it was within a stone's throw of the stadium, it was always jumping on game day. He walked into the bar, which was bursting with music and voices so loud he could barely think. The pregame from the radio broadcast blaring over the ceiling speakers only added to the chaos. He scanned the room and spied Paris sitting against the wall at a table with another couple. He took a deep breath and headed over, feeling like he was stepping up to his own major leagues as he passed by the images of Yankee greats on the walls.

Paris flipped her hair and turned toward him, her face lighting up in a smile. He tried not to let his knees buckle.

"Hey! You made it."

"I'm here," confirmed Mark. "Sorry, I'm late, the four was packed. I had to wait for two trains to go by."

Paris scooted over on the bench to make room. "Mark, this is my sister Paige, and her boyfriend, Cary."

Mark sat down and shook hands with each of them. "How ya doing?"

Paige was pretty, but had darker hair that was cut short under her ears. Cary was wearing a dress shirt and tie that looked expensive. His hair was short and spiked up in the front. They both looked to be in their midtwenties, making Mark guess that Paige was Paris's younger sister. He thought he remembered Paris being thirty from the paperwork she'd filled out.

"So Paris was just telling us how you two met," said Paige.

"Probably a short story, since it was just this morning." Mark gave a nervous laugh and turned to Paris. Her knee brushed his thigh under the table and a tingle ran through his body. "I'm glad you called, though," he added.

Paris smiled. "Me too. This should be fun. You said you were a Yankee fan. We can always use some more support in our row. Cary here is a Mets fan, if you can believe it."

"Boo!" said Paige, jabbing him in the ribs good naturedly. She leaned over and kissed him quickly. "But we still let him come."

"Hey, you can't control who you love, right?" said Cary.

Mark nodded as a thought flashed through his mind, but faded before he could catch it.

"Oh, I nearly forgot," said Paige, leaning into the table toward Paris. "You won't believe who I just saw in Nordstrom when I was doing my returns yesterday."

"Who?" asked Paris.

"Jane Warner! Do you remember her from Terry's wedding? She was standing right in front of me."

Mark zoned out for a second, trying to get the thought back that had floated through his brain a moment ago, but it was gone.

"Did you talk to her?" asked Paris, leaning in.

"Sure, I talked to her. I don't know if she was too happy to see me, though."

"Why not?" asked Cary, trying to act interested in the girls' conversation.

Paige feigned embarrassment and patted Cary's shoulder. "Well, I kind of started dating her boyfriend after that wedding."

Paris's face brightened in recognition. "Oh, yeah!"

"You're terrible," said Cary, eyebrows raised. "Why did you do that?"

Paige laughed. "Don't worry. I'm with you now."

Mark tried to think of something to contribute to this conversation of people that he didn't really know. He shot out the first thing that came to his mind. "Yeah, but for how long?"

There was a nervous pause as the three of them just stared. Paris's jaw dropped in surprise. Then everyone burst out laughing.

"Dude, you're cold as ice," exclaimed Cary across the table. He gave Mark a high five. "Nice one, Mark."

Paris grinned and shook her head.

"I think you're going to get along with us just fine," laughed Paige.

Mark blushed. "I'm sorry, that was rude."

"Not at all," said Paige. "I probably had that coming."

They drank a pitcher of beer and wandered across the street and into the stadium just before game time.

CHAPTER TWENTY-NINE

Paris handed everyone tickets as they walked in gate four, through the concourse of the Great Hall, and into the surround of the field. Mark still marveled at the difference between the old and the new stadium, despite being at the new one now many times. The old stadium was a maze of narrow concrete interior passages, with little in the way of concession stands. You didn't see the field until you emerged from a dark tunnel, when suddenly the great expanse of green field was in front of you, like a dream. The new park was much more grand, with dozens of food choices every twenty feet, and it gave a clear view of the field from all the concourses. It lacked, though, that old-style charm and ambiance of the old park, and the ongoing debate among die-hard fans was often over which version was better.

Paris led them down the row of seats toward the field on the first base side, stopping just three rows behind the home team dugout.

"Wow," Mark marveled. "These are great seats!"

"She has connections," chuckled Paige, before her expression turned down as she glanced at Paris. "Oh, sorry, maybe I shouldn't have said that."

Paris waved her off. "It's okay. I told him."

Mark smiled. "I think it's pretty cool, actually."

They settled into their seats just as the fielders were warming up. "So why aren't you still with Jack Best?" asked Mark. "Is it because he was traded to Cleveland?" He decided he might as well use the opening to get some more information.

Paris shrugged. "It was a lot of things. Cleveland was part of it. It's a whole different lifestyle, dating a pro ballplayer."

"Different, bad?" asked Mark.

Paris tilted her head. "Not necessarily bad...there are obviously a lot of positives, a lot of perks." She paused, seeming to search for the right word. "Just different. I think it's harder to feel like you're living in reality sometimes when the fame component is lurking in the background. On one hand, you're pinching yourself, on the other you're always looking over your shoulder for whoever else might be trying to glob on."

Mark thought it was hard to imagine a girl like Paris having to look over her shoulder. A man would be crazy to pass her up. But he supposed there were a lot of competing interests in the life of a major leaguer.

The game began and the Yankees pitcher started strong, striking out the side. The crowd was already getting into it, standing in each two-strike count. Mark watched the players file into the dugout just feet in front of him. It was a nice view. He stared over at Paris in the seat next to him. He was feeling a little surreal himself right now.

"Didn't you say you used to play baseball too?" asked Paris.

Mark nodded. "In high school."

Cary leaned over. "Oh yeah, what position?"

"Pitcher," answered Mark.

"Did you play in college?" asked Cary.

"No..." Mark had told this story so many times over the years, he knew the lines pretty well by now. "I blew out my arm the end of my senior year."

"Lefty?" asked Cary, grimacing.

Mark nodded, quietly.

"How did you know he was a lefty?" asked Paris.

"I saw you rubbing that elbow when you said you blew out your arm," answered Cary.

Mark chuckled. He didn't even notice anymore.

"Were you good?" asked Paris.

"Yeah. I was pretty heavily recruited. There were pro scouts at most of my starts senior year. Coach thought I could have gone in the third round, maybe the second..."

"Ouch," said Cary. "That sucks."

"Yep." Mark faked a smile. "But hey, that was a long time ago."

The Yankee shortstop hit a long drive off the left field wall. The crowd erupted as he burned around the bases, sliding into third headfirst for a triple. They stood up and screamed. Paris reached over and gave him a double high five in the excitement.

By the bottom of the third, the Yankees held a two-run lead. Cary and Mark took food orders and walked up to the concourse between innings. They lined up at Carl's, which Mark was convinced had the best cheesesteaks in the city. They weren't exactly what you'd call good for you, but they were delicious.

"So Paris, huh?" said Cary, smiling.

"Yeah..." answered Mark, not exactly sure what to say.

"She's something. Believe it or not, she's pretty particular about the guys she dates."

"Besides the ballplayers?" laughed Mark.

"Yeah, well, I think that was a one-time thing," Cary stepped up in the line. "And besides, you seem to qualify for that category too, no?"

Mark scoffed. "Not quite."

They hauled their cheesesteaks and four plastic beer cups back down the aisle, attempting to settle back into their seats without spilling all over everyone.

"Thank you, sir," Paris said as Mark handed her a drink.

"Sure," said Mark. "This is fun. Thanks."

"I'm having fun, too." She paused, like she had to say something more, but didn't.

"What?" asked Mark.

"I'm glad you came. I was a little worried I was being too forward."

"It's still early in the game, give it time." Mark laughed and dug into his cheesesteak. A generous helping of peppers and onions slid out the back of his roll and landed on his pant leg.

Paris handed him some extra napkins. "Smooth."

Mark felt his face turning red, but tried to relax. "See, I told you there was still time for things to go wrong." She smiled, wiping the corner of his mouth with a napkin.

The next few innings moved quickly without any base runners. Mark tried to enjoy watching the game from such good seats, while still taking advantage of being with Paris. By the eighth, the Yankees still clung to their two-run lead. "This is not going to end well," Mark muttered out loud.

"No?" asked Paris, turning her head, quizzically.

Mark saw her expression and laughed. "No, I don't mean this..." he gestured at them both. "I mean the game. This is always where they give it away. We have no middle relief."

As if on cue, a long ball rocketed off the bat of the visiting team's first baseman, landing softly in the bullpen in left. Mark shook his head. "See what I mean?"

"There's still time," said Paris.

The next batter was a lefty, a big slugger that looked like he could hit the ball all the way to the scoreboard. The Yankees manager stepped out of the dugout in front of them, making a slow walk to the mound. He raised his arm, signaling for the lefty specialist.

Paige leaned over from down the row. "Is this good or bad?"

Paris shrugged. "Mark seems to think it's bad."

"But nothing's happened yet," said Page.

"He doesn't trust their relievers," explained Paris.

The next pitch came in hard, and the ball was popped up to

the first base side. It was looping in a high arc right toward where they were sitting. Everyone bolted out of their seat, scrambling to figure out where it would land.

A big guy in the seat behind them started to lean in, pushing Mark to the side just as the ball came down. The other man missed, and the ball bounced high off the concrete between them. Mark raised his arm and leaped, snatching the ball from the air.

"I got it!" he screamed, suddenly aware of his voice sounding much more high and shrill than he'd want it to be.

"Hey! Way to go!" shouted Cary.

Paris snickered, but put her arm around him and squeezed.

"I mean," said Mark, "I got it," this time in a much deeper voice.

"Look guys!" Paige screamed, pointing to the outfield. Mark's and Paris's faces filled the giant video board in centerfield. A big heart was superimposed around their heads. Mark's heart started racing, but Paris just smiled and leaned over and kissed him. Everyone in the seats around them cheered.

Mark took a deep breath and smiled as Paris squeezed his arm playfully. "I take it back, this pitcher is doing a great job." He raised his other arm in a cheer. "Come on Rojas, bring it in there again, just like that one." Paris laughed as they sat back down in their seat.

The next pitch was a weak grounder to second to end the inning. Paige and Cary stood, gathering their things. "We're going to head out," said Paige. "Cary's got an early morning deposition."

"Oh," said Mark, looking at Paris. "Do you want to go, too?" He glanced at the scoreboard. It was a close game, but he wasn't going to raise a fuss since he was her guest.

"Are you kidding?" said Paris. "We have to see who wins!"

Mark smiled. That's what he was hoping she'd say. "Okay."

"Mark, it was great to meet you," said Cary, shaking his hand as they squeezed past in the row.

"You too," said Mark.

"Be nice to my big sister," said Paige, leaning in for a quick hug. She looked at Paris and whispered, "I like him," loud enough for Mark to hear.

For once, the bullpen held, and the Yankees made it out with a victory. The crowd cheered as a soft fly to right brought the final out, and the customary tune of Sinatra singing *New York, New York* echoed over the loudspeakers.

"You should have more faith in your team," said Paris, as they filed out the concourse.

"I guess."

"You're not one of those glass-half-empty kind of guys, are you?"

Mark shook his head. "I think things are pretty good."

Paris smiled. "Me too. Come on, get me home safely."

CHAPTER THIRTY

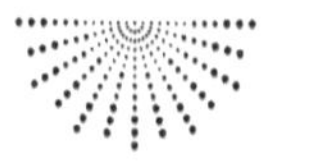

They squeezed onto the subway, packed as always after a game. Mark didn't mind, since it meant he and Paris were pressed tight against each other amongst the crush of navy blue dressed revelers chattering all around them. She rested her head against his shoulder as they rode in silence on the express line.

When they filed out at the stop near her apartment, she pulled him into a corner deli. "Let's get a bottle of wine."

Mark nodded, his mind trying to keep up with the implications of what walking her home and buying a bottle of wine meant. He picked out a bottle of moderately priced Pinot Noir from California he thought he'd seen before. While Paris was still browsing in the back, he quickly threw a pack of Trojans on the counter and paid before she came up. He was the last one to be presumptive, but if this was leading anywhere close to where he thought it might, he didn't want to be caught empty-handed. He slipped them into his pocket before she came around the corner.

"Ready?"

"I am," said Mark, smiling.

They reached her apartment, still familiar from the morning. His head was spinning at all that had happened in one short day.

She took the bottle into the kitchen and poured two glasses. "Mmm, this smells good."

They settled next to each other on the couch. Paris held her long-stem glass up for a toast. "To surprises."

"Surprises." Mark wondered what kind of surprises she had in mind as he clinked his glass against hers. He tried to make sure he didn't surprise her with a wine spill on her black leather couch, but he still couldn't help grinning.

"Why are you smiling? You should know I don't usually invite guys up that I've just met."

"That's good, because I don't either. I mean, get invited up to girl's apartments that I just met."

"Good."

"Except for the pretty ones," Mark added. "That happens all the time."

She laughed, taking a slow sip of wine.

He looked around the apartment. "So I know you like the Yankees, you have a sister named Paige, and had an aunt named Doris. What am I missing?" He paused, giving her a knowing glance like it was her turn to fill in the blanks.

"Hmm, you want more, huh?"

"Yep. You're busted."

"Well," said Paris. "I think you know a little more than that from all that paperwork you had me fill out. And I told you where I work."

Mark took a sip of his wine. It was good, or maybe it was just the company. Sometimes when he drank something, it felt like every pore in his body was absorbing it to its fullest. He sensed this might be one of those times. "True. I'm sorry, but tell me more. How did going by Paris instead of Donna happen?"

She sighed, but then shared how she grew up on Long Island, that her dad was an investment banker, her parents were semi-retired now with an apartment on the Upper East Side and a house in the Hamptons. She spent her high school years in a boarding school in New Hampshire, went to college at NYU while modeling part-time. She started pre-med, but decided she couldn't bear that many more years of school and switched to general science. Near graduation, several people she knew were getting recruited as drug reps, so she stepped into that. It wasn't too hard. Doctors seemed to like having her come to their office. Sure, she was playing a bit on her looks too, but she also knew her science and wasn't just some dumb blonde.

"And the name?" Mark asked again, when she seemed done speaking.

She waved her hand and smiled. "It's silly. When I was at NYU, I got it in my head that it would be glamorous to be called Paris. My family had spent a summer there when I was in high school and it always stuck with me. Have you ever been there?"

Mark shook his head. He hadn't been out of the country, unless you counted Canada. "I haven't. It sounds exotic."

She nodded. "It does, doesn't it? So that's how it started, and then it just kind of stuck." She stared into his eyes. "You don't think it sounds too haughty, do you?"

Mark frowned. "No, it's cute," he said, while thinking to himself that it did seem a little haughty. "It's like New York, New York, but Paris, Paris." He took a sip of his wine and placed it back on the coffee table. "It is a little confusing, though."

She laughed. "I'm worth it though, right?"

Mark nodded, happy to be there with her. "So what are you going to do with the life insurance money? If I may ask."

She chuckled. "Well, you just did, so I guess you can. It's okay. I don't know, actually. It's not that I'm not appreciative, but I don't really need the money. I'll probably put most of it away, maybe donate a portion of it. I like to support the downtown women's shelter when I can."

"Wow, that's...admirable."

"What? Is that bad?"

"No," answered Mark. "I'm just trying to find a flaw. So far you're too good to be true."

Paris reached for the wine bottle and refilled their glasses. Mark couldn't help but notice she didn't volunteer any flaws, either.

"You know, sometimes I feel like all of this isn't worth it." She stared off out the window.

"What, the apartment?" He was starting to wonder where this was heading. Maybe it was the wine.

"No," she answered. "Just all this life in the big city. Running around, trying to be a part of the trendy crowd, making lots of money."

"I know, I just *hate* that," said Mark, making a face.

She tapped him on the knee. "Stop it, I'm serious. Don't you ever wonder if you'd be happier living out in the country, a little barn by a pond with fields and horses?"

Mark tried to follow along. "That sounds like something out of a movie."

"Yeah, but it sounds nice, doesn't it?"

He shrugged. "Sure, it sounds great. But I wonder if it's really as great as it looks in the magazines pictures and in the movies. There's probably a lot of shit to deal with too."

"You mean not being happy?"

"No, I mean the shit. Literally. From the horses. That's a lot of work."

She laughed, setting her wine glass down on the table. She leaned toward him and planted a delicate kiss on his lips.

Mark felt his pulse race as he kissed her with his eyes open wide. God, she was gorgeous. How was this happening? He closed his eyes, trying to take in the sequence of the last couple weeks. Images of his father flash before him. Then for a moment, he saw the image of Amy from the street at the veterinary clinic, only this time she turned around so he could se her face. Then she waved at him through the window.

He opened his eyes, pulling back from Paris slightly. That was weird. He hadn't thought of Amy for a long time, certainly not when he was kissing someone.

"What's wrong?" asked Paris.

He took a deep breath. Get it under control. He stared into her eyes, noticing for the first time that they were almost green. He marveled at the gentle curve of her face, counting five tiny freckles scattered across the bridge of her nose. He tried to force the distracting thoughts from his mind.

"Nothing," he replied, reaching up and running his hand through her hair, pulling her closer, and blocking out any other thoughts. This was better. This was now. This was really happening. There was no need to think about things that happened long ago. He moved his hand to her thigh, caressing her leg, her skin as soft as velvet. "I'm glad you called me," he muttered between kisses.

"I'm glad you came."

He pressed his lips harder against hers, their mouths parting slightly, her tongue dancing against his. He pulled back for a short breath. "This isn't because I just gave you a hundred fifty thousand dollars, is it?"

He felt her lips turn in a smile. "That wasn't you. It was my Aunt Doris."

"True." He tried not to think about some old lady named Doris. "So that's not why we're doing this?" he asked again.

"Doing what?" she panted, moving her hand against his back.

"This..." He leaned down, kissing her tenderly between her breasts along the top of her shirt.

"Maybe." She giggled softly.

He pulled his head back up, raising his eyebrows.

She smiled playfully, then stood, reaching for his hand. "Come with me."

Mark froze. "I don't know," he deadpanned. "I should be going."

She rolled her eyes, placing her finger to her lips. They walked down the narrow hallway to her bedroom. When they entered, she pushed him gently down onto the edge of the bed, then slowly lifted her shirt over her head.

A GARBAGE TRUCK down on the street woke Mark from a crazy dream. He stretched his legs, his foot hitting an unfamiliar metal bar at the end of the mattress. He opened his eyes halfway, the sunlight streaming in the window, his head feeling slightly sore. He looked around at the empty bed next to him, slowly remembering where he was.

Wow, it wasn't a dream. He heard the shower running in the next room. The details from the night before slowly start seeping back into his mind, but they were a bit hard to fathom. The water stopped, and his eyes opened wide when the bathroom door opened. Paris entered the bedroom, her hair falling around her face. Her body, glistening wet, was wrapped in a white towel, her breasts squeezed magnificently together along the top.

If this was a dream, he didn't ever want to wake up.

Paris grinned slyly. "Good morning."

"Morning to you."

"I was glad to see you were still here."

"What, you thought I'd sneak out in the middle of the night? 'Wham bam, thank you ma'am' kind of thing?"

She shrugged.

"Oh, I'm sure you get that a lot."

She smiled again, bigger this time. "I told you. I don't do this a lot."

Mark propped himself up on an elbow. "Well, the truth is, I tried to leave early this morning, but your floors are really squeaky, and I was afraid I'd wake you. You really need to get those fixed."

She laughed and batted her eyes, pulling a brush off the dresser and working it through her long hair. "I have to work today, unfortunately."

He realized what she was saying and eased his legs over the side of the bed. "Oh, right...so I should probably get out of here." He was having a hard time taking his eyes off her body.

"Sorry," she said. "I had a really good time."

"Yeah, that was a great game. I can't believe that catch Green made in left field."

She frowned. "That's not what I was talking about."

Mark feigned a confused look. "Oh, well, obviously the cheesesteak was amazing too. I don't know how I could have forgotten that."

She opened her mouth wide. "Shut up!"

He laughed. "Oh, you mean that...well, yeah, that was pretty good."

"Pretty good? What?" She ripped off the towel and threw it over Mark's head. He moaned and pulled it off dramatically, then caught his breath at the view. She climbed onto the end of the bed and leaned toward him.

Mark's head began to spin. "Okay, I take it all back. What baseball game?"

"That's what I thought," said Paris, lying next to him on her stomach. Mark followed the line of her back into the curve of her perfect ass and tried to control himself. She reached out and placed her hand on his thigh, slowing inching upward. "Think you can handle a double header?" she whispered seductively.

"Um...I think today's an off day."

Paris slid up closer to him against the top of the bed. She took a firm hold of his manhood, leaning in and kissing his chest. "Are you sure?"

"No," Mark moaned softly, gasping for breath. "I'm...I'm not sure.

"Mmm," she said, moving her lips up to his neck. "That's what I thought."

CHAPTER THIRTY-ONE

The next couple weeks saw Mark and Paris spending a lot of time together. She seemed to find him fun to be around. Clearly, he was a bit different than her normal jet-setting crowd, but she kept saying that he was wholesome. He never would have considered himself wholesome, but whatever she saw in him, it seemed to be working.

Against his better judgment, he even took her out with Percy and Tyler to Chelsea Piers to hit some golf balls at the driving range. They quickly discovered she was on the golf team in high school in New Hampshire, and she made them all look pretty bad. Of course, Tyler got mad and started dumping his rental clubs over the edge of the three-story hitting platform, and they had to make a run for it before they got kicked out, but other than that, it was fun.

Shortly after that, Paris had to go on a week-long trip for business to Barcelona for a European Cardiology meeting with her company. Mark asked what that entailed, and she explained it was primarily a lot of standing around an exhibit hall and smiling at doctors who came by. The evenings consisted of endless dinners entertaining those same doctors to convince them to prescribe her company's drugs to their patients. In between was a major boondoggle, with many of the overly attractive sales reps drinking and hooking up. Of course, she said that wasn't her kind of thing, and Mark was pretty sure he believed her, but he couldn't help wishing he could come along, even if it was just to tour Barcelona.

She'd called him twice in the evenings, but it was tough to coordinate the times since that part of Spain was five hours ahead of New York. The first call he'd missed when he was in a meeting at work, but on the second they'd had a short but good talk. He was looking forward to seeing her again, and he didn't think it was just because of the sex. He really liked her. How much and how serious, he wasn't sure, but it was nice to have someone to spend time with and a new relationship to sink himself into.

He'd had a few casual relationships here and there with other girls in Boston and in New York, but they hadn't lasted more than a few dates. Work was boring, he still felt oddly numb with everything going on with Dad, and if he was honest with himself, he didn't want to think about his trip to Harborwood, his conversation with Mr. Holland, or any prospects of seeing Amy.

On the evening that Paris was to return to New York, they'd planned for her to come over to his apartment for a nice dinner. It would be the first time she'd spent any significant time at his place, other than once when they'd bounced by for fifteen minutes on the way back from a bike ride in Central Park.

He'd left work two hours early since he needed more time to finish cleaning and tidy up. She would surely expect his kitchen to be tidy, even if he was bringing in take out from a bistro around the corner. He suspected there was a decent chance she would spend the night, so that meant clean sheets, clean bathroom—basically he had to clean the entire apartment. Luckily, the place wasn't as big as hers, but he was a guy, and spotlessness was not usually his main priority.

She texted him when she landed at Kennedy, saying she'd be to his place around six once she dropped off her suitcase, showered, and changed. He suggested she just come there, and he'd be more than happy to help her with both the showering and the changing, but she said she really needed to get home first after being gone for a week.

Mark conceded, and it was probably for the best, since it gave him a little more time to get the table set and everything in order. He was behind schedule, mostly because he'd spent more time than he should have agonizing over a playlist on his computer for the evening's music. His wireless speakers were positioned strategically around the apartment for maximum impact and just the right mix of chill and romantic tunes to keep the night flowing in the right direction. Honestly he didn't know what the hell he was doing with someone Paris's caliber, but so far, winging it seemed to be working, so he wasn't going to change anything now.

At ten minutes to six, the street door buzzed.

Shit! She was early.

The water was boiling on the stove for the pot sticker appetizer he had decided to make at the last minute so he didn't look entirely lame by serving only take out, he hadn't lit the candles on the table, and the music wasn't even playing.

He rushed over to the panel on the door and buzzed her up without even answering. He jumped over the couch to turn on the music, nearly catching his toe on the top of the cushion and tumbling into the bookshelf. That would not have been good.

As the music came on, a knock sounded at the door. He hustled over, pausing to run his hands through his hair in the mirror and straighten the collar of his cotton polo.

He did a few short fake smiles to loosen his lips, then threw the door open. "You're early," he exclaimed.

But it wasn't Paris.

"Hi, Mark."

It was Amy, staring back at him with an uneasy smile.

For a moment, he thought his jaw had actually fallen on the floorboards, or that his heart may have stopped beating. He blinked his eyes. Amy was standing in front of him. In New York.

At his apartment. His face probably said all that and more the way she looked back at him and his stunned silence.

"Amy..." he finally forced himself to answer.

"I know, this is crazy to just show up like this at your front door, but I just had this feeling that I needed to talk to you." She looked past him to his apartment. "Can I come in?"

"Uh, sure," he managed, as she walked past him. "How did you even know where I live?"

He didn't remember saying his address to her dad. He couldn't even be sure if he'd mentioned that he lived in Manhattan. He forced a smile, slowly gathering his footing.

"My dad told me about how he ran into you on the boardwalk the other week in Harborwood. I couldn't believe he'd seen you."

"Yeah," Mark nodded. "It was crazy."

"Anyway, he kept talking about it, he mentioned about your dad..." She paused and looked into his eyes. For a few seconds, high school came flooding back. He hadn't really seen her close up in twelve years, but time had been good to her; she still looked nearly as youthful as she had as a senior in high school. Her hair was a little shorter, maybe she wore a little more makeup around her eyes than she used to, but it was the same Amy.

"I'm so sorry to hear about it, Mark."

"Yeah..." he replied. He didn't really want to talk about that. He didn't really know if he wanted to talk about anything right then. Not with her. "You know, things were always complicated with Dad."

"Yeah," she said. "So I called your mom. She gave me your address. She said she thought it was a great idea for me to stop up and see you since it isn't that far from the shore. I know it's probably a shock. I should have called, but I tend to get ahead of myself with these kinds of things if you remember."

Mark nodded. He did remember.

"After Daddy told me he'd seen you...I just, I know this sounds stupid, but I couldn't stop thinking about you. I felt like there were a lot of things that never got resolved that we might need to talk about."

He tried to think of something to say. She was right, there were a lot of things unresolved, but that was mostly because they'd been apart for twelve years. And she'd moved to California. Oh, and she'd gotten married.

Something started making a sound in the kitchen. He turned his head to see his pot boiling over just as the door buzzed again. His stomach did a somersault.

Paris. He'd forgotten all about her with Amy standing there.

He tried to organize a plan in his mind, but nothing was coming. "Hang on," he said to Amy, as he walked back to the door and pushed the speaker button. "Hello?"

"Hi, it's me," answered Paris's cheery voice.

Mark just stood there, frozen.

Amy shook her head and closed her eyes. "Oh my gosh. I'm so sorry, I was so caught up in seeing you I didn't even notice." She scanned the room. "The table, the music, you're even cooking dinner. You have someone coming over and I'm here in the way."

Mark tried to say something, but the door buzzed again and interrupted him. He pushed the button again.

"Mark?" came Paris's confused voice.

He didn't know what else to do, so he buzzed her up.

"I'm so embarrassed," continued Amy, turning and walking back out the door. "I should have called." She threw her hands up in the air and began moving faster down the hall toward the elevator. "I should have called! I can't just barge in here after God knows how many years and just expect you to be ready to talk to me."

"Amy..." said Mark, following her out the door but stopping at the edge of the hall.

The elevator dinged and Paris stepped out, almost bumping into Amy, who paused, stared at Paris for a moment, and then back at Mark. She shook her head, brushed a tear from her eye, then marched into the elevator.

Paris hesitated a second, trying to make sense of what just happened, then looked up at Mark in the doorway and smiled. "Hola, stranger!"

Mark smiled back weakly and hugged her in the doorway, feeling dazed. He looked back at the elevator just in time to see Amy's face disappear behind the closing door.

"What's the matter?" asked Paris. "You look like you've seen a ghost. I haven't been gone that long, have I?"

"I, uh...sorry," he replied. "I think I'm trying to do too many things at once." He pulled her closer and kissed her gently as they walked back into his apartment. "How was your trip?"

"Oh my God, it was amazing. It was like traveling back in time, you know?"

"Yeah," he answered, looking back into the empty hallway as he shut the door.

CHAPTER THIRTY-TWO

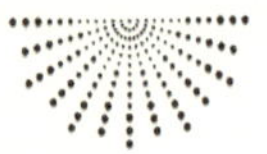

Amy burst out the doorway and into the busy street. She just started walking, not even bothering to look at which way she was going.

"How could I be so stupid?" she screamed, ignoring others near her on the street. She figured they were used to crazy people yelling to themselves in the big city, and that's surely what she was. Crazy.

It was Dylan all over again. The only difference was that with him, she'd actually gone through and married him. Not that it did her any good.

What did she think was going to happen this time? That she'd just waltz into Manhattan to see Mark out of the blue after twelve years apart? Sure he talked with Dad, but he was probably still in shock from his own father dying. It was ridiculous. He hadn't come looking for her. He didn't know she lived in Harborwood. He didn't even intend to see her dad.

So why did he go to Harborwood, anyway? That was the question she'd been wondering about for the past several weeks. It wouldn't leave her mind, actually, and was ultimately what drove her to Mark's doorstep, hoping to find out.

But she didn't. All she learned was that the woman getting out of the elevator was clearly coming to see Mark for a date. Probably a model or something. She was gorgeous. Mark had obviously moved on after all these years, and from the looks of it, he was having some pretty good luck in New York, despite what his mom had told her on the phone about him being single and not seeing anyone.

He probably didn't even think about her anymore. He'd made it pretty clear they were done at the end of high school when he let her drive away from his house. Dating someone that looked like the elevator woman would be enough to keep Amy out of his mind, that's for sure.

There was a time when Amy thought that her life had worked out pretty well, despite Mark's unexpected curve. Her heart had been broken, for sure, but she'd picked herself up, determined to make her own happiness. After graduation, she took the scholarship to veterinary school at Oregon. She knew Mark stayed in Virginia working for his dad, but thought she heard he moved somewhere else with someone from school after that, but didn't know where.

For a while her parents asked her about him when they talked, passed on any news they heard around town, but after a few months the questions and the news ended. She'd even tried to call him a couple times over her freshman year, tried to stay in touch, but he didn't respond. She'd found his profile online over the years but he didn't seem to update it often so she didn't learn much. Clearly he'd meant what he said that he was better off without her. Time passed and she moved on.

She met Dylan Roberts at Oregon. He was a few years ahead in med school. Stupidly, it was his name that got her attention before she even saw him. She bumped into him in the hall, his name tag on a white lab coat the first thing that stared her in the face. His last name was written first, and she'd giggled at the thought of his having the same name as the folk singer. When she raised her head and caught a glance at his dark hair and steely good looks, she could sense she was already halfway to trouble.

Dylan had seemed like a good idea, sort of, when things got started. The truth was, despite her best intentions, she was still reeling from being rejected by Mark. It had caught her by surprise, those last few weeks in high school. She had long decided Mark was the one, that they were meant to be together 'til the end. Well it was the end—the end of their relationship—but not the end of their lives like she'd planned.

Early on, Dylan seemed to be all the things that Mark was not: confident, charming, successful. For a while that felt like a good thing. But life got serious really fast, before she even realized it. She lost herself. Then she got pregnant.

They got married very quickly, mostly due to pressure from his parents to keep up appearances, but then she lost the baby. At the time, losing Mark had seemed like it was the worst thing in the world, but when she lost the new life growing within her, she felt as though her soul had torn in two. Looking back, she wondered if it may have been for the best, as terrible as that sounded. She was so young, and a marriage with Dylan would have been no way to raise a child. But it had left a mark, pulling her just a bit more inside of herself than before.

Every time he touched her, which wasn't often, she died a little bit inside. Like a flashlight whose batteries were going bad, the glow that once poured from her eyes seemed to be gradually fading. Amy saw it now when she looked in the mirror. She'd just passed thirty, and hell, she still felt in her mind the same as she did as an eighteen-year-old, but the lines creeping in around her eyes, much more than the other women she knew her same age, told a different story.

Those three years in high school with Mark seemed like a hundred years ago as Amy thought back on them, but also like yesterday. She supposed most things seemed like that as she got older. Ugh, maybe it was a hundred years ago. Thirty was a long way from sixteen when she first met Mark on the boardwalk. She'd once had so much hope, fire that seemed to exude from her being, that's what Daddy used to tell her.

After the miscarriage, she and Dylan just stared at each other for a while, wondering what they'd gotten into. He took a residency at a prestigious plastic surgery clinic down in Santa Barbara. She joined him after she graduated, taking a job at an animal hospital.

It was good—sometimes. But mostly they seemed like they were leading two separate lives. They both stayed distracted by digging into their respective work until she started suspecting he wasn't spending all his extra time at the office. He'd be late for dinner. Again. She almost didn't even notice anymore, it had become such a norm. He was reviewing patient charts, or out for drinks with his partners, or sometimes away all together at a medical conference. He couldn't call since it was late. His phone was almost out of battery. Sometimes he didn't even provide a reason.

They didn't talk about it. In some ways, that was easier. It wasn't fun to bang your heads together, trying to argue around the fact that you were stuck in a loveless marriage and didn't see a way to call it quits. He held on because his parents would be mortified and couldn't face the social disgrace from their country club friends, and she'd told herself she wouldn't let go again, that she'd find a way to make it work like Mark hadn't.

Dylan was just discrete enough not to leave anything incriminating, yet she still knew. She knew he didn't love her. She knew he wasn't faithful. She knew he was pouring his affections into someone else, maybe more than one. She was left with the scraps, the dredges, the frustrations. All the shit and very little that was good.

Her life hadn't turned out the way her sixteen-year-old self had expected. She wondered why she was still there, lost in a rut in the side of the road that she couldn't get out of. Somehow bad had become strangely normal. She didn't think she deserved it, although it was just as much her fault as his. She could have said no, she could have seen the warning signs back in college, but she chose to ignore them.

That's how it was until one weekend almost three years ago when she decided on a whim to surprise him at a meeting in Vail. She'd told herself it would be fun, that they could stay a few extra days after the meeting and ski, but the moment before she opened the door to his room and found him with some bimbo with a body from a magazine, she asked herself if she really did know what she was doing. If she was just pushing down the accelerator to bring her sad little marriage to its ultimate conclusion.

Not surprisingly, he immediately tried to deny that anything serious was going on, that this was the first time, that it was an isolated incident, that the girl had come on to him in a bar after the convention. It was so hard, he said, working with so many beautiful women.

She didn't buy it, but didn't know what to do. So she took an unexpected weeklong vacation from the clinic and flew home to Virginia see her parents. Mom hadn't been doing well. Her cancer, which had faded into remission for several years after high school, had returned with a vengeance three months prior. She was fighting it, of course, and there was some new kind of therapy that seemed to be working, but it was anyone's guess as to how much longer she'd be with them.

Amy hated that she lived a continent away and barely got to see them. Dylan said he didn't like to fly over the holidays since he traveled so much for work already. So on the few occasions when she did get back east, she flew home alone while he stayed back in California doing God knows what.

Well, now she knew, and it was finally clear that it was the end. Her marriage was over, and truth be told, she was relieved.

AFTER AN HOUR WANDERING THE CITY, Amy hailed a taxi to Penn Station to catch the Long Branch line of NJ Transit back to

Harborwood. It was funny, Mark had only been a couple hours away ever since she'd come back east, but she hadn't even known he lived in New York. She tried not to cry, but the tears streamed down her face all the way through the train station. The man behind the ticket counter had asked if she was okay. She probably looked a wreck.

"Thank you, I'm fine," she whispered with a rather unconvincing nod, then slinked away to the train platform.

Why did she always have to put herself in these positions for dramatic confrontations? Was she subconsciously trying to sabotage herself by showing up unannounced at Mark's door? Sure, she'd called him on the way up, on the number his mom gave her, but she just got his voicemail and didn't leave a message. Did she think he'd smile, sweep her off her feet, and carry her off into the sunset? It was pitiful.

She was almost thirty-one years old. She should have learned by now that life doesn't work that way. She used to pride herself on being free-spirited, uninhibited, but as she got older, those qualities only seemed to send her headlong into painful experiences from which she couldn't fully recover.

Life used to feel like a vibrant dream, like when she stood at the railing on the boardwalk with Mark, the salt-tinged breeze blowing through her hair. Everything seemed possible. But now she'd learned that such thoughts were just a fairy tale.

Life was hard.

CHAPTER THIRTY-THREE

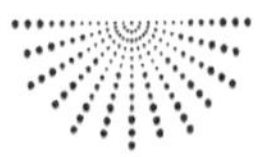

The landscape whisked by as the train made its way down the coast to Harborwood. It was the local, and it seemed to stop in every small village it passed along the way. Amy tried to sleep but couldn't. She checked her schedule on her phone—Maureen was closing up the clinic tonight. She regretted not walking right to the train. If she'd gotten back earlier, she could have helped close. It would have helped get her mind off things.

Working with the animals had always calmed her. Mom always said that animals had a peace about them, an ability to sense human pain and anxiety. That's why comfort dogs worked so well for the elderly or those with chronic illnesses. Dogs seemed to sense when people needed consoling. God knows there was plenty of consoling to go around in her life. Living with only the animals might be an easier way to go.

The train was late, but Amy stopped by the clinic anyway. She entered quietly through the back door, keeping the lights low. She checked on things, talking to a few of the dogs that were spending the night, two that were boarded, one recovering from a surgery, another older girl that might not make it into next week. The animals, mostly dogs, were all shapes and sizes, but it did her soul well to tell them goodnight when she could.

When Amy finally got home, she was exhausted. She realized she'd never eaten dinner, so she heated up some leftovers from the fridge, ate them quietly at the kitchen counter over a magazine, then ran a warm bath and soaked in it until she was nearly asleep. The water, too, always comforted her. It reminded her of sitting by the ocean, listening to the waves.

She emptied the bath, dried off, and slipped into bed. She tried not to think about the day behind her, but images of Mark still flooded her mind and later, her dreams.

THE CLINIC WAS BUSTLING the next morning.

"Thank God, you're back," said Tanya, her receptionist.

Amy smiled. "Miss me?"

Tanya lowered her head, peering over her glasses. "I don't like it when you're gone." She looked over her shoulder into the exam rooms. "And I don't think the patients like it either. They know someone's missing."

Amy laughed.

"I'm serious," said Tanya. "I go in there to try to take their temperature or look them over and they just stare at me, like, girl, whatever you think you're about to do to me, don't."

"I've never noticed that," said Amy. "I'm sure it's your imagination."

"Nope, it's true. You've never noticed it because you're the one with the diploma on the wall. I'm the one with the phone on my ear and the pen in my hand. They're onto me, I'm telling you. Sometimes I wonder if they're all going to revolt. You know, like those books where the rats all join up and take over the world. Or was it monkeys?" She narrowed her eyes, then waved her hand. "Doesn't matter, it would be bad news, I'm telling you."

Amy laughed again, shaking her head. "I think you better see who our first patient is for the day, Tanya. I'll keep an eye open for any industrious rats back there in the meantime."

Tanya turned in her chair toward the computer. "Yeah, I better do that. You know, the next time you decide to parade out of town for the day unannounced, please make sure it's on a day when we don't have a full slate of patients. You're just lucky that Dr. Maureen was here to help out. Otherwise it would have been chaos."

Amy chuckled and pushed through the swinging door to the back exam room hallway.

"Chaos!" she heard Tanya yell again.

Tanya had a flare for the dramatic, to say the least. But she was reliable, and in a beach town like Harborwood, where most of the eligible workers often seemed more interested in surfing or working on their tan, reliability counted for a lot.

Tanya and Maureen kept things doable. Maureen was a part-time vet who helped out three days a week. It was just enough to keep the workload manageable for Amy, and she was a solid doctor and a good friend. God knows she could use a few of those in her life.

Amy took a deep breath and tried to clear her mind before the first patient of the day. As she pushed open the door, she pursed her lips and put on a happy smile as she stared at the file for appointment number one, a routine vaccination for a 140-pound Great Dane named Rosco. Things didn't slow down until an hour later after two cats, a yellow lab, and a golden doodle that was having trouble eating.

With a spare moment, Amy snuck back to the lab room to exchange a few cultures in the incubator. Maureen had come in through the rear entrance to review some medical records. She looked up at Amy with raised eyebrows. "Are you just going to stand there, or are you going to tell me what happened?"

Amy rolled her eyes and tried to think of what to say. She'd mentioned where she was going before she left, and Maureen had already pried most of the backstory out of her.

"It was a disaster," she said bluntly, not knowing where to start. There was no use sugar-coating it. And she needed to tell somebody.

"Oh, no," said Maureen, walking over and placing a hand on Amy's shoulder.

"Yep, I surprised him at his apartment, and he seemed absolutely shocked. Then some perfect-boobs supermodel showed up for a date with him."

Maureen covered her mouth with her hand. "You're kidding?"

Amy nodded. "And the worst part is I should have known better." She looked up pleadingly at Maureen. "Shouldn't I have?"

Maureen frowned. "Don't beat yourself up about it. He doesn't know what he's missing. I thought his mom said he wasn't seeing anyone?"

Amy shrugged. "She did, but what does she know? I don't think he goes home much."

"So what did you do?"

"I got the hell out of there, that's what I did. It was terrible."

Maureen sighed. "I don't want to say I told you so, but..."

"I know, it was stupid." Amy threw her hands up. "I just thought it was a sign, him showing up and running into my dad like that out of the blue. On the boardwalk where we first met." She tried to keep herself from getting emotional again. She'd be a wreck for the rest of the patients if she did. "I guess I just wanted it to be, but maybe sometimes a coincidence is just a coincidence. It doesn't have to be fate."

Maureen shook her head. "Maybe you deserve to find someone to make you happy. Did you ever think of that?"

Amy thought about it all right. Every day. She wanted it, too, but she was growing convinced it just wasn't in the cards.

CHAPTER THIRTY-FOUR

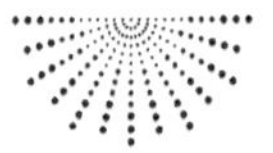

The busy pace of the clinic took it out of her by closing time on most days, but today she felt completely fried. Her emotions were frayed and she needed a release. The last appointment of the day canceled, so she let Tanya go home and Amy locked up early.

She drove home, changed into her running clothes, put in her ear buds, and walked to the boardwalk just as the evening sky was beginning to blush. The air was relatively still for near the ocean, and she took her time stretching against the boardwalk railing.

The music in her ears muffled out the noise of the passing crowds—families pushing strollers, and small packs of teenagers happy to escape the reach of their parents. Her mind wandered over all that had changed in her life. Leaving Dylan and moving back to Harborwood was healthy for her in so many ways, but it also brought back a flood of emotions that she often didn't know how to process.

Running usually helped. She'd always been athletic, always swam throughout school and eventually lifeguarded at the beach. She wanted to be fit, for sure, to stay in shape, but getting the blood pumping through her body seemed to just feel right. The harder life got over the years—when Mark pushed her away, when times with Dylan were at their worst, when Mom lost her battle with cancer just three months after Amy had moved back—running seemed to clear her mind, filled it with oxygen and breathed life into her soul.

As she finished stretching, then set off bouncing in a rhythm along the familiar wooden boards, she found herself pushing harder than normal. As if running fast and hard could force out all the hurt and make the memories fade. It never worked completely, but it helped.

She didn't look up until she reached the end of the boardwalk, past the shops and the stores to where the boards narrowed and the space was tighter. She remembered as a girl being just barely big enough to ride her bike without training wheels. She'd get up early in the morning and make a ritual boardwalk ride together with her parents, often ending up getting doughnuts at Groves. They'd rest their bikes against the railings and Daddy would treat for her favorite warm cinnamon powder doughnut. She saw it as clear as if it were yesterday.

That memory drew a straight line to that day she ran into Mark, or he ran into her, rather. He'd surprised her, she really *hadn't* seen the bike coming her way. It was fun teasing him that she didn't believe him, but of course she'd seen it go past after he pushed her. He was so cute in his "save the damsel in distress" kind of way. Unassuming, yet kind and charming. He just seemed right, and she thought he'd burrowed a spot into her heart from that very first day.

Staring out across the beach, Amy almost laughed out loud remembering how she used to scribble his name on her notebooks at Cooper High. How they'd go on long walks after school, making out under the extra tall tree behind her house just out of view from the street and the kitchen window. It was perfect, for a time.

Ever since she'd met him on the boardwalk at Harborwood that summer after their freshman year, she never saw Mark happier, more at peace, more himself, than when he was pitching. And when they were together. But after his injury, he wasn't the same person. He wouldn't open up to her, he just seemed crushed and unable to climb out from underneath the blow.

It was as if he couldn't believe she'd still love him if he wasn't a star baseball pitcher. Of course, he wasn't a star pitcher when she fell for him. It had never been about baseball. But she thought he never really did believe that. It was always like he had to prove himself worthy, to her, to his father, maybe even himself. Maybe it was hearing about his dad's passing that made her act so impulsively. After what she'd gone through with Mom, she felt like they might relate on that level, that things might be different now.

She leaned over and pulled off her sneakers and socks, carrying them as she walked down the nearest steps onto the beach. At the water's edge, she turned and slowly headed back the direction she'd come. The waves, full of foam, lapped up on the sand, gently pulling at her toes as they reached the end of their strength. The sand was soft and shifting beneath her feet, but she didn't move up higher to more solid ground where it was easier to step. She liked the feel of the water reaching out to her and then retreating. A slight breeze hit her face going this direction and it felt cool to her warm skin, still sweating from the run.

As the sky began to darken, she recalled that night when she and Mark had swam together in the ocean. She'd caught him so off guard. A giggle and then a tear slipped out as she remembered how alive she felt back then. The world seemed open and inviting —she didn't need to be guarded or place locks around her heart. Mom had always taught her life was something to be embraced, not feared. Lived to its fullest, not just endured.

Did she still feel that way? Had these past years jaded her optimism? Certainly Dylan stole much of her joy, but was it irreplaceable? Could it still be hiding somewhere inside her again, waiting to be found? Was it ever too late to get back on the right track, no matter how far off course you had turned?

CHAPTER THIRTY-FIVE

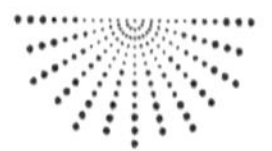

When she reached Fourth, Amy walked back up the boardwalk, pausing to gaze down at the street where she'd spent so many summers and where her dad now lived. It was funny how even a house could remind her so much of her youth. She'd gotten her own small house in town, happy to be near him but still wanting her privacy and independence. They were both going through a lot, and while they relied on each other for support, they also needed some space to figure it all out, if that was even possible.

She wandered down the lane and up the steps to the second floor porch, dark, but glowing from the light inside the house. As she opened the screen, her dad's chocolate lab, Gus, greeted her, tail wagging.

"Anybody home?" she called inside.

"Depends on who's asking," Dad's warm voice answered back.

"How much would I have to pay you for a glass of lemonade?"

"For you, nothing at all." He came out on the porch and kissed her on the forehead. "How's my little bear?"

She groaned without answering, plopping down in the soft-cushioned wicker chair, leaning back and resting her legs up on the railing. Dad settled into a chair a couple feet away, lighting a candle on the table, its flame slowly flickering in the dark.

For a while they just sat, silently sipping their lemonade, the hum of the lazy beach town drifting along the street below like a puff of smoke moving through their subconscious. An old song she recognized from college played from a car half a block away and she smiled.

She reached down and rubbed Gus's ears as he snuggled against her leg. He'd been a patient at the clinic a while back until his family never came to retrieve him. She'd taken a liking to him, and Dad decided he might be a nice companion.

She suddenly had a yearning for a drink, although she knew there wasn't any alcohol in the house. Dad hadn't had a drink since Mom got sick. He said he didn't think it was fair since she couldn't anymore. They loved each other so much.

"So how's it going, Bear?"

Amy didn't answer, she just shook her head and started to cry.

"Why does it have to be so hard, Daddy?" she said, finally.

He nodded, smiling through the candlelight. "I don't know."

"I miss Mom." She hated saying it in front of him, she knew he missed her just as much as she did, if not more, but she couldn't help it.

He just nodded again, silently.

"I don't think I'm doing very well, Daddy." She told him about her trip to New York, the blank look on Mark's face when he opened the door, running into the other woman. She finally looked up at him with moist eyes. "What was I thinking?"

"I think you were trying to find your joy, Bear. I worry about you. That light that used to shine so bright, it's hiding from your eyes. I miss that. You're still too young. When your mother was your age, you'd just been born, it was the beginning of things. We were a happy family. I'd love to see you happy."

"I want that too, Daddy."

"You can't force it, sweetie."

She looked over at him through the shadows. "But how is it

going to happen? I feel like I messed up, like I made the wrong choice, that I missed my chance."

"Are we still talking about Mark?"

Amy shrugged. "I don't know. Maybe. Maybe I'm just talking about life in general. About being happy."

"And you think a man can solve all that?" He grunted, leaning back in his chair. "Honey, things are still tough with a man. Sometimes tougher."

"You don't have to remind me about that Daddy. I was married, remember?"

"That's what I'm saying."

"What are you saying?" She valued her father's wisdom, but sometimes you had to dig through it a bit to understand where he was going.

He stared at her. "That it's not just about having someone. Your mother and I, we were happy, right?"

"It seemed like it to me," Amy answered.

"Sure, and we were, but do you think that we never had tough times?"

"I don't know, probably I guess." She thought about how long Mom was sick and felt stupid. "Of course, I mean when she got sick, I know it was hard. It was awful."

Dad nodded. "Sure, but not just that. Even before. We had them, but we worked through it. We were committed to each other. We had to have that decision." He paused, staring out into the darkness for a while. "Do you remember when you were little, when we used to swim in the ocean together here in the summers?"

Amy smiled. "Of course. It was great." She thought back to the fun times of playing in the water. Long before she started lifeguarding, she used to pretend she was a dolphin and had grown a tail that could take her to anywhere she'd like to go across the ocean. Dad would chase her through the surf and throw her far into the waves.

"What happened when the current was stronger if you weren't paying attention?"

"It pulled me down the beach. I had to keep walking back up toward you."

"That's right. If your feet weren't firmly planted in the sand, you drifted. Then you had to correct. But you had me there, watching and waving you back."

"When I got older," said Amy, remembering, "I looked for our umbrella on the beach. You always had an orange one so it would stand out from the rest."

"Yep, you course corrected and kept your center in view. That's how it is with life, you know. You have to have a center. You have to know what you stand for, who you're connected to, where you're headed. There's a saying that if you don't have a destination in mind, you'll never get there."

"You'll always be lost."

"Exactly. Where are you headed, Bear?

"I don't know."

He reached across and took her hand. "Think about it. It might help you."

SHE SAT out on the porch for a long time, well past when Dad kissed her on the forehead softly on his way in to bed. She sat still, as she had many summer evenings on that same porch across her whole life, listening to the mixture of sounds floating up from the street and the boardwalk and the ocean beyond.

She found herself thinking less and less about Dylan and her life in California. It had been hard at first to put aside the wreckage of what had happened, to forget the hurt and betrayal. She didn't know if she would be able to forgive, and she hadn't forgotten, but she was moving on. She could feel it.

That was part of why she thought of reaching out to Mark's mom and going to New York in the first place. She needed to start over, but it also felt right to connect to something else from her past, before the mess that Dylan had become, back when Mom was still here, when things seemed right. And Mark always seemed a big part of that.

She did wonder, sometimes, if it was just a way that her mind played tricks with her memories of the past, glamorizing things from long ago to feel like it was always greener than the present day. She still didn't know the answer to that question, but she had felt enough of a glimmer of hope that she went to Manhattan looking for it. What a mess that turned out to be. She mentally whipped herself again for that bad decision.

Try as she might, however, the longer she sat out on that porch, the more her mind kept drifting back to memories with Mark. She dozed for a little while, listening to the sounds, the memories so thick she could taste them like salt in the air, wandering through a past that seemed so close but yet so very far away.

CHAPTER THIRTY-SIX

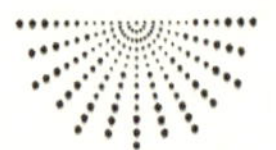

Mark shifted anxiously in his seat as the taxi edged through Columbus Circle on the west side of Manhattan.

"Remind me again how you talked me into this?" he asked, leaning down to see the lights of Lincoln Center up ahead.

Paris smiled and kissed him on the neck, nibbling lightly on his earlobe. "Because it's fun and you enjoy being with me."

Mark titled his head indifferently. "Uh huh."

"And because you know I'm not wearing anything underneath this dress," she whispered, biting down on his ear again, but harder this time.

He stiffened against the seat with a wince and a smile. "Oh, right." He turned and stared into her green eyes, then kissed her on the lips. "I suppose that could be a reason."

"If you play your cards right, you might get a peek before this night is over," said Paris, running her hand up his thigh.

"Lincoln Center," the cabbie called over the divider.

Mark raised his eyes, catching the taxi driver glancing at them in the rearview. He nudged Paris off his neck. "Come on, stop, we're here."

He paid and they climbed out the door and onto the steps of the famous concert hall. A large banner with the name of Paris's pharmaceutical company stretched across the front of one of the buildings on the side of the courtyard. Mark half expected to see her name on it, but it wasn't.

"So this is work for you, huh?" he joked.

"It's rough," replied Paris, taking his hand. "Come on, I want you to meet some people. They won't bite, I promise."

"That's what you said in the cab," said Mark, rolling his eyes as he followed.

As they walked into the lobby of the building, Mark couldn't help but wonder what he was doing there. He glanced at Paris, her natural face sparkling like it was being drawn in by the spotlight. She literally glowed from head to toe, and in between was a curve-fitting dress that didn't leave much to the imagination. Mark still found time to imagine it, however, and her comment in the cab had only fired up his brain more.

Fancy parties weren't really his thing, but Paris had insisted since it was her big awards banquet for her drug company and most people were bringing a guest. Rumor had it that she was going to win the big award for highest percent to goal or something like that and she was beyond excited.

"Paris!" a voice called across the room with the hint of a French accent. A middle-aged man with curly graying hair charged her with an embrace and a kiss on both cheeks. He stepped back and looked at Paris's dress, drawing in a deep breath. "You look simply ravishing, darling. This is going to be a big night for you, I think." He put his hand over his mouth in mock surprise like he'd let out a secret. "Oops, did I say that out loud? Silly me."

Paris giggled in a way that seemed to Mark a bit too rehearsed. "Oh, Philippe, you always know just what to say." She leaned in closer to him. "But I hope you're right!" They both cracked up again.

Philippe turned to Mark. "And who might this be? Is this the famous baseball player I've heard so much about?"

Mark felt a shot of adrenaline through his body as his face flushed red. He gave a nervous laugh.

He thought he saw a trace of something flash across Paris's face before she said, "No, Philippe, I told you that was all over. This is Mark. Mark, Philippe was my district manager years ago before he became a big cheese."

Mark extended his hand and tried to regain his confidence. "Mark Parsons. Nice to meet you."

"I'm sorry, Mark, my apologies," answered Philippe. "It's very nice to meet you. You have my respect and admiration on the arm of this beautiful woman."

Mark gave a thin smile. "Thanks." He wondered if this was how it was going to be all night. He tried to think back to what Paris had told him about how long it had been since she and Jack Best had broken up. In his mind it had been a long time, but now that he thought about it, he couldn't remember her saying exactly how long it had been. Short enough that Frenchy here still thought about it.

They greeted several other of Paris's friends and colleagues in the lobby until a woman with a handheld xylophone walked through chiming lightly, which seemed to signal the program was about to start. Everyone filed into the hall, which had been set up with nearly a hundred round tables scattered around a huge banquet room with a stage and lights up front.

They sat with five other couples, two of whom Paris knew already. Mark casually introduced himself, listening again to several gush about how they'd heard Paris was a shoo-in for the night's big award. Paris blushed demurely, but Mark could tell she was eating it up. It was interesting, watching her preen in front of a captive audience. There was no denying she was a natural, and they were eating out of her hand.

He could imagine how a poor defenseless physician would be no match for Ms. Paris waltzing into his office to share the benefits of whatever heart medication she was hawking. He wondered how many doctors might have had to increase the dosage of their own prescription after she stopped by. He looked around and noticed how many of her fellow reps were young, attractive females. Nothing like a little eye candy. Not that Paris didn't have the brains to match, but a little bit of skin and good looks never hurt things.

The first course came and went, as did his cocktail from one of the several open bars in the corners of the room. Mark had followed it with a bottomless glass of Pinot, one named after a flower, he thought, that was getting refilled so regularly by the waiter that Mark lost track of how much he'd had.

A comedian Mark remembered seeing once on *Comedy Central* warmed up the crowd with jokes that were pretty funny for half an hour. After a short break, the stage lights flashed and changed colors as the VP of Sales marched out with a wide grin like he was hosting the Oscars. It seemed it was time for the major awards of the evening. Mark glanced over at Paris, who sat up straight in her chair, hands on her lap, head tilted slightly lower at an angle that reflected the light off her cheekbones just right. He wondered if she'd learned that pose when she modeled back in school.

After a string of lesser regional awards, the lights dimmed further and the sales guy turned serious, as if he was about to announce the cure for cancer right there from the stage.

"Now the moment we've all been waiting for. We have the award for the representative with the highest percentage to goal for the year." He paused dramatically, then picked up the microphone from the stand and walked out to the front of the stage. "And for this prize, ladies and gentlemen, we have something a little special this year..."

The audience buzzed with excitement at this juicy tidbit. Paris reached over and squeezed Mark's arm nervously. He tried to smile, but his head was feeling a bit heavy and he was starting to get weary of the whole scene.

"It can be tough to catch a cab sometimes here in the Big Apple," the man continued, "so we thought we might assist with some alternate transportation..." He stretched his arm out to the left of the stage as a car slowly rolled out from the wings. Several people screamed and the audience started buzzing loudly. A silky black Porsche stopped mid-stage, sparkling underneath the lights.

"Oh my God!" Paris exclaimed.

Mark closed his eyes. This was out of control.

"And the winner of the Porsche Cayman 2017, and representative with 179 percent to goal. Ladies and gentlemen..."

Mark didn't have to listen to what came next. Somehow he just knew.

"Donna Paris!"

The room erupted, a spotlight shot across the ballroom to their table, resting on Paris's beaming face, her hand on her chest in presumably modest surprise.

"Oh my God!" she screamed again, rising from her seat and walking up to the front of the room, the spotlight following her every move, a few hundred eyes watching enviously, and likely for more than just her award.

Despite his head already starting to swim a little, Mark took another long drink of his wine as Paris posed for pictures with the VP, then moved across the stage and climbed behind the wheel of the Porsche, flashbulbs popping.

After several minutes, the dinner plates were cleared and music began to blare more loudly with a dance beat. The left side wall suddenly slid into itself, revealing an adjacent open ballroom with a dance floor and disco lights blazing. The throng of beautiful faces spilled into the new space, buzzing with excitement, and began moving to the music.

Mark realized Paris might not be returning for a while, so he grabbed her small purse she'd left on the table, and walked up toward the stage, finally spotting her surrounded by a group of men in expensive-looking suits. He caught her eye by dangling her purse in the air while leaning against the back of a chair with his other hand. She nodded, but kept talking to the group, her smile still lighting up the room.

Mark groaned and wandered to one of the open bars in the

back of the room. A couple of bourbons later, he was feeling pretty plastered. He wondered if this was how the real world with Donna Paris would be—a side note to the beautiful girl in the tight dress who got stuck holding her purse. Perhaps this was how the significant others of Hollywood actresses felt. He wasn't sure if he was cut out for this.

"Nice purse," a guy next to him at the bar tapped his shoulder, raising an eyebrow. "Yours?"

"Yeah, you like it?" replied Mark, shaking his head wearily. "My girlfriend's." He lazily scanned the room for Paris, but didn't see her. Perhaps she was still basking on stage in accolades, or maybe she'd been swept onto the dance floor and forgotten about him completely.

"Ah, sure it is," laughed the guy, thrusting out his palm in a well-rehearsed move. "Darren Fisher."

"Mark Parsons," he answered, shaking hands.

Darren pointed up toward the Porsche that was still on the stage. "Quite something, huh? Nice wheels."

Mark nodded.

"And that girl who won was something else, wasn't she?" He flashed Mark a wide smile. "Nice tits."

Mark rolled his eyes. He was getting tired of this.

"What's the matter, you more of an ass man?" Darren continued, slapping Mark on the shoulder roughly, clearly more than a little intoxicated himself.

"That's my girlfriend, okay, so take it easy." Mark tried to ascertain if his own speech was garbled, but it was hard to tell. He knew this conversation wasn't heading anywhere good. He should step away before he said or did something he regretted.

"What?" Darren laughed, his mouth hanging open. "The tits girl came with you?"

"Hey, that's enough, alright?" said Mark, a little more forcefully.

Darren tapped another guy at the bar on the shoulder and

nudged him over to their conversation. "Listen to this, Tony." He pointed at Mark. "This guy's girlfriend is the one who won the car up there on stage."

Tony nodded and raised his glass in the air dramatically. "Hey, well done, buddy."

"But," Darren continued, emphatically, "she's up there on the stage, probably getting it on with the CEO, and he's sitting back here holding her purse!"

Mark took a final swallow of his bourbon and set the glass down on the bar. He'd had enough. It was time to go.

Darren grabbed Mark by the shoulder. "I should have won that car, Mark, not your floosy girlfriend. Did you know that?"

"Yeah, well maybe next year." Mark answered, tugging away and taking a step from the bar. "I'll see you, guys."

"You know your problem, buddy?" Darren called to him.

Mark paused, his body tensing, a familiar rush flowing through him. He turned back and looked the man in the eyes. "No, what's my problem, Darren?"

He gave a crooked glance to Tony, and then grinned. "You're a pussy!"

Darren was on the floor before he knew what happened, Mark's fist still clenched in its follow through. The bartender started yelling for the hotel management, who quickly scurried around the edges of the room. Before Mark knew it, he was sitting in a chair out in the hallway, his knuckles throbbing.

He flagged down a woman from the wait staff and handed her Paris's purse to deliver up to the stage. "Just look for the beautiful woman everyone's talking to," he explained, after showing a picture of Paris from his phone.

He stumbled down to the lobby and then out into the night air, the sound of the city suddenly filling his ears. He flexed his left hand, his pitching hand, he remembered, then walked around the corner to a bodega and paid for a bag of ice. He flagged down a taxi and muttered Paris's address to the driver, but after a minute changed his mind and said his own apartment instead. He was asleep before they even got there, but somehow he managed to pay the driver and drag himself up to his apartment where he fell asleep on the couch in his clothes.

CHAPTER THIRTY-SEVEN

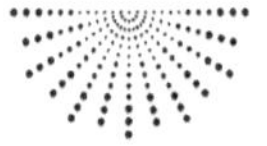

Schedules were busy for both him and Paris the next couple days, but Mark felt like keeping his distance, so it was just as well. She'd been confused as to what had happened at the banquet and why he'd left alone without telling her, but he'd made up a lame story about feeling sick and not wanting to interrupt her big night, which was partially true.

He didn't want to get into how he'd slugged Darren, although he figured the story would reach her eventually. She seemed to buy it, but then proceeded to gush for thirty minutes about winning the award, the Porsche, and all the attention she'd received. After that a few short texts replaced what had become their normal daily conversations and time together. So when Joe called and pushed him once again to fly down to Virginia for a weekend visit on a Super Saver fare out of LaGuardia, Mark finally gave in. He checked out at lunch on Friday, much to Marvin's dismay, but didn't even tell Paris until a brief text on his way down the jetway.

As the plane rose into the sky, the tall buildings of the city fading off into the distance, he looked down at the sea, stretching into the endless horizon. Before he realized it, his mind drifted back to the Ferris wheel with Amy, staring out into the night. He remembered how nervous he'd been, afraid to even touch her, the smell of her hair. In a way he could still smell it, even though it seemed a lifetime away.

***

JOE HAD OFFERED to pick him up, but Mark never confirmed his flight time, so he just hopped into the lone airport taxi parked outside baggage claim. It dropped him off next to the familiar mailbox a few yards in front of the box hedges of his childhood home. The bushes seemed more unkempt than usual, the mulch wasn't refreshed, and weeds poked around the corners. Mom's flowerbed was partially overgrown, not full of its usual colorful display, carefully selected to keep something in bloom through the entire season.

Mark's first thought was someone was going to catch hell from Dad for letting things go to pot, but then he remembered, of course, that Dad was dead. It still hadn't fully sunk in that he was gone and not coming back. Somehow the largeness of his personality seemed to make it harder to believe. He wondered if people who were more laid back and easy-going when they were alive left the same effect when they died.

He reached for the screen door just as it was opening, Mom standing in the doorway.

"You're home!" She enveloped him in a hug and didn't let go.

"Hey, Mom."

She squeezed even tighter. "It's good to have you home, honey."

Mark breathed deeply as she finally let him go. He didn't really blame her for being emotional. He knew it hadn't been easy for her.

"How was your trip?"

"Good."

"Well, come in, come in," she urged, pushing him into the

foyer. "Bring your bags up to your room. I'm making dinner. Pork Chops with stuffing, just as you like them."

Mark nodded, moving up the stairs. He knew she would probably overdo things, trying to make him happy. That's how Mom was when she was nervous or really wanted something to be perfect. He supposed there were worse faults than trying too hard to please, and sometimes it wore on him, but it had always been such a contrast to Dad's attitude that it normally came off as refreshing.

He splashed some water on his face in the bathroom, then looked up when he heard a door close. He poked his head around the corner, only to be ambushed.

"Welcome home, little brother!" Joe grabbed him in a bear hug.

"Hey!" Mark squirmed, swinging his arms and breaking free much easier than he had when they were younger. He looked over at Joe and frowned. "What the hell?"

"Sorry, I couldn't resist." Joe stepped back into the room and sat down on the bed. "Doesn't it just take you back, being in these rooms, like we were still twelve years old?"

Mark smiled, sitting down in his old desk chair. The room was still covered with his posters from high school—Derek Jeter, Pearl Jam, Green Day—they were all still as he'd left them. He couldn't believe Mom had never taken them all down. The crack in the sheetrock where Joe had banged his head next to the closet and knocked himself out cold was still there too. He'd seen it all after the funeral but he'd been in a fog and hardly paid attention. He finally cracked a grin. "It *is* crazy."

"How was your flight?" Joe asked, lying back on the bed.

"Fine."

"No delays?"

"Nah." Mark waited for it to come. He knew that Joe had more than one reason for having him come back home for the weekend. He'd hinted on the phone about needing more help in the office. He'd tried this tactic before, but it really didn't interest

Mark. It was a different vibe, with everything with Dad going on in the background now, but there was always something that didn't feel right. The last thing he wanted was to be in some stuffy low-tech office selling insurance, even if it was with Joe. There were so many better ways to run an operation letting technology work for you, but he doubted Joe would ever go for it.

"How's work?" Joe reached for a tennis ball on the nightstand and tossed it in the air.

Mark shrugged. "It's fine, you know how it is."

"Not really loving it?"

Mark rolled his eyes. "Dude, why don't you just say it?"

"Say what?"

"You want me to work at the firm. I know you do, you don't have to hide it."

Joe acted shocked. "You? At the firm?" He shook his head. "I don't think that's such a good idea."

"Sure."

"Although, if you were looking for a change, there are some things we could talk about."

Mark pointed his finger at Joe. "And there it is."

Joe grinned. "But not here at the firm."

"No?"

"Nope. You're a city man, from the north now, I can tell. This southern life would be too slow for you."

Mark tilted his head, trying to figure where his brother was headed with this. "Is that right?"

"Yeah." Joe paused, then looked back up. "But..."

"Aha!"

"I was going through the files last week and I noticed something very interesting."

"Since when are Dad's files interesting?"

Joe frowned. "They're not Dad's files anymore. They're ours."

Mark shook his head. "You mean yours. I just told you, I don't want to be in the firm."

"You didn't say that, but it doesn't matter. Let me tell you what I found. Dad opened up a ton of policies in New York, New Jersey, Connecticut, even Pennsylvania."

Mark raised his eyebrows. "I thought most of the business was down here in Virginia?"

"It is, most of it. But the firm grew pretty big, plus all those years going on vacation in New Jersey, he signed up a lot of new customers."

Mark nodded. He could see that. Dad couldn't keep his mouth shut. He never met someone he didn't think was a good candidate for a policy. "Okay, there's a lot of policies up there. So what?"

Joe sat back down, leaning forward toward Mark. "So, I was thinking. We could really use more coverage up in that area. Maybe even a branch office." A grin broke out over his face. "Which would need someone to run it."

Mark put his hand over his face. He hadn't seen this direction coming, despite knowing something was up. "I don't think so, man."

"Hear me out, Mark." Joe stood and paced the room. "It's a really good idea, if you think about it. It's a stable job. You're not going anywhere in that job of yours now anyhow. What's the name of the boss you hate?"

"Marvin? Oh, he's not so bad," Mark lied. "There's nothing wrong with my job."

"Listen, you don't have to decide right now, just think about it, okay? It would be good to insert some new ideas, some fresh blood into the place. I know you've got some great concepts just waiting to break free in that brain of yours. You already know the basics of the business. Just like the other week when you helped out with that claim to that woman. What was her name?"

Mark looked down at the floor and scratched his head at the reference to Paris. He realized he hadn't thought about her since he'd taken off. "Paris."

"Paris?"

"That's what she goes by," Mark explained. "Her name's Donna Paris."

Joe smiled. "So she was good-looking, you said?"

"Uh huh."

"And you guys have been seeing each other?"

"Yeah."

Joe raised his eyebrows. "But what? Trouble?"

Mark sighed. "I don't know. She's fine. I mean, she's great. She's smoking, fun to be with—in a lot of ways, she's perfect."

Joe laughed. "I can see the problem."

Mark frowned, standing and paced the room. "It's hard to explain. She moves in a fast crowd, if that makes any sense. I'm just not sure we're made to live in the same circles."

Joe was quiet for a moment. "Okay, well that's cool. But think about what I said, alright?"

"Boys, time for dinner!" Mom's voice called from downstairs. A chill ran down Mark's spine, like he was back in grade school.

Joe's eyes opened wide. "That was weird, no?"

"Totally."

"I feel it sometimes, even when I just come over here myself. With the kids too, it's strange. Like an upside down universe."

"Yeah," said Mark, again. He'd been feeling that a lot lately.

CHAPTER THIRTY-EIGHT

"It's so nice to have you here, honey," said Mom, as she pushed a platter full of mashed potatoes in his direction. Typical Mom, acting as if he hadn't eaten in a year.

"Yeah," Mark replied.

She nodded at Joe, who quickly got the hint and agreed mid-bite. "Right, it's real good to have you, little brother."

Mark frowned. It was one thing to be here, another to be fawned over.

"It fills my heart to have both my boys around the table for a meal." She looked off into the distance for a moment. "Your father would have liked it too."

Mark finished his bite and tried to really look at her. She seemed the same, but different. Older perhaps, the lines on her face more pronounced. "You doing okay, Mom?"

She nodded faintly, wiping her mouth with a napkin. "It's very quiet around here. I never realized how much space your father's personality filled. I don't think that's something you can just replace."

"It'll get easier, Mom," said Joe.

She looked at him and smiled. "I know, dear. And you and

Lauren and the kids have been such a great help. I don't know what I'd do without you all around."

Mark looked down at his plate, avoiding her eyes, although he could still feel them bearing down on him across the table.

"Anyway," she suddenly proclaimed, apparently deciding that it was time to move on to a new topic. "Mark, you won't ever believe who called me the other day."

He opened his eyes wide, but said nothing, already guessing what she might say.

Joe looked up in interest. "Oh, yeah?" Mark tried to silence him with his stare, but this time he didn't get the hint. "Who's that, Mom?" Joe continued.

She placed her fork down on her plate and stared directly at Mark with expectant eyes. "Amy Holland!"

"Really?" said Joe.

"Can you imagine that, honey? How long has it been since you've seen her?"

Mark squirmed a bit in his seat, then concluded he had no choice but to talk about it. "A couple weeks ago," he muttered.

Joe smacked his hand down on the table. "What?"

"Joseph, please," Mom scolded. She turned back to Mark. "Is that true, honey?"

Mark nodded. "She showed up at my apartment unannounced." He lowered his eyes. "You should have told me she called you, Mom."

She shrugged. "I gave her your number and address; she didn't call you first?"

"No," Mark replied.

She ignored him, charging forward in her questions. "So how did she seem? Did you talk with her? I think it's just wonderful you two are talking again."

Mark shook his head.

"Uh, oh," said Joe. "That doesn't sound good."

"We're not talking, Mom, and it was kind of a disaster. She and Paris both showed up at the same time."

"Paris?" Mom asked.

"This girl he's been dating," explained Joe. "She's a model."

"A model?" said Mom.

"She's not a model," said Mark.

"Oh, sorry, she just looks like a model," said Joe.

"Oh, no," said Mom. "What happened then?"

Mark shook his head, remembering the scene. He could still see Amy's nervous, confused eyes as she realized he was expecting someone else at the apartment. "She took off and I didn't see her again."

"Oh, crap," said Joe.

"Didn't you go after her?" Mom asked, hopefully.

Mark rolled his eyes. "No, I didn't go after her," he said, raising his voice a bit. "I told you, she took off."

"It sounds like she needs to talk to you, honey."

Mark spread his hands out. "Well what was I supposed to do? Paris was right there, she had just come home from a trip to Europe, and we hadn't seen each other in a week. If Amy wants to pop in out of the blue to talk after twelve years, maybe she could have called me up or contacted me like a normal person."

Mom frowned. "Mark..."

"What?"

"I just...I just thought maybe this could be a new beginning for you two," she said.

"Yeah, well, that sounds like a nice story, Mom, but I don't think that is going to happen in the real world." He pushed his chair back and stood up from the table. "I thought I only got interrogated in this house by Dad."

"Hey," snapped Joe. "That's not cool."

Mark ignored him. He didn't look at Mom as he marched out the back door. He sat stewing on the porch for a while. He didn't know how long, but it was enough for Joe and Mom to do the dishes and clean up.

Joe walked past on his way out to his car. "I'll talk to you tomorrow." He stepped off the porch, then paused and turned around. "Just take it easy on her, okay? She's still not quite right."

Mark took a deep breath and nodded. He knew Joe was right, he just didn't like it. After Joe's car pulled away, Mark heard Mom's footsteps coming closer in the kitchen and then the porch door creaked open. She sat down on the other side of the cushioned patio chair in silence.

He gave in first. "I'm sorry. I shouldn't have gotten upset."

She flashed a weak smile. "It's okay, I shouldn't have pushed you. I know you're going through a lot of things too." She leaned back, taking a deep breath. "I guess it's a tough time for all of us."

Mark nodded, softening his stance. "I know you miss Dad."

She leaned against him, taking his hand. "Don't you?"

Mark breathed in deeply. "I do, but it's complicated, Mom. I just don't know how to explain..." He stopped, feeling his eyes well up with tears. She squeezed his hand tighter.

"It's okay, honey. I know you two didn't always see eye to eye. But he loved you very much. I hope you know that."

"Uh, huh."

"It's true. He would gush to me about how proud of you he was, how much he respected your quiet way, even if he didn't understand it all the time."

Mark looked over at her in the growing dusk. "Are you sure you're talking about Dad?"

She nodded. "He just didn't quite know how to relay it to you for some reason."

Mark frowned. "He was certainly able to relay some things to me just fine." He decided against going into any specifics with her; it wouldn't do any good at this point. He knew she saw them fighting, but didn't know if she ever really chose to notice exactly how bad it was, or knew what Dad said to him in private. "But I thought he could talk to anybody?"

"I didn't say it made sense, I'm just telling you what I know. And I know he cared for you very much. I prayed for a long time that the two of you would find a common ground to be able to relate to each other better." She looked off into the distance.

"It's okay, Mom." He sighed. "I did know, it just was so difficult. I wish it was easier to have talked to him."

She patted his knee. "I know. We can't always choose the way someone else loves us. Sometimes it's just enough to know that they do, and then how you deal with that is up to you."

Mark nodded silently. It *was* complicated.

"And I didn't mean to push things about Amy. I know those things were a long time ago."

Mark wiped his eyes, then recounted his stop to Harborwood after the funeral, how he ended up speaking with Mr. Holland on the boardwalk, and then saw Amy in the window of the veterinary clinic. "It's crazy, Mom. It just kind of happened."

They were both quiet for a minute. "You know, dear," she eventually said. "We always thought Amy was going to be the one for you, even though you were so young. Your father and I met just after high school too, we fell in love, and look how things worked out."

"I just don't think I can go back to that, Mom. This Amy stuff really hit me out of left field. She's divorced, living back in Harborwood, and with all these memories rushing back, it's hard to know what to do. Whether it was a mistake to end things with her or not, it's been so long, I wouldn't even know where to begin, you know?"

She nodded. "That period of time after you two broke up is when you seemed to lose your way a bit, honey. Maybe going back and starting over could be good for you."

Mark shrugged. "I don't know."

"What about this Paris girl? Is that really her name? Paris, like the city in France?"

He shook his head. "It's Donna, but people call her Paris."

She nodded. "Well, what about her? Do you love her?"

"I don't know," he answered with a sigh. "Truth is, I think she might be a little too fast for my pace. She's great and all, and fun to be with, but I don't know if I can keep up with the glitz. She seems to thrive in it."

Mom chuckled. "Reminds me of someone else we know."

He gave her a puzzled look. "Dad?"

"As you know he was quite the personality. It can be a lot to take in, believe me."

He thought a moment. He'd never considered the similarities before, but maybe Mom was right. "You should have seen the way she lit up under all the attention and ogling at this banquet we were at. She was definitely in her element."

"And you didn't like that?"

Mark forced a laugh. "I got drunk."

"Oh, honey. I hope you didn't do anything foolish."

"I don't want to talk about it." He turned and looked out into the woods behind the house, the trees in which he and Joe used to climb and play games. "I don't know what to do, but I really think I need to decide."

He slept in late the next morning. As weird as it felt to be sleeping in his childhood bed once more, it also felt good, which was different than after the funeral. He puttered around the house, helping Mom with some odd chores until mid-afternoon when they drove over to Joe and Lauren's to see the kids and cookout. After about a hundred pushes on the swings in the backyard, the little ones ran inside for a snack.

"I don't know how you do all that," said Mark, leaning against the side of the yellow plastic slide.

"Do what?"

Mark gestured at the backyard. "All of this. The kids, the wife, being around for Mom."

Joe chuckled and handed him a cold beer. "Still don't think you're ready to be a family man?"

"Not this week."

"Well, you're not getting any younger."

"Yeah, yeah," said Mark. "Don't rub it in."

"Everything alright with you and Mom?"

Mark nodded. "We talked on the porch." He grabbed one of the swing chains, twisting the metal in his hands. "Sorry about all that."

Joe patted him on the back. "It's okay, little brother." He broke out in a grin.

"What?"

"So I crunched the numbers again last night, and that pocket of policy holders up near you is even bigger than I thought. It could make a whole lot of sense."

Mark sighed, shaking his head. "When are you going to give that up?"

"What are you doing up there, anyway? Admit it, you don't like that gig you have, other than the hottie thing. But look at it this way, there could be ten more like Donna Paris out there holding policies, just waiting to be romanced."

Mark laughed nervously. "I don't know if I could keep up with more than one of her."

Now Joe shook his head. "I don't even want to ask about the sex."

"No, you probably don't," Mark answered, grinning.

Joe gave the swing a shove, knocking Mark off-balance. "You're killing me."

Mark chuckled. "What? You're Mr. Family Man, happily married with a lovely wife and two perfect kids. No?"

"Right," said Joe. "It's all like a dream." He stopped and shook his head at the ground, then took a step toward the house. "Listen, just think about it."

Mark held up his hands. "Okay, okay. I'll think about it. God, you're like a broken record."

"Can you stay for a while and watch the game after dinner?" Joe asked as they walked inside. "The Yankees are playing Cleveland this afternoon. I finally talked Lauren into letting me get the package that gives me all the games, even down here."

"You don't need one of Dad's satellite dishes?"

"Ouch," grimaced Joe. "That was bad." He turned back to Mark. "So you'll stay?"

"Sure, that sounds fun, at least for a while. I'm heading back to the city early in the morning."

"Why so soon? You should stay a little longer. It's nice having you around."

Mark shook his head. "I don't want to cut it close. I read a storm coming up the coast is not looking good. I'm going to try to get standby on the earlier flight. I've had enough problems flying out of here before. But thanks."

"Okay, but I want a solid six innings from you. I don't get to watch the games with guys around here very much. Mostly just Disney movies with Lauren and the kids."

Mark nodded. "Deal."

CHAPTER THIRTY-NINE

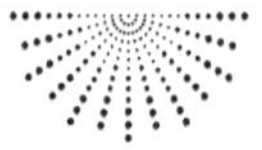

It was a short flight back to New York. Mark studied the familiar shapes of the skyline from the back of the taxi as they approached the Midtown Tunnel. Every time he entered the city, he marveled at how despite the crush of people all around him, he had a deep-seated feeling of being alone. As the sky slowly faded into crimson behind the stacks of concrete and millions of nameless faces, he made a decision. A choice to start fresh. To let go of the past, embrace the future, and do what he knew was inside him.

Despite all his pestering, Joe was handing him a plum opportunity. The chance to manage a branch at the successful insurance agency was too good to turn down. When Dad was running things, it wouldn't have worked, but now with Joe in charge, there would be less butting heads. He'd be a fool to say no, particularly if he could do it his way. He'd take some of the programming skills he'd perfected at his current job to modernize the systems Kingfisher had been using, likely the same ones Dad had instituted twenty years ago.

Mark had also worked through a mental list of his concerns about Paris on the flight home, but then caught himself laughing out loud. The disastrous ending at the banquet had really been more about him than her. He'd had too much to drink and that asshole, Darren, was just pushing his buttons. Mark just needed to get used to dating a beautiful and successful woman like Paris. It didn't mean they weren't right for each other. How could he even be thinking she was too much trouble? Most guys would give their right arm for trouble like that. Sometimes life handed you something great and you just had to take advantage of it.

He decided to surprise Paris and didn't text her that he was back in town. Instead of going straight to his apartment, he got out of the taxi in Herald Square, dragged his roller bag right into Victoria's Secret and picked out something sultry. His mind quickly wandered to the image of Paris filling out the thin fabric with her curves. Traffic was heavy so he took the "D" train up Central Park West to the familiar entranceway of Paris's building, buzzing the door.

"Yeah?" a voice answered. It was static-filled as always, but it didn't sound like Paris.

"Oh, sorry," said Mark. He must have pushed the wrong button. He bent down closer and hit Paris's apartment number. This time the door buzzed right open without an answer. Striding up the staircase, the gift-wrapped box tucked under his left arm, he hardly noticed the inconvenience having to haul his suitcase. He pictured Paris smiling in the lingerie, imagined her surprise, the perfect beginning of a romantic evening together.

At the top he rapped rhythmically on the wooden door. It opened, but Mark did a double take as a familiar-looking man stood in front of him, a towel around his waist.

"Shit, sorry," Mark said, instinctively stepping back and glancing around the landing. "I must have knocked on the wrong door..." He turned his head, gazing past the man into the room. Paris's room. Behind Paris's blue door. He wasn't at the wrong apartment. His heart now pounding, his head slowly computed that he was staring uneasily at Jack Best, star second baseman for the Cleveland Indians.

"Are you okay, man?"

Mark stared blankly at him, caught in a surreal moment he wasn't expecting. "I, um..." His head was suddenly foggy.

"Was that the door?" Paris's voice called from inside. She came up behind Jack, then froze upon seeing Mark in the hallway. "Oh, Mark..."

A pain in his gut nearly doubled him over. He was going to be sick. He spun on his heel, lifting his suitcase off the ground, and headed back down the stairs. He didn't know what else to do.

"Mark!" Paris called behind him. "Dammit. Wait..."

He kept moving, descending into the entranceway, suitcase in one hand, gift box in the other, the sound of Paris's steps following. He stepped out on the street, the door quickly opening behind him.

"Will you wait a second?" urged Paris.

Mark stopped, half turning, and looked at her sideways. He didn't say anything, his head a jumble of thoughts.

Paris caught her breath. "Listen..."

He raised his eyebrows, motioning with his hands that he was still there.

"I know this looks bad."

"Do you?"

"Mark, I didn't expect to see him. I was out after the game, we ran into each other, I had too much to drink, and one thing led to another."

"Are you sure he wasn't selling you an insurance policy?" said Mark, forcing a laugh. He waved his hand. "Hey, whatever. You don't have to explain. I get it. Your old boyfriend, the professional baseball player, swept back into town, knocked you off your feet, and the rest is buried in the sheets. It's your business..." His voice trailed off. He didn't know what he was even saying.

"I didn't mean to hurt you," Paris said, looking sincere, but also not quite as torn up about things as he was. Probably because she just hooked up with a pro ball player. Again. Versus Mark, who had just hung out for the weekend with his mom and brother, decided Paris was the one for him, only to come home and find she'd just been with another guy.

He tugged on the bar of his rollerboard. "Good luck with things, okay? I'd tell Jack I hope he strikes out, but from the looks of things, he's already cleared the bases."

"Mark..." Paris began as he moved down the street. She didn't say any more, since, really, what more could be said. It was pretty obvious what had happened.

When he turned out of sight, he remembered the gift box under his arm and tossed it in the trashcan on the corner. As he stood waiting for the light to change, he stared at the red bow on the box, blowing in the wind and stuck out at an angle on top of some discarded coffee cups, looking oddly out of place. He knew that feeling.

CHAPTER FORTY

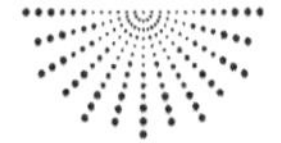

Mark called Percy and Tyler from the taxi on his way home. They were both tied up but agreed to meet him at DJ's in a bit. Not a problem. Mark was more than happy to arrive early and get a head start drowning his sorrows. He dropped his bags off at his apartment and headed straight for the bar. After downing two quick beers, he pulled out his phone and texted the guys to hurry up. Drinking alone was fine, but he felt like he needed to tell somebody what had happened.

He flipped through his contacts, then his missed calls, noticing a number he didn't recognize. It was from nearly two weeks ago. He knew 804 was a Virginia area code, but what was 805? He decided to call it back, his curiosity outweighing his inhibitions already well softened by the alcohol. He listened to several rings before it went to voice mail. He was about to hang up, when his heart froze.

"Hi, this is Amy, leave a message."

He quickly hung up before the beep. She'd called him? How had he missed that? It must have been the day she showed up at his apartment. How could he have overlooked it? Probably since she wasn't in his contacts. He often let unfamiliar numbers go to voicemail so he didn't have to talk to some guy trying to sell him something. He started walking through the implications of what it meant in his mind, hardly noticing Percy and Tyler walk in to the bar. Percy asked Zach, the bartender, for two cold ones.

Tyler looked disappointedly across the bar. "Where's Kelly?"

"She's off on Thursdays," replied Zach.

"Oh, that sucks," said Tyler, despondently.

Zach raised his eyebrows, to which Tyler quickly added, "Sorry, dude, no offense, but you know what I mean."

Zach nodded, showing he clearly did know what Tyler meant, then walked to the other end of the bar. Mark felt bad for him, but figured he got that a lot. It had to be hard to compete with the perky barmaid. Mark felt a twinge of disappointment too. For once, he wouldn't have minded a little of Kelly's flirting to cheer him up.

"You're such an ass," said Percy, shaking his head.

"What?" answered Tyler, trying to look innocent. "You'd rather look at him than her?"

Percy grinned. "Hey, I'm a married man."

"Yeah, yeah," said Tyler. "Well some of us are still on the market." He tapped Mark on the shoulder. "Right, buddy?"

Mark groaned, talking another swallow of his beer.

"So what happened?" Percy asked. "Paris isn't as lovely as it seemed?"

Mark frowned at the lame joke, then told them about coming face-to-face with Jack Best at her apartment.

"Ouch," grimaced Tyler. "I don't know if I could even compete with that one." He looked at Mark seriously. "Honestly, buddy, I don't know how you tapped into that situation in the first place. You have to admit, it was pretty out there."

Mark frowned again. "You're just jealous."

Tyler laughed. "You're damn right I am."

"Oh, man, game's canceled," moaned Percy, nodding at the TV on the wall. The field at Yankee Stadium was covered in a tarp and a message along the bottom announced the final home game in the Cleveland series was postponed due to tropical storm Bethany rapidly rolling up the coast.

Mark had been glad he'd left Virginia early to beat the storm, but now he wasn't so sure.

"You know," Tyler continued. "Now that old Jack Best is leaving town again, if lovely Paris is available..." he let his voice trail off like he was imagining some deviant tryst in his mind.

"Will you shut up," said Mark, nearly shoving Tyler off his stool.

Tyler glanced at Percy. "Too soon?"

Percy shook his head. "Just a little."

Tyler pursed his lips and looked back at Mark. "Sorry."

"So what's next?" asked Percy, shaking his head.

Mark looked up. "For what?"

"For you. Paris is over, what's next?"

"Yeah, you can't just sit around here and feel sorry for yourself," said Tyler.

"I don't know," said Mark, shrugging. He hadn't gotten that far. "Joe wants me to come work for him in the business."

Percy raised his eyebrows. "And?"

Mark frowned. "And, I haven't decided yet."

"Aren't you the guy who hates his job?" said Percy. "The one who was ready to find something new three months in, which was three years ago?"

Mark raised a couple fingers. "Two years ago."

"Whatever."

"Dude, you need to get out of there," added Tyler. "Even I can see that."

"I told you I don't know," said Mark, waving to Zach for another glass. "It's complicated, okay?"

"Because of your dad?" asked Percy.

"Yeah, but—"

"And he's gone now right?"

Mark glared at Percy. "I get it. I don't need a lecture."

"Do you?" asked Percy. "I don't mean to be rough on you man, but it sounds like a pretty great opportunity, if you ask me."

They all looked up as a group of girls entered the bar, nearly tumbling through the door with the wind and the rain that had started falling out on the street. Through the front window, Mark saw groups of people running for cover under the storefront awnings and clamoring down the entrance to subway station.

"This storm is really moving in quick," said Percy.

"Those girls are soaked," laughed Tyler, sliding from his stool, a sly grin on his face. "I think they might need someone to help dry them off. I'll be right back."

"So I have to mention the elephant in the room here," said Percy.

"Oh yeah, what's that?"

"None of this has anything to do with Amy, does it?"

Mark chugged another swallow of beer. "Who?"

Percy smiled. "I can't help but notice a bit of symmetry in what happened to you, and what happened with her and Paris."

"Uh, huh," said Mark, rolling his eyes. "What's your point?"

"Just that sometimes things happen for a reason."

"Which is?"

"Got me, but suddenly she's back in your life—showing up at your door, in fact. Maybe you should go talk to her."

"And say what? I just got dumped, so now I'm desperate?"

Percy grinned. "Dude, she's the one that showed up at your apartment, remember? She wants to talk with you. It's not that hard to figure out."

Mark shook his head. He knew Percy was probably right, but he felt like there was an invisible wall keeping him from going back. How many times could he head down a road before it closed? Then again, what other choice did he have? He thought about finding her missed call on his phone history. That was twice she'd tried to speak to him. That had to mean something, didn't it?

"Boys, this is Trina, Anna, and Britney," announced Tyler,

walking up behind them with the three wet girls smiling next to him. They seemed like college girls, probably from NYU, or maybe Hunter, this far up the East Side.

"No, it's Bethany," the third girl giggled, "just like the storm." She pointed out the window at the rain pounding against the building.

Tyler flashed a smile and wrapped his arm around her shoulder. "Isn't that wild? The same name as the storm. How about that?" He put his other arm around Mark's. "Ladies, this here is Mark, and he's had a really tough day. His lady friend just dumped him and he's pretty upset about it. And this one's Percy, but he's married, so don't worry about him."

Percy shrugged and held up his ring finger. "It's true."

The girl named Trina smiled at Mark. "That *is* a rough day."

As Tyler pulled up stools for the girls to join them at the bar, a gust blew against building, sending the door flying open. Menus scattered from the tables and the girls all screamed.

"Holy shit!" Tyler yelled, just as the power went out and everything went dark.

CHAPTER FORTY-ONE

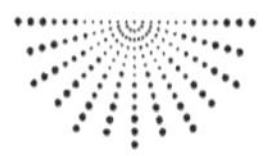

Amy turned the deadbolt on the rear door to the clinic. The radio on the counter by the sterile syringes chattered ominously about the tropical storm moving up the coast past the Carolinas. There was disagreement among the meteorologists over which of the six possible paths the storm might take, but two of them had the storm, Bethany, it was called, making landfall on the coast of New Jersey later that evening.

It wasn't expected to be as severe as Hurricane Sandy several years back, but you never could tell how a storm would develop and track. Local residents were preparing for the worst. Amy hadn't lived in Harborwood during Sandy, but Dad told her that thankfully most of the town managed a lot better than what the world saw on TV of other parts of the shore towns. Some of the older homes had flooded, but for the most part, things survived intact, particularly the boardwalk.

She glanced out the window at the wind already picking up, blowing in gusts in from the sea. She wondered if they'd all be as lucky this time.

"Why do they name these storms after people?" complained Tanya, as she walked past Amy with a green bag of dog food under each arm. "Nobody I ever met wanted to be named after a damn tsunami, or whatever this thing is."

Amy chuckled. "That's a good question."

"They can sense it, you know?" said Tanya.

"Who can sense what?"

"They can." Tanya pointed toward the kennel room where the dogs were kept overnight. "Just like when you're gone. They don't like that, but they really don't like bad weather."

"Could be." Amy knew from her classes at Oregon that some studies showed animals could sense danger. She looked back out the window at the darkening sky. "Hopefully this one will miss us."

"Uh, huh," said Tanya. "I can sense things too, and I think this is going to be a doozy."

Amy frowned. "Let's try to stay positive. We're prepared."

Tanya paused at the door. "Maybe you're prepared, but I'm not prepared to face anything except a nice sunny day at the beach. Bethany can just turn her ass around and go back to the Atlantic, the Pacific, or wherever else she came from." She pushed through the doorway back to the reception area with a huff.

Amy sighed. She always tried to see the positive side of things, but she had to admit, this one was making her a little nervous too. Her pocket buzzed, and she pulled out her cell.

Time to get home, Bear, a text read.

Daddy was more than a little overprotective since she'd moved back, even when there wasn't a major weather event. But this time he was probably right. As a result of the storm, she was closing the clinic at three so everyone could get home and stay off the roads. The last weather report showed the storm had indeed shifted inland, suggesting the path of Tropical Storm Bethany could be much more serious than previously announced.

She did one more check on the animals, then when she was sure everything was locked securely, she walked Tanya out to her car. Rain was falling now, the wind pushing against them hard enough they had to lean into it as they made their way across the parking lot.

"Stay safe!" she called to Tanya, over the growing squall.

"You too, baby!" Tanya answered as she scurried into her car.

Amy pulled onto Atlantic Avenue as a few remaining beach-goers scurried along the sidewalks to their cars, chairs over their heads for cover, finally giving up on their optimism that their vacation could be salvaged.

Amy could feel the gusts push against her car, the rain now coming down in buckets, only minutes after it had begun. She looked up at the blinking traffic signal, rocking back and forth on a wire hanging over Ocean Avenue. Had the power already gone out? It was hard to believe things were deteriorating that fast.

She bent forward over the steering wheel, straining to see through the blur of the water on the windshield her wipers couldn't fully clear. The line of trees next to the drugstore on Eleventh Street were dancing back and forth like one of those nylon blow-ups outside a car dealership with a big sale.

She approached the intersection, hands tightened on the wheel, when her cell phone buzzed in the passenger seat. Probably her dad checking on her again, wondering why she wasn't home yet. She glanced at the phone quickly and caught her breath. "Mark" lit up on the screen. In the beat of a wiper blade, she wondered whether she was imagining things, but then she recalled how she'd put his number in her contacts list after speaking with his mom. She'd called him on the way into Manhattan, but he hadn't answered. Why was he calling her now?

She braked, lingering in the intersection, barely making out the yellow signal, then without thinking any longer, reached over and tried to swipe the phone on with her right hand. It didn't take, so she leaned a bit further to hold it more carefully. She didn't want it to stop—

The silver SUV slammed into the rear driver's side door, crumpling it in like a punctured soda can. The sound of metal on metal thundered through the intersection like two old trash can lids smashing together like cymbals. Broken glass, shards of metal, and mangled plastic shot into the air, mixing with the rain and wind.

Amy never saw it. She passed out on impact, the white airbags pounding against her flesh like a boxer's glove, certainly lessening the blow compared to the fist-like steel of the oncoming SUV, but by no means gentle. Her body was tossed against the seat belt and interior of the car like a dozen oranges in a bag.

Her red Nissan spun tightly toward the far curb, only to slam into another oncoming sedan, ripping the front bumper completely off in a burst of water spray and spiraling upside down onto its roof, spinning like a top amongst the broken glass and debris. The noise of the impact subsided until there was a moment of nothing but the rain and the wind pounding against the motionless automobile.

Several stunned onlookers gaped from beneath umbrellas at the scene, then quickly joined the driver of the sedan, who jumped out of his still-functioning door and scrambled to Amy's mangled coupe. She hung upside down, unconscious, suspended in the air by her seatbelt and surrounded by half a dozen airbags, deflated like empty white balloons. Huge puddles formed around her broken car, buffeted in the rainstorm like a stranded vessel in the middle of a raging sea.

CHAPTER FORTY-TWO

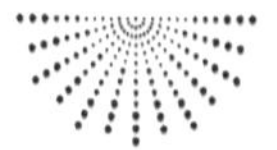

When the power was still out at DJ's after thirty minutes, most of the patrons started heading for the door. Zach and the other bartender had stopped serving, and without any sports on the TVs, people were getting bored just talking. The only thing that had kept them around for that long was the nasty weather outside.

Somehow Tyler had convinced Bethany that his place would be a good venue to ride out the storm, and Percy was headed home to his wife. Once Mark made it clear to Trina that he wasn't interested in her or anyone else right now, she and Anna left together. Mark sprinted through the downpour across the street into the subway, soaked to the bone in just seconds, and headed back to his empty apartment where the power was surprisingly still on.

His head was slightly heavy from the few drinks, but he felt better than he'd expected to. The radar on *The Weather Channel* showed the storm had, in fact, turned dramatically inland after narrowly missing the Outer Banks in North Carolina. Bethany was now jumping across the Chesapeake Bay and pounding the southern shoreline of New Jersey in earnest.

The screen changed to a reporter striking the familiar pose of braving the raging wind in front of a sand dune on a beach. He was reporting from the town just south of Harborwood, predicting widespread flooding that could erode many of the dunes. Mark thought of all the time he'd spent on Harborwood's beach over the years, how it had looked just a few weeks before when he'd talked with Mr. Holland. He fell asleep, stretched out on the couch, the glow of the television dancing around the walls of his otherwise dark room, trying to process all the thoughts in his mind—Paris, the storm, Harborwood—but when he awoke, the dream that remained was of Amy.

LIGHT STREAMED through the window of Mark's apartment when he woke on the couch, head pounding. His cell phone buzzed, probably what had stirred him in the first place, and he picked it up to read an alert from CNN reporting that power had been lost to five hundred thousand homes along the mid-Atlantic coast, most significantly in southern New Jersey. The towns of Sea Bridge, Sanderling, and Harborwood were reported to be the most severely damaged.

The phone buzzed again, this time a text from Joe.

Call me. Storm causing all kinds of damage. I'm heading north. Need your help.

Mark groaned, then eased himself up, his neck aching from sleeping wrong on the couch. He used the toilet and fumbled with a bottle of Advil before heading to the window. It was still cloudy, but the sun peeked through in spots, the storm seeming to have blown past them through the night and back out to sea. He poured some water and turned up the volume on the television.

The news was all live from the Jersey shore. He clicked through until he found a station reporting directly from Harborwood. He sat on the couch and stared at images of the dunes, which had so long protected the town, but were now nearly washed away in places. Huge swaths of the streets along the ocean were covered in sand piles that looked like tan-colored snow drifts. He recognized a few storefronts and houses he used to ride past on his bike.

The camera panned to the news lady standing on the boardwalk, just outside of Groves. Mark felt a pit in his stomach when he saw the blown out windows, sand piled up against the building, and entire sections of boardwalk missing completely. He picked up the phone and dialed Joe.

"Hey," Joe answered.

"What happened down there, man?"

"It's crazy. The governor just declared a state of emergency. Harborwood was hit as hard as anywhere. I've been combing through the policies all morning. Did you know that thirty percent of the policies that Dad sold in the tri-state area are actually *in* the town of Harborwood? It's unbelievable. I think he must have sold a policy to every guy he ever went on a fishing trip with. We're going to be busy, little brother."

Mark was silent, his mind going back to his fishing trip with Dad. He felt the sickness again, the bombast of his father shaking hands, grinning from ear to ear, slapping guys on the back and talking them up about their insurance needs between fish stories.

"Mark? Are you with me?" asked Joe. "I need you, brother."

And then something clicked. Mark wasn't quite sure why, but suddenly he just knew. It became clear that this was what was next, to follow his dad's footsteps, even though he was gone. Maybe that was the only way it ever would have worked out. It was time to stop screwing around with his dead end job, to do something worthwhile with his big ideas and not just coast. That wasn't the kind of life he'd dreamt of for himself, regardless of whether there was a baseball diamond or not.

His mind drifted to Paris and whatever she had been for him, a temporary diversion most likely, and then to Mr. Holland on the boardwalk, and Amy at his apartment door. He wondered where she was now, amidst all of the chaos in the storm? He felt a yearning to see her, to talk to her, to hold her and make sure she was all right.

"Okay, I'm in," he finally answered in the phone.

"Wait, you are?" Joe answered sounding surprised.

"Yeah, but I have some conditions."

"Okay, name them."

"I need some say in the operations, okay? We'll make things better, update the technology platform. That's the kind of thing I can help you with. I'll meet you there this afternoon, okay?"

Joe paused. "Okay, Mark. Thank you. I think Dad would be happy, you know?"

Mark smiled, feeling differently about that statement than he had in a very long time. "Yeah, I think he would."

CHAPTER FORTY-THREE

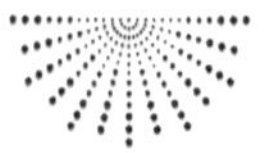

Amy opened her eyes, the images blurry around her. She saw a room fading in and out, people darting on the edges of her view like puppets. The pounding in her head, from behind her eyes, was excruciating. She didn't know where she was, but before she could think about it further, she faded out.

When she woke again, her vision was a little clearer, although she must not have her contacts in since everything was still blurry. As she slowly scanned the room, it dawned on her that she was in a hospital.

A man sat in a chair. Who was it? Her husband? No, it was her father. She stirred, tried to extend her hand, to make a sound, but nothing happened. She resorted to blinking her eyes, hoping to attract his attention.

He finally glanced up from his book, looking her way. His face softened as he leaned toward her.

"Hey, Bear," he said.

She knew that was what her father called her, but couldn't remember why. She tried to speak again, but couldn't. It felt like her jaw was wired shut. The pain in her head dug deeper into her brain like someone was hitting it with a pickax.

He reached over and squeezed her hand tightly. She saw his eyes grow moist, a tear flow down his cheek. She wanted to squeeze his hand back, to tell him she was okay, but she couldn't.

She wondered why she was there, lying in a hospital bed. Had she been shot? Attacked? Did she have cancer? Was there an accident? Her mind slowly turned, but wouldn't find anything, like a car engine that wouldn't start. That's it—she was driving. There was a storm.

Memories from recent years flooded through her brain like hitting the rewind button on the TV remote—Dylan, Vail, the divorce, moving back home, her mom, the clinic. It was all a colorful blur, filled with ups and downs, but mostly downs. She felt Dad's hand squeeze hers, his other wipe a tear from her cheek. Then she remembered something else.

She'd gotten a phone call in the car. From Mark.

Then everything went dark again.

CHAPTER FORTY-FOUR

When the taxi drove Mark into Harborwood from the train station, he could hardly believe what he saw. It looked almost like a different place from just a few weeks ago, not the quaint little beach town he'd grown to love. The closer they drove to the oceanfront, the more damage he saw. Water filled the shoulders of the roads, still standing from backed up rain gutters. Puddles in the alleyways behind the rows of beach houses had now become like miniature ponds. Pickup trucks, work crews, even dump trucks and back hoes were everywhere he looked, working hard to salvage the worst hit areas.

He'd packed light, leaving by noon after Joe had called him, an eerily similar call to the one the morning of Dad's heart attack. Mark felt a sense of urgency to get to Harborwood quickly because of everything that was happening. He remembered enough about the insurance business to know that when a major accident or disaster occurred, all hell broke loose, and one of the first thing customers needed was to review the status of their policy, determine how to collect, and often times come to the sad realization that they were underinsured.

Probably not the customers Dad had hooked. He was known

to have the tightest sales coverage in the industry, sometimes, as Mark knew too well, to the point that he overinsured people. But in cases like this, there was no company you'd rather be connected with than Kingfisher. Mark understood why Joe needed his help, and if there was ever a time that the agency needed a technology upgrade and automation to help keep things afloat, it was now.

Mark had the cab drop him off at the small motel three blocks back from the beach that Joe had rented him as a place to crash until he got his bearings. It appeared undamaged by the storm, other than a few pieces of siding missing from one of the end units. While a few residents of Harborwood had fled their flooded homes for local hotels, much of the town was empty since tourists were not exactly flocking to the beach rentals after the storm. It would be a while until things got back to normal in Harborwood.

Mark met Joe for coffee, reviewed how he could immediately help out the most, formed a basic strategy for the next forty-eight hours, and then Joe left for a meeting at City Hall with the town council's emergency response team.

Mark walked up to the boardwalk and stared out at the ocean, now calm, but with the evidence of its former fury all around him. It was hard to believe so much could change from a single storm. He gazed down to Fourth Street, then back to Atlantic, wondering the best strategy to approach Amy. He contemplated stopping by her clinic, but decided to swing by her father's house first. He'd said he now lived permanently in the house he once rented for the summer. Chuck felt safer somehow after speaking with him on the fishing pier.

Stepping down Fourth Street, Mark remembered that first time he'd walked Amy home, their clothes sopping wet, his young heart a crazy jumble of hormones and emotions. He paused at the corner where they'd talked before she retreated to her house, remembering how he floated on air the whole way back to his beach rental that night.

He climbed the stairs to the screened porch, rapping on the spring-tight wooden door. When there was no response, he moved onto the porch and knocked on the inside door, but again, everything was silent. It looked like no one was home.

He took a deep breath, knowing he'd have to face Plan B and go to Amy's clinic directly, his chest tightening at the uncertain prospect of standing in front of her again. It had been so long, other than the incident at his apartment door in the city, and that was such a disaster. Surely it couldn't be worse than that, he decided, walking down the stairs to the street, thinking through which direction to turn for Atlantic.

"If you're looking for Chuck, you won't find him up there, I'm afraid," a craggy voice said from behind him.

Mark spun around to see an elderly woman bent down, pulling at the ground in a flowerbed. Small stacks of weeds and twigs were grouped behind her on the narrow path between the beach houses.

"I'm sorry?" he answered.

"You looking for Chuck Holland?"

"I am, but it looks like he's not home."

The old woman shook her head slowly. "No, he's not, I'm afraid. You a friend of his?"

Mark hesitated, then smiled. "A family friend from a long time ago. Do you know where I could find him?"

"Afraid he's at the hospital since yesterday."

Mark's heart sank, thinking of all the things that could have happened to him in the storm. Mr. Holland wasn't that old, but then again neither was his own dad. "Did something happen to him in the storm?"

The woman nodded her head solemnly. "Worst I've ever seen, even nastier than Sandy, at least in Harborwood."

"Was he injured?"

"Chuck? Aw, he's fine. It's his daughter, I'm afraid, that was hurt."

Mark's heart stopped. No, God, not now. Not after all this. "Amy?" he said, barely uttering the word.

She nodded, pointing up the street. "An awful car accident.

Had a collision at the start of the storm up on the corner of Ocean and Eleventh. Other driver hydroplaned when he tried to stop, hit her broadside and flipped her car straight onto its roof. Firemen had to pry her doors open with a machine. Would have airlifted her to the hospital too, I think, but the storm was too strong. I haven't seen Chuck since it happened." She looked up at Mark, likely noticing his face turning pale. "Did you know her, dear?"

He tried to breathe, but didn't think any air was entering his lungs. He simply nodded slowly.

"She's such a sweet little thing. She's been in my prayers all day."

Mark managed to find his voice enough to ask which hospital she had been taken to, then turned and walked away from the house. He barely remembered calling Joe, borrowing his car, and finding his way across the causeway to the regional hospital several miles outside of town.

When he pulled into visitor's parking, he froze behind the wheel, his mind racing. What would he say to her? What was he going to find? He refused to think he was too late, that Amy was already gone, that she'd slipped away from him just as he was ready to find her again. He couldn't bear losing her a second time.

The scene of her walking away from his house that very last time in high school played in his head. He'd thought about it a million times, how he should have acted differently. He remembered how badly he'd wanted to ask her to stay, to bury his head in her arms, to tell her how much he needed her, how crushed he was with his dreams falling apart, how the only thing he feared more than never playing baseball again was being apart from her. And yet somehow he did the opposite, he pushed her away.

He opened the car door and climbed out. He wasn't going to let that happen again. He only prayed he wasn't too late.

CHAPTER FORTY-FIVE

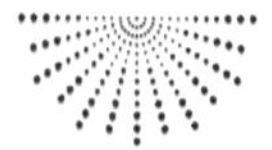

Amy was thirsty when she opened her eyes again. Her arm felt weighted, like it was tied down. She stretched her head forward enough to make out the surrounding hospital room. She faintly remembered it from her last period of consciousness. The pounding in her head that she'd felt before had subsided, but she was still sore and groggy.

There was noise to her right, and she slowly inched her head. Someone was sitting in the chair. Their head was turned toward the wall away from her, but they weren't moving, although she heard a strange sound. She realized it was a man snoring. She glanced toward the window, and despite the drawn shade she could tell it was night. She turned back to the man in the chair. It must be her father. He'd been there before. She narrowed her eyes to try to gain focus. When he stirred in the chair, turning his head toward her in his sleep, she lost the little breath she still had.

It was Mark.

The monitor's stead beat next to her bed picked up slightly in tempo in the otherwise quiet room. She closed her eyes, then reopened them, trying to determine if she was still dreaming. She knew she was in the hospital, but she'd forgotten again what had happened to her. Maybe she was hallucinating. She knew it was possible when doped up on enough painkillers, but it felt like she was thinking clearly. Maybe her brain was playing tricks on her.

Whether it was a dream or not, she coughed and tugged at the IV in her wrist. The metal bed rail rattled. The man, who she was growing more certain by the second was not her father, but indeed Mark, stirred and opened his eyes. He smiled.

That's when she knew it was truly him. Some memories simply do not fade. The gaze Mark used to cast at her that made her feel like she could fly was there again across the dim room. She felt goose bumps run down her arm, IV and all.

"Mark..." she whispered, her lips still barely moving. "Is that you?"

He leaned forward, sliding his chair up to her bed. "Hey there, stranger."

"What...what are you doing here?"

"I came to see you." He reached his hand out, brushing a strand of hair from her face.

"How did you, I mean, how could you know I was here?" She turned and glanced slowly around the room. "Why am I in the hospital?"

"You had a car accident."

"I did?"

Mark nodded. "During the storm." He explained to her how she'd been blindsided by the oncoming car.

Amy scrunched her eyebrows, trying to concentrate, but it was hard and all very confusing. "Am I in New York?"

He shook his head. "You're in East Bay Memorial, right next to Harborwood. I came down yesterday after the storm to help Joe. There are tons of policy claims coming in, people we need to help dig out of the mess. The agency covered a lot of them."

"But how did you know I was here?"

"Your father. He told me."

"You saw him?"

"I came to look for you when I got to town. His neighbor told me he was here, so I came right away. You were asleep."

Amy felt her eyes welling up with tears. All of this at once was almost too much to take in. "Is he okay? Was Daddy in the car too?"

Mark smiled comfortingly, shaking his head. "He's fine. You were the only one in the car."

She tried to raise her arm again, looking at the tubes and the monitors all around her. "Am I going to be okay?"

"Physically, they tell me you should be fine."

Amy looked at him questioningly.

Mark grinned. "I mean, emotionally, I don't know how you're going to be." He let out a nervous laugh. "At least if you're feeling anything like I am." He reached out and took her hand. "I've been thinking about you a lot."

Amy's heart warmed as she tried to process Mark's words. She didn't know what it meant that he was here, that he had come looking for her, that he was waiting in the hospital room for her now. She closed her eyes. "I'm so tired," was all she could manage to say.

"I'm sorry," said Mark. "I don't mean to bring up all this stuff. You're not in any shape to deal right now. You need to rest." He tried to pull his hand back, but Amy held it tight.

"Stay," she whispered, feeling herself drifting back toward sleep. "Don't leave me."

She felt Mark's hand rest in hers, heard him slide back in the chair.

"I won't," he answered softly as her eyes fell shut. "I won't ever leave you again."

CHAPTER FORTY-SIX

"Kingfisher Insurance, please hold." Mark juggled three different phone calls, trying to keep up with the pace of things in the rented storefront serving as a temporary office. The storm had indeed brought chaos to the region, worse even than what many had feared. Reports said Bethany had been the second worst hurricane to hit the Jersey coast in fifty years, right after Sandy. He was quickly discovering Joe hadn't lied—Dad really *had* sold policies to half the town, the older places at least. There was a reason why it had always seemed like Dad was working. He was.

Mark made it through the morning and well into the afternoon until Lucy, the temp they had helping out part-time, came in for the rest of the day to cover the phones. Joe had been right about another thing too; he did need Mark, desperately. Mark didn't know how they'd have functioned without him. As it was, Joe was spending half the week in New Jersey, the other half back home with his family in Virginia. How long that would need to last was anyone's guess.

Mark had put in for a leave of absence at his job in New York, although he knew deep down it was as good as a resignation.

Marvin might not realize it yet, but Percy had been right, that job was a dead end, an easy way to hide from moving on with his life. Joe's proposition could be a gateway, and whether it ended up being a long-term solution or not, it was the push Mark needed.

He carried a sandwich up to an undamaged section of the boardwalk and sat on a step facing the beach. It was good to be out of that office, even if only for thirty minutes. The rumble of a bulldozer echoed across the sand from the south. Already, earth-movers of assorted shapes and sizes had descended on what was left of the dunes, attempting to craft the mounds of sand back into their previous barrier forms. The fact that the dunes did their job was one of the main reasons the damage to the town wasn't even worse.

He really did feel for all the people who were hurting. Whether they'd lost everything or only had partial damage, speaking to their insurance agent was high on people's list. As much as he didn't understand his dad, Mark had to give the old man credit. He'd built a strong business that was now helping a lot of needy families.

Nearly a week had passed since he'd spent the night in Amy's hospital room. The office had become so busy, it was difficult for him to get away. He'd stopped in to say hi twice, but for the most part, Mr. Holland was keeping watch over her. She'd been cleared to go home two days ago after spending her first thirty-six hours fading in and out of sleep. The doctors had monitored her until the end of the week, but thankfully concluded that she'd made it out of the crash with just a concussion and a broken collarbone. The fact that she was recovering nicely made it easier to keep his distance and mull over where things might be headed next for them.

He wondered if she was thinking about the same things. Just because she had tried to see him and now he was back in town, it didn't mean that they were automatically going to spend lots of time together. Whatever was going to happen moving forward would need space to develop. The last thing he wanted to do after all these years apart was rush things. Her recovering from the accident only made that more true.

Once she was released, they'd traded some text messages, ultimately agreeing for him to meet her at the veterinary clinic just before closing time that night, then go for dinner and spend more time catching up.

Even though he couldn't really afford to be away from the busy office, Mark cut out early, leaving Lucy to manage the chaos until morning. He went back to the short-term rental he was staying at now, a cozy third-floor efficiency in an older beach house a little further down Atlantic, near Tenth.

He showered, shaved, and changed, feeling more nervous about dinner than he thought he should. The tingle in his chest was different than anything he'd felt for a long time, even from the excitement of dating Paris. Looking back, he sensed his time with her had been a curious mixture of anxious expectancy, lust, and who knows what else, but truthfully, he recognized now that it wouldn't have led to anything permanent. Even after a couple of months together, things had stayed fairly surface level. They didn't seem to have that deep connection, not like the kind he'd had with Amy years ago.

At five thirty, he hustled down the back steps and walked up Atlantic toward Amy's clinic on Seventh. He took a deep breath as he pushed open the door and stepped into the waiting room. Other than his time in high school dating Amy, he'd never spent much time around animals, unless you counted Tyler, so he felt a bit out of place in the veterinary clinic. He reminded himself it was probably a lot like a regular doctor's office, just hairier.

There weren't any other customers, but several balloons hung along the ceiling with *Welcome Back* and *Feel Better* printed across them. Mark hadn't considered how the clinic must have fared during Amy's hospital stay—he wasn't sure if there were other veterinarians or just her—but it was nice they welcomed her back so heartily.

"Forgetting something?" a woman behind the front desk asked, looking up at him above her glasses.

"Excuse me?" answered Mark, turning his attention from the balloons.

"Most folks come in here with an animal of some kind, sugar. You have a dog, a cat, an alpaca with a cold maybe? Or do you just like to look at balloons?"

"I, uh, actually, I'm here to see Amy Holland."

The woman stood up from her chair. "Are you Mark?"

He nodded, trying to decide if she would was pleased or alarmed by that fact.

Thankfully her face brightened, grinning wide like she'd just won the Pick Six. "Well why didn't you say so! I'm Tanya. Dr. Amy's told me all about you."

Mark felt his face flush and tried to look nonchalant as she bounded toward the door to the left of reception. "Dr. Amy, you have a visitor!" she yelled, then turned back to him, looking him up and down like he was under inspection. He wondered just how much Amy had shared with her, or if she was just being friendly. The door opened and Amy stepped into the office.

"Hey," she said, smiling. Her hair was pulled up behind her neck, her left arm hanging securely in a cloth sling over the top of her white lab coat.

"Hi." Mark grinned back. "It's good to see you up and about."

Amy let out a long breath and nodded. "Tell me about it."

"It's good to see her up and about for a man, that's another good thing," Tanya added.

Amy opened her mouth in shock. "Tanya, you need to settle down a bit, I think."

She smirked at Amy and shook her head. "I am going to say whatever I want to say on this fine day, now that you are safe and out of the hospital and about to spend time with this fine man here." She nodded at Mark. "She's been a lonely girl."

"Tanya!" Amy exclaimed, shaking her head.

"Well, it's true."

Mark laughed and helped Amy slip her lab coat off from under the sling.

"I think we better get out of here," said Amy, wincing as the coat passed over her left hand. "You're okay locking up, right Tanya?"

"You know I'm fine, now get out of here."

"Okay, then, let's go." Amy flinched again as she adjusted the strap on her sling. "Slowly."

Mark nodded, holding the door. "You got it."

CHAPTER FORTY-SEVEN

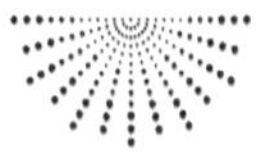

They walked together along Seventh Street toward the ocean. Waves of deja vu swept over him as they tried to make small talk. At the intersection, he let out a chuckle.

"What?" Amy asked, glancing up at him.

"This is really...strange."

"Strange, bad?"

"No, just strange. Isn't it?" he asked, as they crossed Ocean Avenue.

"Yeah, I guess I know what you mean."

"It's just that after all these years, we're suddenly back in Harborwood together walking toward the beach." He paused. "I never would have thought it was possible."

Amy nodded, and they continued quietly until they reached the ramp to the boardwalk. Mark had talked with the owner of *Barry's by the Sea* that morning about a policy, another of Dad's old fishing buddies. He'd learned they were still open, despite their storage basement flooding. Nothing fancy, but it was right on the boardwalk and he remembered them having some of the best fish around, which was saying something for a town on the water.

They seated themselves at a small front table that faced the ocean. The air was warm, but not muggy, with the slight breeze that always seemed to be present at the shore. He flipped casually through the menu out of habit, even though he knew he was going to have the crab. "Do you want anything to drink?"

Amy shook her head. "Not with the meds I'm on. We don't want this to turn into a scene when Amy goes crazy on a drug-induced episode."

Mark chuckled, "Probably not the best way to try to kick things off again."

She stared over at him. "Is that what we're doing? Kicking things off?"

He looked down at this menu nervously, then thought better of it, and looked back up at her, stopping a beat to marvel at the view. God, it was hard to believe it had been twelve years since he'd sat down with her like this. She'd changed, they both had, but the memories were flooding back to him, like the little way she pulled her hair from her eyes, or how she bit her lip just slightly when she was trying to decide what to order. That sparkle was still there, the magnetism that had pulled him so hard all those years ago. She was still sexy as hell, even with her arm up in a sling.

"I don't know," he finally answered. "I feel like I've veered off course for a while...but this seems like it might be right. What do you think?"

She nodded. "I know what you mean. This didn't seem like it could still be a possibility anymore. I'd tried to move it out of my mind, but I don't know if I ever really did."

"Maybe it's where I wished things would end up," said Mark, looking out at the boardwalk, "but not the way I'd imagined it happening."

He noticed her faint smile. "What are you having?" he asked, deciding to change the subject before things got too weighty too fast.

"I think the flounder, what do you think?"

"The crab. I miss that from the summers eating here," he said.

"Surely there are lots of great restaurants in New York, no?"

"Yeah, but not like this. Sitting outside, smelling the salt air."

"Better than taxis and honking horns?"

"Just a little."

The waiter glided over and lit the small votive candle on the table.

"Better than California?" Mark asked.

It was Amy's turn to look out toward the sea, gazing at the waves for a moment before nodding. "Things didn't work out so great for me after high school."

He nodded, waiting for her to say more.

"I thought Dylan was a star I could attach to, and he was, but he burned too brightly and I wasn't enough to keep his attention, it seemed."

Mark studied her lips, the curve of her chin. "I can't see how that is possible." She was still beautiful. He knew why she'd grabbed his heart from the very start, he just couldn't believe he was so stupid to let her go.

"Yeah, well, it happened."

"I think that sounds more like his shortcomings than yours." She shrugged, and he decided not to press the subject. "So you moved back here with your dad?"

Amy nodded. "The divorce was finalized eighteen months ago, but it was over long before that. It's funny, as soon as I left, I knew it was right. I just don't know what took me so long to figure it out."

"It's easy to get caught up, I guess."

"So what about you?" asked Amy. "It seemed like you were getting on pretty well with the ladies there in New York."

"About that..."

"Was that your girlfriend? She was gorgeous."

Mark thought about the best way to answer the question. He still wondered himself how that had happened the way it did. "We were dating, but it's over."

"Not because of me, I hope?"

"No, more like because of an Indian."

Amy frowned. "She ran off with an Indian guy?"

Mark laughed. "In a manner of speaking. He was from Cleveland."

Amy's face said she still didn't understand.

"A Cleveland Indian," Mark explained. "He was a baseball player."

"Oh! Ouch, that's tough competition."

"Yeah, that's what my buddies said." Mark thought about where he wanted this conversation to go, where he wanted it all to lead. "It made me think about us," he said finally, deciding to go for it.

"It did? How?"

He took a deep breath. "I realized a while back that it was my fault that we broke up."

Amy listened silently.

"I don't know why things happened the way they did, but I certainly made them worse. When I blew out my arm, it just sent me spiraling in the wrong direction." He shifted nervously in his seat. "It sounds stupid now, but I really didn't think I was good enough for you."

"Mark..."

"No, let me finish. It didn't hit me until after Dad's funeral. It's weird, but I think it took his dying to make me realize I'd been trying to live up to his expectations all these years."

Amy reached across the table and took his hand. "Those were his expectations, not mine. I never cared about baseball, other than because it made you so happy to play."

Mark nodded. "I know, that sounds obvious now. But it was a little harder to understand when I was eighteen."

Amy shrugged. "Sometimes it's hard to realize what's going on. The whole forest through the trees thing."

Mark laughed. "I never really understood what that means."

"Yeah, but it sounds good."

"Right."

"I've often thought that part of the reason it was so easy for

Dylan to sweep me off my feet was that I was still reeling from losing you."

"I'm so sorry I hurt you." He squeezed her hand gently, watching the reflection of the candle dance in her eyes. In that moment, she seemed exactly like the girl he'd loved so many years ago. There was no twelve years, no marriage, no funerals, no heartbreaks. It was just her and him, young and in love across the table from each other.

After they ordered and dinner arrived, they broke from such deep topics and settled into an easy conversation, just like old times. He paid the check and they walked along the boardwalk. When they came to a break, a section where the boards had been washed away in the storm, Amy smiled and took his hand, gently leading him onto the sand. "Wanna go for a walk?"

Mark felt his heart flutter, visions of years ago flashing through his mind. "Hell, yeah."

She laughed and nodded at her sling. "Don't get too excited. I don't think I'll be doing any late night swimming this time."

They pulled off their sandals and wandered down to the water's edge.

"You threw me for quite a loop that summer," said Mark. "I was so nervous, walking out here on the beach with you. I thought I was going to pass out from excitement when you stripped off your clothes. I'd never done anything like that with a girl before."

Amy looked down at the sand, smiling coyly in the fading light. "I sometimes got a little too carried away with the whole free-spirited thing. I think I've learned my lesson the hard way. Divorce will do that to you, I guess."

Mark reached out and took her hand. "I loved that about you."

She smiled and they continued along on the sand. He felt the warmth of her body next to his. Twelve years had changed so much, and yet somehow they were back where they had started, albeit with a few more scars.

"It feels a little easier to breathe since the funeral," said Mark, wading the conversation back into the deep waters. "That probably sounds stupid."

"No it doesn't."

"The ironic thing is that, of course, now I miss him."

"You do?"

"Yeah, I think so. I wonder if it was my fault, if I should have done more to stay closer to him than I did."

Amy nodded. "I wish I had some more time with Mom too."

"Your dad told me when I ran into him on the boardwalk. I'm so sorry. I know she meant a lot to you."

"Thanks. She'd been sick for a long time. We didn't want to see her suffer, but it was just so hard to not have her around. I miss seeing her smile. She was so fun. It's been hard for Daddy, too. I know he's lonely, but it's been good for me to be back, keep him company a little."

"I don't know which is better," said Mark, "to have it happen so suddenly like my dad without any chance to say goodbye, or have them gradually fade away."

"I don't know," Amy answered solemnly. "I think both ways pretty much suck."

Mark nodded. He knew he still hadn't had time to fully process everything about Dad. Maybe he never would. It was complicated, but he didn't know if it would be any better if it had been drawn out. He looked back at Amy, trying to focus on the moment. "But how's it going here now? It seems like you have a nice thing going at the clinic. Do you like it there?"

"Sure," she answered. "Actually, it's been wonderful in a lot of ways. It's amazing how different the rest of life could be when I wasn't consumed with wondering what Dylan was doing, or who he was doing it with."

"That bad?"

Amy nodded. "Pretty stupid, huh?"

Mark scoffed. "On his part, yeah."

"Thanks."

They spied a lifeguard stand, somehow still upright despite

Bethany's best attempts. Amy grinned as he pointed to the steps and they climbed up next to each other.

"This seemed bigger back when we were in high school, didn't it?" He wrapped his arm gently around her shoulder, careful not to push too hard on her injury.

"I don't think we cared back then," said Amy. "We were just so happy to be off on our own, away from our parents, spending time together."

"It's still nice."

"But not such a novelty as it was." She leaned her head down onto his shoulder.

"Yeah, we're so much more experienced now. For better or worse, I guess."

Amy chuckled to herself softly.

"What are you laughing at?" asked Mark.

"Nothing."

"What is it?" he asked again.

"Do you remember the time you tried to come see me when I was babysitting for the Patrick kids?"

Mark scrunched his eyebrows, trying to remember. "What? When was that?"

"I think it was our junior year, remember, because you'd just gotten your license."

"You were babysitting? What happened?"

Amy giggled. "I'll give you one hint."

"Okay."

"Mrs. Pasquale."

Mark's jaw dropped open. "Oh my gosh. I'd totally forgotten about that. What made you think of her?"

She smiled. "I think climbing up the ladder here. Don't you remember? You tried to surprise me when I was babysitting, but you went to the wrong house."

"Yeah, that's putting it mildly," said Mark, thinking back. He'd attempted to come and see her at the house she was working at, but when he tapped quietly on the front door well after dark, there was no answer. A television glowed in the upstairs window, and he somehow got a fool's notion to climb the porch post up onto the roof and rap on the glass.

Unfortunately for him, he'd picked the wrong house. Amy was three doors down, and he caught old Mrs. Pasquale getting ready for bed. She saw his shadow outside her bedroom window and let out a scream that nearly sent him toppling off the roof. He luckily caught himself on the edge of the rain gutter and jumped the rest of the way to the ground before sprinting back to his car and high-tailing it home.

"Did you know there was a police car patrolling my neighborhood for like a week after that?" Amy laughed. "Mrs. Pasquale was convinced a serial rapist was roaming free."

Mark shook his head. "What a disaster. You didn't ever tell your parents it was me?"

Amy smiled. "No, I promised I wouldn't, but I still think Daddy would think it was funny."

"Yeah, well I didn't want to press my luck. I used to have nightmares about falling off a roof and that old lady chasing me. I can't believe I forgot." He squeezed her tight with his arm. "See, you always were trouble."

"Ouch," she moaned.

"Oh geez, sorry," he said, realizing he'd pushed too hard on her arm. "Are you okay?"

"Yeah," said Amy, resting her head back on his shoulder. "I'm good."

They snuggled there for a while, listening to the surf, soaking in the moment.

"So . . ...." she said at last, breaking the silence.

"So?"

"What is this?"

There were so many things he could say. "I'm not sure," he started. "But when I found out you'd been in an accident, I thought I might have been too late. It was like I'd lost you all over again, just when I thought I might have another chance."

Amy nestled closer into his shoulder. "You were worried about me?"

Mark chuckled. "No, I just felt really bad for your dad."

She pulled back from his shoulder and poked him in the ribs. "Shut up!" They both laughed. "And now that you know I'm okay?"

He laid his chin against her head. She still smelled like apples. "I'm so glad."

Amy turned her head slightly toward the water, "Do remember when we were on the Ferris wheel, staring out at the ocean, and you saw that cruise ship in the distance?"

He nodded. "I remember."

"I think about that a lot."

"You do?"

"Uh, huh. I think about where that ship was going, out into the open space, the unknown, all the possibilities that could have laid in store for the passengers. It feels like that was how you and I went, out into the darkness, not knowing where we were going."

Mark smiled. "Maybe it can be a new start for both of us."

"I'd like that," she said, raising her head. Mark could feel the electricity in the moment, the tingle that had been so real years ago on that same beach. He paused, staring into her eyes through the shadows, trying to relish the reality of being next to her, then he leaned forward and kissed her, gently, but long.

They held each other at the top of that lifeguard stand, soaking in the warmth of their bodies next to each other, listening to the rising and falling of the tide, staring into the sea that had once seemed so inviting, but which they each now knew was so deep and full of consequence. And somehow, Mark could sense things were going to be all right. That his ship was coming into port, leaving the darkness and the depths behind, and heading toward the light.

CHAPTER FORTY-EIGHT

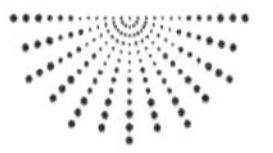

"Oh my goodness," Tanya snickered from across the waiting room.

"What?" replied Amy, looking up from the window that she'd been staring out absentmindedly into the clinic's parking lot.

"Somebody had a good date."

"Stop it."

"What? I'm serious. You're practically glowing."

"Tanya, please."

"Don't please me, I know a girl in love when I see one. Tell me with a straight face that you didn't have a great time with that handsome man."

Amy rolled her eyes and stopped in the doorway and grinned. "Yes, we had a great time."

"I don't have to be a doctor to figure that out, honey." Tanya looked up from her computer and smiled at Amy. "I'm happy for you. You deserve it."

"Thanks, Tanya."

Amy pushed through the door into the lab room, knowing that she was wearing a constant smile on her face for everyone to see. She couldn't help it. The night had been magical, there was no other way to describe it. Mark had walked her home just before eleven, both of them seeming to have a hard time letting the evening come to an end. They'd both hesitated, lingering at her doorway like a couple of awkward teenagers again, both seemingly unsure of whether his coming inside was the right step. She wasn't sure if not having a waiting father inside made things easier or harder. Eventually he said goodnight, perhaps acting on a bit of experience and maturity, something twelve years will do for you, she supposed.

She hadn't fallen asleep for a long time. The soreness in her shoulder made it hard to lie on her side as was her custom, and the pain behind her eyes still drilled through her head if she forgot to take her pain meds soon enough. But even without the pain, her mind was whirling.

Some nights in the past months, but not as many as it had been, she would wake up and still think she felt Dylan next to her. Then she'd remember that those days were past, and she'd burrow down into the pillow, trying to sleep, but more often weep, wondering how things had gone so far wrong.

But last night, she had lain eyes open, sleep not close to coming. She still felt the real warmth of Mark's arms around her in the lifeguard stand, the taste of his kiss on her lips. She tried to imagine what it would be like to have him sleeping next to her on the sheets. He seemed different, but the same. Older, more experienced, a little more sure of himself, sure, but deep down, he was the same boy she'd fallen in love with in high school.

She also realized how different he was than Dylan. She'd always consoled herself that Dylan was more cutting edge, more exciting, but she knew deep inside that Mark was much more her pace—steady, despite some turmoil. Baseball may have been the incident that derailed him, but she understood that Mark's struggles were as much about his father as they had been about any ballgame. With his father gone, he seemed to be more at peace, and she sensed a readiness to finally branch out and be himself.

Daddy always said that to be truly alive, you had to be forged in the fire like iron. She knew she had been burned a little in her own fires, but she'd made it through them. Perhaps it was the same for Mark. It was strange to consider, but maybe now they were more ready for each other, scars and all, than they ever had been before.

She woke in the morning, a fresh dream from high school still vivid in her mind. It had been their very first fight. They'd been dating for several months into the school year following that memorable summer on the beach. It wasn't "the" fight, the one that ended things, that wouldn't come for many months later. This was a small one, but it was the first, and those always seemed more intense.

It had started with something about Mark seeing her talking with another boy at school and getting jealous. He started acting all cocky, nearly aggressive even, not toward her, but just in his general demeanor. Seeing him act like that made her mad, even though it mostly just made him look stupid. It had sparked the fight. They didn't talk for two days, which at that time, after only three months of dating, was the longest they'd gone without speaking to each other. It was ironic, thinking now about how often she'd gone days at a time not speaking to Dylan, even when they lived under the same roof.

After the two days, Mark had tried to reach out to her, but she was out at the mall with Julie Ackerman. Not to be dissuaded, he drove over to her neighborhood, parked his car down the street from her house, and then ran in circles around the block, maybe fifty times, until Mom finally realized who it was and invited him in for lemonade. When Amy returned home an hour later, they had a long talk, he apologized, and she made fun of him for all the running. Then they made up. She still remembered the kiss he'd planted on her in her backyard that made her insides turn upside down.

She'd asked him some time later why he he'd run around her house all those miles instead of just waiting in his car or even on the porch. "When would you have stopped running, if Mom hadn't come out and seen you?" she'd asked him.

"I don't know," he'd replied. "But I couldn't stand just sitting there doing nothing. I missed you and I wasn't going to leave."

Mom spoke kindly of him that evening as she was telling Amy goodnight. Amy had been gushing about him, but also was confused over why a boy would act that way, why all boys act the way they do, and what it would all mean. Mom had told her acting foolish was sometimes just a man's way of showing he cared. She said she often knew that her father loved her tremendously because of so many foolish things he'd done over the years. That all seemed odd to Amy, but she trusted Mom's wisdom and knew she was probably right.

Her cell phone buzzed in her lab coat. She pulled it out and smiled at Mark's name on the screen. "Hello!" she answered.

"Good morning."

"I was just thinking about you."

"I haven't stopped thinking about you."

"Really?"

"I need to see you."

"You just saw me."

"I want more, I'm greedy," said Mark. "I need to see you again."

Amy grinned. "I'm here for you."

She heard him let out a long breath through the phone. "I'm glad. Look outside."

She turned to the window. Mark was standing on the sidewalk outside the clinic, phone to his ear. She smiled and bit her bottom lip, feeling a warm glow from deep within her.

"I'm glad too," she answered.

CHAPTER FORTY-NINE

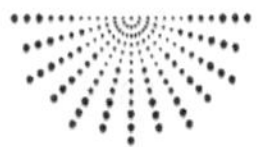

Mark set the final box into the U-Haul truck and stood on the bumper. He thought to himself that at thirty, he should probably have more possessions than just what could fit in a ten-foot truck. Sure, everyone lived small in New York City, but he sensed something was missing.

Joe had known some of it, surely part of the reason he'd pushed so hard for Mark to work at the firm. Whether Hurricane Bethany had been providence intervening in his life or something smaller was more than Mark was prepared to speak to, but the storm and its impact on the Jersey shore, on Harborwood, had been the final push he needed to step out into something different.

With all of the damage to the coast, he and Joe had decided there wasn't a better place for the new branch office than in Harborwood itself, and Mark was set to begin running the operation. He had already mapped out new plans for how to handle the onslaught of policy claims from the storm, and Joe had been very receptive to his ideas. Mark felt invigorated to have something meaningful to sink his energy into, and was happy to finally tell Marvin to take his boring job and stick it.

Amy's accident was a scary complication, but thankfully a short-term one. She was recovering nicely and no longer had her arm in the sling. Dogs and cats of Harborwood were back to being fully cared for. She and Mark had spent as much time together as they could, and it had been interesting. As much as some things hadn't changed, they were clearly different people than they'd been in high school. She seemed more guarded with certain things than she used to and developed an odd obsession with online puzzles. She seemed genuinely interested in his big plans for the agency and his willingness to work with Joe.

More than anything, they both seemed to be nervously expectant about what lay ahead of them. He knew in his heart that he wouldn't let the same fate follow them this time. From everything he'd seen so far, she seemed to share the same desire.

His phone buzzed.

Gone yet?

Mark chuckled. *Almost. Missing me already?* he texted Percy back.

Get the hell out of here will U? Percy quickly replied.

Mark jumped off the bumper and swung the doors shut. As he closed the latch, the clang of the metal rang through the street with certainty. He knew he'd still see Percy and Tyler occasionally being only a couple hours south, but life was changing. As familiar as Harborwood was from his youth, it was very different than the big city.

He started up the truck, crept his way through the busy Manhattan streets, through the Lincoln Tunnel, until soon he was cruising south down the Garden State Parkway. He rolled the windows down, the breeze blowing through his hair, and thought about sitting on the beach with Amy. But this time, he wasn't thinking back to high school, to those first moments together, but rather about now, and how she'd come back into his life in such an improbable way.

As he turned the truck off the exit, the cool salt air reaching his face, he felt that pull again, like the tide yanking at your toes in the sand. But instead of pulling him out into deep water, it was leading him into shore, bringing him back in the right direction, back to where he belonged, back to Harborwood, back to Amy. And he sensed that maybe a new chapter, a permanent chapter, in his life had begun.

ACKNOWLEDGMENTS

This story has been brewing for a while. Many a week over the summer of my youth and now adulthood has been spent at New Jersey shore towns like Ocean City and Ocean Grove. It's surreal to bring my children, a fourth generation enjoying the sand and waves.

Raised in northern New Jersey and later living and working in Manhattan, I spent more than my fair share of time at Yankee Stadium, old and new. Working on the fringes of the pharmaceutical industry for nearly twenty years, I knew the Porsche story would someday find a way onto the page.

I should point out how lucky I am to have a loving and supportive father who does not sell insurance nor sit beneath a stuffed marlin. And while I may have drawn from some faded memories of a teenager straining to be on his own, I'm so grateful for a dad who has taught and nurtured me into the man and father I am today.

Thank you to my own three boys, Matthew, Josh, and Aaron, but especially to my wife, Mary, for her patience and understanding as I dove headlong into writing about these romantic waters. She long ago became the shore on which my heart's longings found its rest. Also thanks for the encouragement from early readers Julie and Ali, Megan for her great direction and edits, Dane for a great cover. Thanks to all the supporters of my writing that has brought me to this place. It's been a joy.

Steven Sawyer is an emerging author of contemporary fiction. After growing up in rural northwestern New Jersey, he now lives with his wife and three sons in Richmond, Virginia. He also writes middle grade mysteries as Steven K. Smith.

As Steven Sawyer

Harborwood

As Steven K. Smith

Summer of the Woods

Mystery on Church Hill

Ghosts of Belle Isle

Secret of the Staircase

Midnight at the Mansion

Shadows at Jamestown

Brother Wars

Splashing in the Deep End (parenting non-fiction)

DID YOU ENJOY HARBORWOOD?

Online reviews are crucial for indie authors like me. They help bring credibility and make books more discoverable by new readers. No matter where you purchased your book, if you could take a few moments and give an honest review at one of the following websites, I'd be truly grateful.

- Amazon.com
- BarnesandNoble.com
- Goodreads.com

I'd love for you to join my **Reader's List** to be notified when I release a new book. Sign up with your email address on my website: **stevensawyerbooks.com**.

Thank you and happy reading!

Steve